TROUBLE

NON PRATT

WALKER
BOOKS

First published 2014 by Walker Books Ltd
87 Vauxhall Walk, London SE11 5HJ

4 6 8 10 9 7 5

Text © 2014 Leonie Parish
Cover design by Walker Books Ltd

The moral rights of the author have been asserted

This book has been typeset in Fairfield and Avenir

Printed and bound in Great Britain by Clays Ltd, St Ives plc

British Library Cataloguing in Publication Data:
a catalogue record for this book is available from the British Library

ISBN 978-1-4063-4769-2

www.walker.co.uk

For my mum, to whom I'd turn in a heartbeat

FIRST

HANNAH

So I had sex with Fletch again last night. It was all right, better than last time anyway, and Fletch is a laugh. And he's not so bad-looking … although not so good without his clothes on. We didn't cuddle afterwards – that's not really how it is with us. We were dressed and downstairs with our History books open by the time his mum came in, although you could tell she didn't buy it the way she gave me evils when Fletch's little brother ran over to show me the crown he'd made at school. Whatever. She might think she knows me by looking at the length of my skirt, but it's her youngest son who's got me sussed. Kids see all the way to your soul. What you wear and how you look mean nothing to them.

I showered as soon as I got in. No one questioned me about it. Why would they? I shower a lot. Mum asked me about my homework, so I lied, but she asked to see it and we had a fight. There was a lot of screaming (her), a few tears (her) and finally a grudging "I'll do it after *EastEnders*" (me – although I wished she'd offered to do it). I never even got started I was so knackered.

This morning I'd planned to get it done before school, but Lola threw a tantrum because she'd already eaten all her favourite cereals from the variety pack. Mum's attempt to make it better by adding chocolate milk to cornflakes was an epic fail and Lola ended up spilling half of it on her uniform as she poured it in the bin. Guess who had to clean it up? I barely had time to grab my cold toast as Robert hustled us out and into the car.

I've no choice but to do my homework now.

Robert holds off for all of five minutes before it starts.

"I thought you did that last night?"

"Well, I didn't," I say, my eyes still on the worksheet I've got flattened on my thigh. Despite Lola's tuneless singing in the back I hear Robert take a deep breath and let it out slowly.

"You lied to your mother."

"No, I didn't. I said I'd do it after *EastEnders* – this *is* after *EastEnders*, isn't it?"

"Don't be so clever."

I nearly point out that clever is exactly what everyone *does* want me to be, but I don't want a fight.

"She just wants what's best for you."

"Mm-hm," I reply, my lips a tight line as I bite down on any more comebacks.

"You need to stop being so hard on your mum, Hannah," he says, tapping the indicator with his middle finger.

"She needs to stop being so hard on me," I reply.

I swear I just heard a sigh.

"It's true," I say. "She's always on at me about something."

"She loves you. She worries about you." It's only because Lola's too young for them to worry about – give her another ten years and she'll be getting the same shit as me.

"Tell her not to bother."

That was *definitely* a sigh. "Perhaps if you tried applying yourself to your school work a little more…"

"What makes you think I'm not?"

"You spend so much time out with Katie and …" I look up to see a frown crease his forehead. He has no idea who else I spend time with and opts for a lame "… your friends. And your marks aren't what they should be."

"Should they be more like Jay's?" I say, changing a "4" to a "7" in my last answer. Now it just looks like a weird Chinese symbol.

Robert rubs the gap between his eyebrows with two fingers – a sure sign he's sick of the conversation. "I don't want you comparing yourself to him."

We all know why. Robert might have the perfect son, but Mum certainly hasn't got the perfect daughter.

I write over the "7" again. It looks even worse now.

By the time we've dropped Lola off at her school and pulled up near the front of Kingsway I've done enough to get by, although I'll get some snarky comment about presentation when I hand it in. I tell Robert that I'll be going round to Katie's after school and open the door, swinging it straight into some boy walking past.

"Sorry," I say once I've got out and slammed the door shut.

"No worries." It's Aaron Tyler, the new History teacher's son. He looks through me, an elastic-band smile stretching tightly across his face for a second before pinging back into nothing as he carries on walking down to the school.

I watch him for a moment. He's quite fit behind that tucked-in shirt and perfect-length tie. Anyone else would get flak for looking so smart, but there's something in the way he wears it that stops anyone – even the basketball boys – from taking the piss. He only started this term, like his dad did, and there are plenty of rumours about why Aaron Tyler's moved schools halfway through his GCSEs. Gideon reckons he's gay and got bullied – I reckon that's just wishful thinking. I asked Katie what she thought, but she wasn't interested in why he'd left, only whether she was in with a chance. Although I know she googled him after that to see if she could find anything. She didn't, but, knowing her, she wouldn't have bothered reading beyond the first page. She's not *that* interested in him.

My phone beeps a text. Katie. Obviously.

U shag Fletch again??? Hes giving ur "homework" session 10/10!

AARON

Like the over-enthusiast he is, Dad's signed up to champion Kingsway's healthy eating initiative and so I, as his son, must set an example and choose one of the flavourless concoctions offered up in the school canteen:

* lasagne made with something that has more in common with cat litter than cat food

OR

* a dish of unknown origin that claims it MAY CONTAIN NUTS.

Interesting how it's more important to tell me what *might* be in it, than what *is* in it. I go for the lasagne just as someone reaches across to grab a bread roll.

"Sorry, mate." It's Stewart Fletcher – Fletch. I don't like him. He spends a lot of time bragging, and the rest checking out his over-gelled hair in any surface that yields the slightest reflection. He's doing it now in the glass screens above the hotplates.

I edge my tray further along and listen in to his conversation.

"She came round to mine last night and we … you know."

Really? I find it hard to imagine why anyone would want to have sex with someone who uses that much hair product.

"… top marks …" His tray wobbles and I catch his bread roll before it lands in my lunch. I hand it back, but he's too busy telling his story to notice. "… not a surprise that Hannah Sheppard knows how to have a good time."

Hannah Sheppard. I've heard that name before now and I've noticed who it belongs to – the girl who tried to take me out with a car door this morning.

"Dude. Why are you telling me this?" It's the boy Fletch is talking to. "What is it about my expression that implies I give a fairy's fart?"

I glance up to see a boy from my class deliver a deadpan unimpressed face. I catch his eye and he winks so fast that Fletch misses it. As I stand and look for somewhere I can read my book and deter anyone from talking to me, Fletch shoves past muttering something that sounds like "useless gay boy".

"That's me he's talking about." Fletch's erstwhile companion pauses next to me. "I'm Gideon."

Usually I see him with Anjela Ojo, who sits in front of me in Spanish, but I've never talked to either of them.

"I'm Aaron," I say, the tray curtailing my handshake reflex.

"I know who you are." He grins quickly as I hear someone call my name from a table behind us. It's a lad called Rex. I was allocated to his bench in ICT and last lesson I sent him a link that made him laugh so hard he cried. It's great that he thinks I'm so funny, only I'm really not. I turn back to say something to Gideon, but he's already gone.

That makes sense. Rex is one of the basketball boys and they're not known for being friendly. I'm surprised he's even acknowledging me, let alone waving me over to sit with him and all his friends. Rex is opposite Tyrone Reed, captain on – and off – the court. Seeing them together, I notice how Rex is practically a negative image of his best friend, right down to the black stud that contrasts against his left earlobe, versus the glittering diamond Tyrone wears in his right. The only thing to ruin the illusion is the fact that Rex is about six inches shorter.

"All right," Tyrone says to me.

"Here." Rex uses his foot to push out the only empty seat and Tyrone gives the barest hint of a nod. I sit down and think better of taking my book out of my pocket. No one here would appreciate the irony of me reading *The Outsiders* in this situation.

There are no introductions. I'm expected to know who everyone is, but beyond Rex and Tyrone, I don't. It's not exactly like I'm interested.

"What's it like having lessons with your dad?" Rex asks as I poke my lunch half-heartedly. The pasta's so tough my fork doesn't even leave a dent.

"I'm not taking History," I say.

"Was he pissed off about that?" Rex again.

"Not really. I'm pretty crap at it."

Tyrone laughs and so do the rest of them. Only someone listening for it would hear the nanosecond time lag.

"You're not so bad, Aaron Tyler." Tyrone slaps me on the back so hard he nearly dislodges the mouthful I was midway through swallowing.

Not so bad? Interesting.

FRIDAY 2ND OCTOBER

HANNAH

Lola isn't eating her beans. They're green, so you can't blame her. Baked wouldn't be a problem. Mum works late on Fridays so teatime's always a little bit ... tense. Despite having raised a teenage son already, Robert has a hard time keeping a grip on his youngest. And me. He manages to get Lola to eat one bean and considers that a win, ignoring the fact that she then eats her pudding and half of mine on top. Afterwards, Lola insists on doing my hair before she starts on her Fluffy Kitty collection. By the time she finishes I'm not sure who looks worse – me or Princess Purry.

Thankfully my grooming session is cut short by a text from Katie: *cu in 10*. Which is code for: *get the drinks in*. I don't have to go far.

Before he left, my stepbrother had a massive party and because Robert is Robert and Jay is Jay, Robert gave him loads of money for it, WAY more than any normal dad would. But Robert likes to flash the cash – especially on his only son. Anyway, Jay overbought on the booze and because I was "helping" him order, he overbought on the sort of booze that *I* liked. I reckon that was the best night of my life...

Worst. Ever. Morning. After.

I might miss Jay, but at least the stash he left me under

his bed means I don't have to miss having someone around to buy me alcohol.

AARON

For the last four weeks the highlight of my social calendar has been the two hours after school on Fridays, when Dad drops me off at Cedarfields, a local old folks' home, where I spend time with some of the lonelier residents. Despite spending most of my time there being teased, patronized or ignored by people who consider the television better company than me, I somehow find it more enticing than the prospect of actually going out.

But I have a deal with my parents, which is that if someone makes an effort to be friendly, I'll make an effort too.

When I told Mum that my lunch on the top-dog table resulted in an invitation to hang out at the park tonight, she threw her arms around me and squeezed until I expired. Dad prised her off, but even then she was so overwhelmed that she started rubbing my back.

"If you're going to act like this every time I go out then it's going to put me off," I said and she instantly withdrew her hand. The last thing she wants to do is jeopardize my reluctant steps towards integration.

"Which park?" (Mum)

"The one by the river."

"Who with?" (Dad)

"Tyrone and Rex and … their friends?" It was more

likely Dad would know their names than me. He's good at his job. Good enough to move into a reasonable position at a reasonable school at a very reasonable speed and get his son into the same school, no questions asked. At least, no questions that I know about.

"The *basketball* lot?" Dad said, his voice incredulous. I'm not known for my sporting prowess.

"It's not like they asked me to take a shot before they invited me along."

"Just as well," Mum replied and I let her give me another hug. I'm doing this for her, after all.

So, now, with my father's blessing and a scarf foisted on me by my mother, I'm standing outside an off-licence which is far enough from our house that my parents won't know about it, wondering if I can pass for eighteen. I don't want to go in and I don't want to drink whatever it is that I buy, but this is what's expected and I have promised my parents that I will try.

HANNAH

Katie is late and all I've being doing since she texted is trying to repair the damage done to my hair during Lola's grooming session. I'm not sure it looks any better than when I started, but my arms ache. She arrives wearing her clothes for the park – that boob tube isn't the wisest choice for someone with a rack like hers, but there's no telling Katie. Once my bedroom door's shut, I hand her a bottle and open one for myself.

"What happened to your hair?" she asks.

"Lola. Is it really that bad?"

"No…" She doesn't look too sure. "Wear your blue skirt and no one'll look at your hair anyway."

Sounds like a plan to me. As I dig about in my wardrobe looking for a top I haven't worn a thousand times already, Katie tips her bag out onto my bed, finds her make-up under tomorrow's clean undies and starts dusting on more powder and grumbling about her skin. To be fair, her skin's pretty bad at the moment, but I'm starting to get bored of hearing her moan on about it. It's not like it stops her from pulling.

"So will Fletch be out tonight?" she asks in the least innocent voice possible.

"Don't know, don't care."

Katie sees right through me. "You're going off him, aren't you?"

"A bit." A lot. He talks too much. And he exaggerates. And, well, I was never "on" him.

"What about Tyrone?"

"What about him?" But I can't stop the smile edging up my face.

"Marcy'll be out," Katie says, and I know it's a warning. You don't flirt with Tyrone when his girlfriend's around – a rule I've been known to break. I'm pretty sure there's a rule about not pulling her boyfriend when she's *not* there, either. No one knows I've broken that one, though – not even Katie. "Watch yourself, yeah? You know what she's like."

I do. But Tyrone's worth the risk.

AARON

The carrier bag feels like it's cutting into my bones by the time I get to the park. Even so, when I see how many people there are, I think about turning round and walking all the way back home again – although I'd have to ditch the alcohol. Might as well persevere. How bad can it be?

HANNAH

We're late, which is a good thing – it's not clever to arrive first unless you're a B-baller or one of their WAGs. I wave away Katie's offer of a cigarette at the gate, but she doesn't move the pack from under my nose.

"Sure? It'll steady your nerves."

"I don't have any nerves," I lie. Katie and I have decided I'm not allowed to go anywhere with Fletch.

"Liar," Katie says, lighting up.

"I'll have one later." I won't be able to say no after a couple more bottles. Never have, never will.

"You can use it to stub out Fletch's boner. That'd work." Katie blows a rubbish attempt at a smoke ring in my face and grins as it mists about me in the cool night air. "Ready?"

Katie tugs her top up, arches her back and sticks her chest out – as if she needs to – before going in. I follow, noticing a stain on my skirt that I'm sure wasn't there when I left the house. There's not much I can do about it now.

The first person I see is Tyrone, standing by the benches. As we walk past I chance a sneaky peek in his direction.

He's watching me.

For a split second I hold his gaze then look away as if I haven't really noticed him. But once we settle on the swings my eyes are drawn back to him; he's got his arm round Marcy. The Brad and Angelina of Kingsway – only Tyrone's the one with perfect lips. I look at his mouth and think about kissing it.

He catches me looking.

There's a flash of teeth between those perfect lips as he grins at me, but I don't let on. Marcy's looking daggers at me already. I get my phone out for something to do and discover a text from Fletch.

Hey sexy. Where ru? Thought ud b @ park? xxx

I look around quickly, but I don't see him anywhere. When I turn to ask Katie if she's seen him I realize she's already got a couple of Tyrone's mates over and the Katie Coleman Show is in full flow. Neither of them really do it for me, but Katie'll flirt with anyone she can see through the vodka veil and when Mark Grey takes a cheeky swig from her bottle, she cuffs him about the ear and giggles. I down my own bottle and wonder how long it'll be before I get myself into trouble…

"Hey there, Han." Fletch's arms wrap themselves around me and there's a wet kiss behind my ear. I want to wipe it off. He walks round and edges one of his legs between mine, hitching my skirt up, hiding the stain amongst the wrinkles. I edge backwards as he leans in.

"Not right now, Fletch," I say, trying not to gag at the toxic cloud of aftershave. He looks confused for a second before smiling and nodding, hearing a promise I haven't made. I want to correct him, to tell him that "not now" means "not ever", but it's got him out from between my legs and that'll do just fine. As he weaves his way across the grass to talk to some girls who will pretend he doesn't exist, I wonder why I ever let him touch me.

My gaze wanders to Tyrone. It's not like I can't do better.

AARON

Since I joined Rex by the picnic tables I've been listening to him complain about his absent girlfriend and quietly trying to work out if park politics are any different from school ones. The only difference appears to be that, for the boys, any girl is fair game, but the girls themselves are locked in a turf war. The cool girls, the ones Tyrone talks to in school, are hanging out by the skate ramp, and there's another group on the far side of the grass. Sitting on the swings, in a satellite group of two, are Hannah Sheppard and her friend Katie Coleman, who look *very* different out of uniform. My dad – whose favourite gripe is the ever-shrinking school skirt – would have a fit if he saw the belt that Hannah's wearing.

I'm having trouble working out where these two fit in. That's why I keep glancing over – nothing to do with the legs that Hannah's got on display.

"Drink?" I hand Rex another beer and remind myself exactly how bad it would be if I opened one for myself. No one wants to meet Drunk Aaron. I'm familiar with his work and I think it's best he stays safely tucked inside a sealed can. Safer for me, safer for everyone else.

HANNAH

I'm bored. Katie's off with Mark Grey and I'm giving her ten more minutes before I leave without her. With Tyrone joined at the face to Marcy, the only entertainment left is playing bitch tennis with Marcy's lot, but with their best player out of the game it hardly seems worth it. Besides, I'm not in the mood.

I check the time on my phone. Katie's been gone over half an hour. Seriously, how long does it take for Mark Grey to get off? I send her a text telling her I feel sick and I've gone home. She has a spare set of keys – this isn't the first time this has happened. In fact, it happens almost every time we go out.

Halfway down the path to the back gate I hear footsteps behind me. I keep walking, listening as whoever it is draws near. Please be Tyrone, please be Tyrone, please be Tyrone…

"Hannah?" Not Tyrone. Fletch. Of course. He's in front of me now, his head cocked to one side, looking me in the eyes, a grin not far from the surface. "Going somewhere more private?"

"Yes. Home," I say, not quite looking at him.

"Yours or mine?"

All of a sudden I feel so tired that I want to curl up in a little ball on the path and go to sleep. But I've got to suck it up.

"I shouldn't have come over to yours again on Tuesday," I say and I sense his smile fading. "It was a bad idea."

"That's not what you said at the time…" He starts to run his hand under the hem of my skirt and I feel a slight buzz at the touch, my willpower wobbling. The way he feels as his body edges closer to mine isn't so bad and the sound of his breathing – slightly too heavy as if he can't wait to reach me – is a turn-on. I open my mouth as he draws closer and let him kiss me with a lunge that makes me gag. This boy needs some serious training in the tongue department.

There are footsteps as someone hurries past and I find myself hoping that it wasn't someone from school.

Stepping back, I put enough distance between me and Fletch to catch the flash of anger on his face. "Look, I'm sorry…"

"Yeah. Whatever." The words land at my feet as if he's spat them and, as he walks away, I fight back an urge to shout out the truth – that he was a pity shag, someone that couldn't disappoint me because I expected absolutely nothing from him. It was what I needed.

Next time it'll be someone I actually want.

AARON

When I return from a trip to the bushes, Tyrone punches my shoulder like I'm one of the guys. He's clearly drunk, since he introduces me to his girlfriend, Marcy, and tells me she's a model for the third time that night, then laughs when I tell him that. Now I've been deemed "funny", almost anything I say gets this reaction – understandable given the company he keeps. His friends are practically interchangeable. All on the basketball team, all in Tyrone's thrall. Beyond Rex the only one I could pick out of a crowd is Mark Grey, and that's only because he's the size of a house. He went missing a while ago with Katie Coleman, which Rex seemed inexplicably aggrieved about.

I find an empty table where I can sit and rest for a moment. Socializing is tiring.

A voice I don't recognize says, "Hey," far too close to my ear for my liking. Glancing round I discover Marcy sitting with one hip propped on the table. It's easy to see why she's a model. She possesses an angular, almost alien, beauty, all cheekbones and jawline – the kind with no warmth. As far from my type as it's possible to get.

"Er, hi?" My voice sounds like it's yet to break and I clear my throat.

Marcy edges close enough that she bumps her arm into mine. For an alarming moment I worry that she's going to sit on my lap, but she doesn't, for which I am grateful – Tyrone would have a hard time seeing the funny side of that.

"Just wanted to say hello properly," she says.

I hadn't been aware that the ones we'd exchanged three times already were inadequate.

"You're cute." Marcy is not the kind of girl that calls me cute. It unnerves me. I glance round, but the nearest person is Rex who's too busy texting to notice I'm in need of rescuing.

"Thank you," I say, then, stuck for anything more insightful, I smile and say, "So. I hear you're a model?"

And that, it seems, is the right response. Marcy talks to me of the woes of modelling, brushing her fingers on my forearm to emphasize points barely worth making and flashing me too many dazzling smiles. Once she's made me sufficiently uncomfortable with her attention, she leaves, blowing me a kiss over her shoulder.

I hiss Rex's name.

"What?" He finally looks up from his phone.

"What was that all about?" I ask. He still looks blank. "With Marcy?"

"Oh." Rex finally catches on. "Marcy. Don't take it personally. She's making sure you know how hot she is. Just tell her she's gorgeous three times in a row and she'll go away. Like the Candyman but in reverse. And fitter."

For the first time tonight I laugh. I'm not sure about me, but Rex isn't so bad. The table fills up as others take up my offer of free beer and there's quite a crowd of us when Fletch comes over, looking alarmingly smug.

"Where've you been?" someone asks.

"For a walk." Fletch retrieves a can of cider from his pocket and takes a slurp. Wiping his hand across his mouth, he says, "That's better. Needed to get rid of the taste of pussy juice."

I blanch. Who talks like that in real life?

"Take it you didn't go for a walk on your own?" Rex says.

I know he didn't – I walked past him and Hannah on my way to take a leak.

"I left alone, I return alone." Fletch makes a zipping gesture across his mouth. Then he makes an unzipping gesture by his crotch and mimes pushing someone's head there, laughing. It takes a moment for me to realize I'm the only one who isn't joining in.

There's a shout of "Bullshit!" to my right but whoever it is gets drowned out by accusations of jealousy.

"Hannah's got standards you know…" Fletch says, swigging his drink.

"Low ones!" one of the basketball guys says.

"Not low enough for you, mate, given how far you got last term!" Rex shouts back and the pack laughs some more. It's like watching a nature documentary.

"Careful, that's Fletch's girlfriend you're talking about," someone warns.

Fletch curls his lip. "As if I'd actually go out with a girl like Hannah!"

"But you'd let her suck you off and tell everyone about it?" I say, concentrating on the crisp packet I've just folded into a triangle. This has nothing to do with me. I have no idea why I'm so irritated.

"Eh?" Fletch looks at me, suddenly noticing the new guy. For a second, I wonder whether I've stepped over the line, but Fletch just laughs. "Man, I've done a lot more than that with her. It's Hannah Sheppard – it's what she's for."

I really do not like Fletch.

SUNDAY 4TH OCTOBER

HANNAH

Today sucked ass. I told Mum I'd get my homework done whilst I was at Gran's but, when I got to the home, Gran was having a bad reaction to her new medication and wasn't her usual self. It seemed better to chat with her and read out bits of gossip from the magazines I'd brought rather than haul out some French verbs. I know she wouldn't have minded – she quite likes me doing my homework while she potters about in the little apartment – but family comes first. School work comes somewhere below taking my make-up off at night and exfoliating once a week.

When Mum picked me up she asked to see my homework and we had a fight. She told me if I couldn't get my school work done then she wouldn't take me to see Gran every week. I went mental until she said something about talking to Gran. I shut up after that – Gran would be on Mum's side. Anyway, I'm doing it tonight whilst Mum and Robert are out and I'm babysitting Lola. We're in the sitting room and I'm halfway through when the doorbell goes.

"Can I get it?" Lola asks, eyes wide and pleading. She loves stuff like that, answering the door or the phone and checking the mail. Sometimes I send her letters so she's got something to open. I cut little windows in the envelope and make the letters look like bills. It means Lola can pretend to study her mail seriously, like Mum and Robert do, except I make the writing really big and decorate the paper with stickers and glitter.

"You can if you pull your top straight, Lolly," I say and I listen as she runs across the hall and fiddles with the chain on the front door.

"Have you looked out of the side window to see who it is?" I call.

"Yes. It's a boy." Helpful.

She opens the door and there's a murmuring voice that I can't quite hear before she *thump thump thumps* back into the room.

"It's for you."

"Did you ask who it is?" Lola shakes her head. There's a reason why you shouldn't send a five-year-old to open the door.

I sincerely hope it isn't Fletch.

It's not.

"Hey, kitten," says the boy on my doorstep. He's not been here since he told me we needed to cool things off but, still, I'm not completely surprised to see him.

"Hi," I say, trying not to give anything away.

"Can I come in?"

I'm not sure that's such a good idea, but I step back and let him come as far as the doormat. I have to lean round him to shut the door, which isn't a good idea either. He smells so good. A warm, clean sort of smell.

But he's not warm. And he's not clean.

"What you up to?" His eyes flash over to the other room, where Lola's leaping around in front of the TV.

"I'm babysitting my little sister."

"She's cute."

I say nothing.

"What's her name?"

"Lola."

He nods his approval. I guess it's habit to think everyone wants his permission for stuff. His eyes turn to me and I feel my clothes stripping from my skin, my body opening up until he can see everything he wants. He knows I want him. He knows I'm no different from everyone else.

"You got a moment to chat?" he asks, his body turning towards the stairs. I get the impression our conversation might take a different path from last time – this time it will be one we follow all the way.

I want to. Oh my God, do I want to.

"Sorry, I can't. Not with Lola here."

He steps forward and his hand goes up to my face, fingers resting lightly on my skin as he traces the shape of my ear lobe with his thumb. We're kissing. Slow, tender and very, very sexy. I close my eyes and let myself enjoy it, let myself sink into him, feeling my hands betray me as my fingers creep along his waistband and trace the dip in his back that leads down…

I pull away.

"I'm sorry," I say again. "I can't, not tonight. Tuesday?" Mum works late at the clinic Tuesdays and Robert takes Lola round to his parents' for tea.

He smiles and nods once, then kisses me quickly before letting himself out. I put the chain back on the door and head back to my homework. Lola gives me a sly look.

"I saw you," she says, screwing up her face and puckering her lips to make a disgusting squelchy kissing noise.

"You shouldn't have been spying," I say, but she shows no shame.

"Is he your *boy*friend, then?" she asks, disgusted at the thought.

I smile and shake my head. "No, Lolly, he's not my boyfriend."

Whichever way you look at it, whatever goes on between me and Tyrone, he is not my boyfriend. He's Marcy's.

MONDAY 5TH OCTOBER

AARON

Although she's in my form, English is the only class apart from PE that I share with Hannah and I watch as she slides into the chair across the aisle from me to sit with Katie. I can't get what Fletch said out of my head – *It's Hannah Sheppard – it's what she's for* – and I find myself thinking that she shouldn't sell herself so cheap.

We're divided into groups to perform the same passage of *A Midsummer Night's Dream* in different styles and my group's given sitcom. I only have a small part that wouldn't be funny if Eddie Izzard turned up for a cameo, so I let the others sort themselves out and watch what everyone else is up to. Hannah and Katie's group has to do theirs in the style of a soap opera. The two girls are sitting on the desk with their books open, but they're not reading their lines.

"… about Friday."

"Don't worry about it. I know Mark Grey's happiness means more to you than mine."

"Don't be like that. I've said sorry."

"I can forgive you for abandoning me. I just can't forgive your bad taste. *Mark Grey?*" I see Hannah wrinkle her nose as she says this and I smile into my book.

"Hello? Fletch." Katie sounds annoyed.

"Yeah, well, we all make mistakes." Hannah sighs just as someone from my group drops his pencil tin in a failed attempt at slapstick humour. I help pick the contents up and resume my eavesdropping.

"... he doesn't seem to be taking it well," Katie's saying.

I've missed something here.

"I know. I feel bad. Fletch is a good mate," Hannah says and I can't help myself from snorting at this. The two girls look up with eyes narrowed and I pretend to be studying my book. No one says anything and when I glance back they're busy with their dramatization.

HANNAH

I wait until he's turned the corner before I hurry after him. I don't tell Katie what I'm up to because she'd only make trouble. She hates people listening in to any of her conversations – which I get – but I want to find out why Aaron Tyler reacted the way he did when I mentioned Fletch and there's no chance of doing that with Katie there mouthing off.

"Hey," I call out and he looks round, confused. He still wears his shirt tucked in, but his tie isn't so neatly knotted and I wonder if he's started trying to fit in.

"Hi," he says, shouldering his bag a bit better.

"Why were you listening back there?"

"I wasn't." But he swallows in the wrong place.

"I'm Hannah."

He nods. "Aaron Tyler." A neat hand twitches towards me as if he's thinking about shaking hands, but it just transfers to his pocket.

"So, why were you listening?" I lean on the wall next to him and cross my ankles.

"I have preternaturally good hearing," he says.

"You what?" I have no idea what he means.

"I have exceptionally good hearing."

I will only decide how much of a wanker he is once he answers my next question. "Why'd you snort when I mentioned Fletch?"

"Erm…"

"Peter Naturally good at snorting are you?" I try out his fancy phrase, teasing him, and I see him hide a smile. Not *that* much of a wanker, then.

AARON

I want to correct her, but I daren't. I don't want her to think I'm laughing at her, because I'm not – at least not unkindly.

"I don't think Fletch can be that good a mate." I shouldn't be getting involved.

"Know him well, do you?"

"No. And I don't want to." I look down at my too-new shoes and think how uncomfortable it is standing here talking to Hannah. I can feel people noticing me, wondering why we're talking; wondering whether she's hitting on me, whether I'm hitting on her.

It's possible I'm over-thinking this.

"So?" she's asking.

I sigh – I've no choice but to tell her. "He said some things at the park that I don't think he should have."

"You were out on Friday?" It's not the first question I'd have asked in her position.

"Tyrone asked me along." Although I'm not sure why I need justification. "I didn't get a chance to say hi. You looked a bit busy with Fletch."

She doesn't react, just says, "We weren't busy for long. I called things off with him."

"Really?" Even I can hear the surprise in my voice. "That's not the way he tells it."

Hannah's looking at me more intently. She's wondering what he said and all of a sudden, I realize I don't know how to tell her. *He told everyone he had pussy juice in his mouth then acted out someone giving him a blow job?* Maybe not.

"He made some jokes about blow jobs and stuff." And because I don't want her to ask for clarification, I say, "Fletch made it clear he'd been with you."

HANNAH

I don't say anything for a moment because if I do it will be an angry thing and it will be aimed at the wrong person.

"Hannah?" His voice cuts through my rage.

"Yeah, look, thanks for telling me." I'm about to leave it at that, but for some reason the truth matters. "I didn't do anything with Fletch, not really."

"I saw you guys kiss—"

I glance up sharply and Aaron stops, as if he regrets saying it.

"So we kissed. That's it." On Friday, anyway.

Aaron Tyler just shrugs as if it's none of his business. Which it isn't. We stand and look at each other and it's awkward, but the moment's broken when a teacher comes out of the classroom and sees us by the fire exit. It's one of the fossils who think any boy/girl contact is about to break in to a lap dance and I know we're about to get moved on.

"See you, Ty," I say, leaving before I get into trouble.

AARON

Teachers gossip way more than the kids.

"What were you doing with Hannah Sheppard at lunchtime?" Dad asks as we start making dinner.

"Talking."

"Why?"

"Er … because that's what us crazy kids do these days?" I hand him the onion I've chopped and watch him add it to the pan. He looks tense.

"What were you talking about?"

"That's our business," I say as politely as I can. I don't like the way the conversation is going and I chop the rest of the veg more violently than necessary.

"There are things I know that you don't."

A bit of carrot hits the floor. The cat's on it in an instant and, in order to avoid the trap my dad is laying, I crouch down to dissuade The Kaiser from eating it before tipping the rest of the veg into the pan. I head to the sink to wash the chopping board.

"I'm trying to help you by making sure you fall in with the right crowd," my father shouts over the tap.

Damn it, Dad, I gave you a chance.

"You're a teacher," I say, hoping a joke might be the way out. "You're more of a hindrance than a help when it comes to making friends in the schoolyard."

He tuts and frowns, deliberately not getting it. "You know what I mean."

"Why don't you spell it out for me? Just to be clear." I can hear the edge creeping into my voice, that porcelain-sharp tone that can shatter any good feeling in a room. But Dad's on a self-righteous rant and there's no stopping him now.

"Hannah's not the sort of girl you should be hanging out with."

"Why?" I say, tightly.

"She's got a reputation as a bit of a … bicycle."

"So?" The smell of burning oil is catching in my throat.

"I don't think my son should be seen with someone like that."

"Your son?" My voice is the other side of angry. "That's a bit of a telling statement, isn't it? Now we're in the same school I'm defined by who my father is?"

"That's not what I said…"

"Er, yes it is." I correct him.

"Still…"

"No, not 'still'. It's not for you to decide who I'll be friends with." I walk past him, trying not to stop in the doorway and say too much, but I can't help myself. "I'm not perfect either, but it's up to me to make my own mistakes."

Dad stands with his back to me, the pan spitting furiously, smoke drifting up across the lights. I think he's about to turn and tell me that he's sacrificed enough already, that the least I can do is keep my head down and stay out of trouble and I wait, wanting to hear it.

Nothing happens. His shoulders sag and he reaches up to turn the extractor on.

"I don't think your mum and I can handle any more mistakes," he says, so quietly that I'm not sure he knows I'm listening.

TUESDAY 6TH OCTOBER

HANNAH

There's a saying that you should fight fire with fire. It's a stupid saying, because everyone knows you should fight fire with water. But I'm sticking with the phrase, because that's how I'm working it.

By lunchtime every girl in the school is talking about Fletch. His cock's bent. He comes quicker than Monday morning. One nipple's larger than the other. His mum caught him trying to give himself a blow job.

Last lesson is PSHE. It's one of the few subjects I do without Katie – this and French – and I enjoy it. Don't get me wrong, I like sitting with Katie all the time. I wouldn't do it if I didn't, would I? But I spend a *lot* of time with her and sometimes it's nice to take a break from being Hannah, Katie's best friend. In PSHE I can just be me.

Of course, just being me means talking about boys and sex with the girls – and boy – on my table. Tilly and Rahni don't really get out much – I never see them at the park. Tilly has a boyfriend, but their relationship brings a whole new meaning to the phrase "taking it slowly". They're practically taking it backwards. I'm not sure whether Rahni has even kissed a boy. It's the same with Gideon, although I know he'd rather it wasn't. Still, whatever our expertise, we're all equally happy talking about it.

"Have you heard about Fletch?" Rahni asks as soon as I sit down and I see a meaningful glance pass between Gideon and Tilly. Rahni was off all last week when I gleefully gave the other two the dirt on my last hook up with Fletch. They don't know that tonight I'll be doing *a lot* better than that greasy little spunk stain.

"What about him?" I ask, as I take my books out. I wonder which rumour she's heard? I hope it's the nipple one, that's my favourite.

"I heard someone say that one of the guys thought he saw Fletch having a" – she mouths the word *wank* – "in the school showers."

Her eyes grow wide and I can't stop myself from opening my mouth in a total OMG moment.

That rumour isn't even one of mine. Operation Embarrass Fletch has officially gone viral.

FRIDAY 9ᵀᴴ OCTOBER

HANNAH

My boobs hurt. They sometimes do around my period and I've checked that I've got some tampons in my bag, but I seriously hope it doesn't turn up tonight.

"You look way good," Katie says glancing not-so-subtly at my tits. I have broken the unwritten rule: Katie does boobs, I do bum.

"So do you." I stare meaningfully at the hem of her skirt swishing up slightly as she walks. There isn't much room for error in the swish.

"Easy access." She shrugs and loops her arm in mine.

"Same here."

Katie finds me funniest when I say something she would and she cracks up at this.

"Do you think Rex has broken up with that posh girlfriend he has?" she says, once she's recovered.

"So that's why you're making such an effort!" I don't know what to make of this. Katie used to be very rude about Rex, but lately I've caught her looking at him thoughtfully.

"No. I don't dress for anyone but me." Katie hands me her bottle as she gets out a cigarette and pauses, turning against the breeze to light it. My hand is cold and my knuckles are white as I grip the glass. Inside is some vodka mixed with a splash of coke. There's another in my bag.

I can't shift the feeling that my best mate is up to something.

"Hello? Calling occupants of Hannah's brain?"

I hadn't realized I'd zoned out. Katie's offering her pack, with a filter beckoning me towards it.

Sod it. May as well.

AARON

I doubt anyone will notice that I'm wearing the same clothes I wore last Friday. I have different boxers on, but that fact is between whatever God there might be and me.

Rex waves me over to the tyre swings. The park is heaving tonight. Almost everyone from our year is here, even the ones I thought would be snubbed. I sit down on the soft rubber of one of the swings and put down a six-pack. There's a chorus of appreciative grunts from the basketball lads and Tyrone slaps me on the back and tells me I'm not bad. Again.

I take one of my own cans and crack it open. Drinking is the fastest way to fit in without having to talk to anyone – and one beer won't do any harm, especially not this piss water I've bought.

Conversations rise up around me and the group starts to unfurl as boys pair off with girls. I scan the rest of the crowd, looking for familiar faces, and I'm surprised to see Anjela Ojo standing with some of the girls from our Spanish class, including Nicole – one of Marcy's friends.

Since Anj is here, I look for Gideon, but he's not around. Neither is Fletch. Not that I'm surprised. Best to sit tonight out whilst the gossip's hot. I don't for a second believe what I've heard about the school showers, but I don't think anyone's interested in the truth – gossip's about the *possibility* of truth.

Note to self: stay the right side of Hannah Sheppard.

That's when I notice that she and Katie have arrived.

HANNAH

We've been here all of five minutes when Katie sees Rex. I count to ten and before I've reached seven, she's left me standing by the roundabout whilst she heads for the swings. Rex is there talking to Aaron Tyler. It's weird how he's hanging round with the basketball lot – I would've thought he'd be above all this clique shit.

Someone bumps into me as I'm staring off into space and half my drink splashes out of the bottle.

"Bollocks!" It's Tyrone, jumping back from the fizz that sprays out over our shoes.

I stay where I am, but then, my shoes cost less than his. I'm not bothered about it to be honest, but it's a good starting point.

"You gonna make up for that?" I say quietly, meeting his eyes. Big, dark eyes and beautiful lips. Lips that feel as beautiful as they look.

Tyrone must be thinking the same thing, judging by the way his eyes dart down to my mouth. I can tell he's thinking about the things we did in my bedroom on Tuesday. So am I.

"Name a time and a place," he murmurs.

I want him here and now, but…

"Tyrone!"

Marcy struts over, her supposedly perfect face set in a scowl. I'm going to enjoy this.

"Hey, sexy." Tyrone turns away from me to try a low purr on his girlfriend, but she's as deaf to this as I would be. Tyrone can charm when he wants to, but it's usually with something more persuasive than his voice.

"I thought you were going to talk to Rex about that thing?"

Tyrone looks baffled. "You what?"

"Never mind." Marcy shoots me a glare. "Hi, Spanner. Going for the Page Three look tonight?"

I glance down and realize my bra's peeping out above my top. And my cleavage is popping out above my bra.

"If you've got it, flaunt it." I shrug. "Or flaunt it anyway, even if you haven't – that's your motto, isn't it?"

But Marcy simply smiles. "People pay me to flaunt what I 'haven't got'. Let me know when you finally get paid for doing whatever it is you think people want you for." She turns away, a perfect dismissal, and lays a hand on Tyrone's arm, leading him away from me.

I hate how Marcy thinks she's so much better than everyone else here. I hate that she thinks she's better than *me*. But I take a deep breath and then I walk away, because, you know, I can. Because I have so shagged her boyfriend.

My first sip of tepid beer tastes like self-hatred. I surreptitiously pour some out, listening to the conversation next to me between Katie and Rex, who seem to have forgotten about his never-present girlfriend.

"… not a regulation-length skirt, Katie Coleman." Rex is buzzing. "Skirt" was almost "shirt". Although her shirt is hardly respectable. It's only done up with one button and that button should have been higher.

"Are you telling me off?"

"I'm just stating facts. Didn't say I didn't like those facts."

Factsh.

"Show me where a regulation skirt should be."

"There." I see him bend down and brush her knee. "Not here." I can guess where he's touching her leg now.

"I'm thinking your hand shouldn't be here either."

"Where should it be?"

This conversation is torture. I do not want to sit here whilst Rex flirts with the girl who by all accounts – including hers – gave his friend an "epic" hand job behind the toilets last week. It's hard not to speculate as to whether "epic" refers to duration or quality – something I'm certain Rex has thought about a lot.

The bin's only a short walk away and I dispose of my beer. It's only after I've done this that I realize it made a good shield from the world. Now I feel naked and aimless.

There is no one I want to talk to. Tyrone is arguing

with Marcy, Rex has his hands full with Katie and the only other guys I know are daring each other to drink a cocktail of cider, Guinness, schnapps and cooking sherry from a plastic cup. There's always the girls from Spanish, but I've only ever asked them about homework before now and that's not going to cut it.

I never knew talking to people took practice, but it seems I've gone so long without any that I've forgotten how.

HANNAH

I'm feeling reckless.

AARON

"Hey, Ty."

I turn sharply at the name of the person I used to be, but it's only Hannah. There's an almost-empty bottle in her hand and she's smiling a slow smile. At me.

She must be drunk.

"Everyone calls me Aaron," I say.

"Does everyone?" She raises an eyebrow. It's a well-practised look. Mark Grey notices us and turns to the guy next to him and nods in our direction.

"So." I struggle for a moment. "What are you up to this weekend?"

Hannah blinks and I notice her lashes are clogged by too much mascara. "I don't know. You?"

"I have plans to write the great American novel." This throws her, but only for a second.

"Good luck with that, being a Brit. I'm thinking those Yanks might not go for your greatness."

She's sharper than Tyrone. Although that's not saying much. The guy's a blunt tool in every sense – he might be the hamster's cheeks around here, but a week of being in favour has left me practically comatose. Tyrone talks about himself all the time, even boasting about Marcy only serves to make him look better. Everyone else's stories and opinions boomerang back to him; he's done everything, or knows someone better than us who has. Only, when I listen, it seems he's got absolutely nothing to say.

"Bored?" Hannah says, reading my mind.

"That's an understatement," I mutter, then worry that I've offended her since she comes here every week. "Maybe it's just me. I'm not in the mood."

"It's not just you. This place is better in the daytime, when the swings are for kids and the roundabout isn't weighed down with drunken basketball morons."

I look at her and wonder what she'd be doing here during daylight hours. She reads my mind once more.

"I come here with my sister a lot." Her face lightens underneath all the make-up. "She's five."

"What's her name?" I ask, surprised to find I'm curious about someone else's life. It's been a while since that happened.

"Lola – although we all call her Lolly," Hannah says,

then glances down at her bottle and chucks it in the bin. "Let's get out of here."

HANNAH

This isn't really how I thought it would go. I'd imagined less talking and more flirting. The two are usually the same when it comes to boys, but this one's different.

I don't want different, though. I want sex.

It doesn't have to be him, but he's new and I want to be the one that gets there first. I don't like the idea of Katie setting her sights on him once she's chewed Rex up and spat him out. Katie and me are different. I like boys. A lot. They're fun to hang out with, they can open jars without looking constipated, they have short hair and they smell good (mostly). Katie does not like boys. She *dis*likes them. When she's after a boy it's about power. Katie is about the hunt and the kill. She's a predator. Me? I'm a tourist. Pick the destination, plan the holiday, check out the best bits, then leave. Thanks for the memories and all that. I've not always travelled so far, but once you've been there and enjoyed it, it's a lot easier to make the journey again. And again. My tourism might look like Katie's shoot to kill, but if I were a boy, I'd rather shag someone who liked me rather than someone who didn't.

As we walk by the slide, I see Anj looking at us and I stick my tongue out and grin. She pretends to disapprove with a roll of her eyes, but when she turns back to her friends she's grinning too. We pass Tyrone and Marcy and I slide my hand into Aaron Tyler's pocket and take out his phone.

"What are you doing?" he asks.

"Nothing," I say, aware that Tyrone has noticed as I tap my number into another boy's phone. "Just giving you my number."

Tyrone watches as I return the phone to the pocket I took it from, linking my arm in Aaron's as I do. I give my audience a sly wink. Tyrone gets it elsewhere, why shouldn't I?

The footpath leads down to the river and turns into a towpath. Neither of us says anything. My arm is still in Aaron's, and I get a thrill from the warmth of his body next to mine. I lean in slightly and breathe deeply. He smells of something vaguely familiar. Something that makes me feel safe.

I can see the bridge. It's a good place, quiet at this time of night and there are some nice dark shadows between the pillars.

49

AARON

Hannah leans into me as a breeze whistles up from the water under the bridge. It feels nice to have someone close again.

Nostalgia for the life I left behind rushes in so fast it hurts: memories of sitting on desks next to my friends, elbows accidentally clashing now and again; the girls not minding if our legs touched as we sat too many on a bench; the lads putting an arm around me and pulling me in for a celebratory hug when I once got between the ball and the goal in a semi-final I shouldn't have been playing in. Here it's different. People apologize when they bump into me, girls and boys seem to occupy different hemispheres and the basketball lads celebrate with high fives and backslaps. They greet each other by punching fists. It's all very passive-aggressive.

The cynic in me suspects that Hannah isn't just being friendly for the sake of it – but I want to believe she is.

I feel her slow her step as we get under the bridge and she pulls on my arm, turning me towards her.

Cynicism one, innocence nil.

For a second I think about it: the way it would feel to have her press that body against mine, how I'd run my hand under the hair at the back of her neck to pull her in. God. It feels like for ever since a girl looked at me like this. Her mouth is pretty and her eyes smile slightly into mine … and that's when I know this isn't going to happen, because there is something about Hannah, something warm beneath the cold, calculating sexiness she spends so much time projecting. Something real.

Real isn't something I'm ready for. And whatever she might think, Hannah is not ready for me.

I duck my chin as she closes the distance between us. Her kiss lands on the side of my jaw, but she's fast and tilts her head so she's in line with my lips once more.

It would be too awful if she tried again, so I step back.

"Hannah, I—"

"What?" There's a shortness to her question.

"I'm sorry, I don't want …" What's the right thing to say? "… to kiss anyone."

"Me, you mean?"

Yes. I do mean that, but I'm not going to say it.

"No, I mean anyone. I'm not … it's not…" Why can't I get the words out?

"I knew it!" She takes a step back and studies me, hands on hips. "You're gay."

It takes a second for me to process her conclusion. I won't kiss her so I'm gay? Wow. That's pretty arrogant.

"I'm not gay."

"It's OK. You can tell me. I won't tell anyone. You'd be surprised at the secrets I can keep." She's grinning at me, inviting me to share, inviting me to tell her something that could form a foundation for friendship.

Why can't I just say that I'm gay? Why can't I just *be* gay? It's not like I'm looking to get lucky with girls any time soon.

"Look, I'm really sorry, Hannah, I'm *not* gay. Really."

We look at each other some more and I see her features change. The open share-with-me expression is closing up and the shutters are coming down ready to protect her from the humiliation of being rejected.

I feel bad for her. It's not as if I intended to lead her on and let her down. I hadn't meant for her to lose face – although it's not like anyone saw this happen. As far as everyone else is concerned, we've done the deed. They saw us leave the park. They know what Hannah's like and they know nothing at all about me. They wouldn't think I'd say no to a plateful of Sheppard pie.

HANNAH

I leave Aaron under the bridge as he fails to find the words to explain why he embarrassed me like that. Screw him. Well, not *screw* him … you know what I mean.

Heading back to the park isn't an option, so I find the nearest bus stop that'll take me where I need to go. It's cold now there's no one else here to keep me warm and I wish I'd brought my hoodie.

I scrunch my eyes tight shut. There will be no tears over this. None over Aaron stupid Tyler.

When I get home I go up to Jay's room and flop into the bean bag like I used to whenever I wanted to vent. The place is almost empty – most of the stuff Jay took to uni came from here rather than his mum's. Even though the walls have been stripped bare and the bed's made up with the wrong duvet cover, it still feels like he's here.

I wish he was.

I get out my phone, leaving a new text from Katie unopened as I scroll down to the last message I had from Jay. Two weeks ago. There's no room in his life for the things he left behind – I've seen the Facebook photos of all the fun he's having at Warwick, surrounded by unfamiliar faces. It hurts, but I've got to get over it. Besides, it's not like he'd want to hear all my problems even if he was here.

MONDAY 12TH OCTOBER

AARON

"Thought you had better taste than that, mate," says Mark Grey, who is sweating all over me as we sit on the subs bench during PE. Despite being nothing short of MASSIVE, Mark is not a particular asset on the basketball court and Mr Prendergast has grown tired of calling fouls on him.

"Huh?" I'm not really listening since I'm too busy wondering when I'm going to be called up. Basketball isn't my kind of sport – not that any of them are – and I can imagine my ineptitude mattering more than it should.

"… Hannah."

That's when I pay attention.

"What about Hannah?" As if I didn't know.

"On Friday. Doesn't take a genius to work out what you were up to."

"Obviously not," I murmur but Prendergast calls me up before Mark has time to process the insult.

I'm on the team that's playing against Tyrone's. Prendergast hasn't given much thought to balancing the teams since mine consists of Gideon, who considers Converse All Stars suitable sportswear, a couple of shorter-than-average girls and a boy who spends a lot of time chatting to the token girl on the other side. Excluding her, the other team are made up of the best basketball players the school's got.

"You left in a bit of a hurry the other night," says the guy marking me, whose name I never quite caught. Might be called Rad. Or Rod. Or neither. He was the one Mark Grey had been talking to in the park and he's wearing an expression somewhere between a smirk and a leer. It's unpleasant. I ignore him, jump to intercept a pass and bounce it on to Gideon, who runs with it to score two much-needed points.

"So, what did you get up to?" Rad/Rod/Neither asks, as Gideon takes a victory lap.

I shrug. I did a lot of shrugging on Friday when Mum questioned me about my night out as a normal teenage boy, punctuating my shrugs with grunts like a normal teenage boy, which seemed to please her. I know how to hide things.

"Saw you left with Hannah, my man," Tyrone chips in as he walks to the centre, head tilted back so he can look down his nose at me. I'm guessing the effect he's going for is gangster, but it's spoiled by a bogey in his left nostril that flutters with each breath. All this attention is unnerving. No one made this much of a fuss over the Mark Grey/Katie interaction and that was so public a live show may as well have been projected into the sky like a Bat-Signal.

The ball bounds in and I track back to try and stop Rex from belting down the wing. I underestimated how good Rex is at basketball; he might be short, but he's fast and springy. He's better than Tyrone, but no one admits this. It is not OK to be better at anything than Tyrone.

"You wanna steer clear of that skank," Tyrone says behind me. I turn around, not understanding the venom in his voice and Rex dodges right past me.

Tyrone isn't paying any attention to the game; he's looking at me, eyes narrowed, then he nods, once, like I'm to obey him and turns away.

FRIDAY 16TH OCTOBER

AARON

Today is the first time that Hannah acknowledges me since she ran off last week.

"Can we borrow your copy of *Jane Eyre*?"

"Of course." I hurry to hand it over, but I don't let go when she takes hold of it. I want to at least *try* and clear the air. I'm frustrated that I've ended up involved in something that didn't even happen. There's been a seismic shift in Tyrone's love for my jokes and I'm certain it's linked to Hannah in some way. "Hannah, about last Friday…"

"Huh?" For a moment it looks like she's forgotten she even knows my name.

"What happened with me and you…?" I prompt.

"Yeah. Let's just leave it there, shall we, Ty?"

I wish she wouldn't call me that.

"I just wanted to say—"

"Leave it, Emo Boy. She doesn't want to talk to you, yeah?" Katie leans round her friend and snatches the book – doesn't even say thank you as she cracks the spine open, and gives Hannah's arm a squeeze.

Did Katie just call me "Emo Boy"?

No one here has a clue who I am. Maybe that's for the best.

HANNAH

Katie's sympathy isn't fooling me. What she really wants is for me to tell her more about what happened. As far as she's concerned it was a really disappointing shag, but she's annoyed that I've gone light on the details. Katie overshares to the point that I could play pick-the-ex by looking at nothing more than snapshots of their penises. Thing is, there's a lot I've not been sharing with her. Whatever I haven't told her about Aaron, or the on/off thing with Tyrone is nothing compared to what she doesn't know about Jay's party.

AARON

Neville chews on the inside of his cheek, reaches for a card, then changes his mind. It's like playing whist with a tortoise – right down to the sagging skin at his neck and the shell of a cardigan he's wearing. I can't see a clock – Cedarfields isn't fond of showing its residents how slowly time moves round here – and I gently twist my wrist to look at my watch.

"Getting bored, sonny?" Neville's voice croaks out amidst his too-loud breathing.

I am, but I don't say anything.

"You don't have to sit with me, you know. I've got plenty to entertain myself. *Countdown* is on in a moment."

"I'm pretty sure you've missed it, Mr Robson," I say.

Neville works his jaw so I can hear his teeth clicking together. Looking down at my cards, I wonder why I'm going to the park at all. After a week of being out of favour I'm certain no one will miss me. And if I "forgot" my sacrificial offering of alcohol, I could get myself frozen out entirely.

"Well, I'm bored." Neville takes the cards out of my hand and works them effortlessly back into the pack. "Every Friday, you come, you spend some time with the loneliest oldies and then you leave. Not staff, not family…" His voice might be timorous, but I can feel his gaze, straight and steady, pinning me down. "What's your business about?"

"No business, Mr Robson, just volunteer work," I reply, standing up to turn on the light.

"Why?"

"Because I'm a Good Samaritan." I try to sound like I'm joking but it comes out a little bitter. I'm not bitter, I just don't want to talk about it.

"Suit yourself," he says, wincing as he stands. I think about helping him, but I'm not sure he'd appreciate it, then I hear him mutter, "Don't mind me," and I hurry to offer him a hand, only to be ignored.

I look at my watch and figure I could leave now. There's a McDonald's on the way to the park and I've got my book with me. Before I even realize what I'm doing, I've got one arm inside my coat and I'm turning to say goodbye.

"Have a g—" I stop.

Neville is standing over the waste paper bin unzipping his flies. I bound across the floor and put a hand on his arm.

"Hey!" Neville shrugs me off, spraying a trail of urine over his bedside table. "Do you mind?" And he swings back over the bin.

I turn away and stifle a laugh as I hear a wet patter on the contents of the bin. Neville zips up and turns to face me.

"Poofter."

I don't bother correcting him – what good did it do with Hannah? – I just say goodbye and leave, stopping to warn someone about the contents of Neville's bin.

"He likes you, you know," the manager says, as she hunts around reception for a set of keys to the cleaning cupboard.

"Really?" I'm not sure Neville likes anyone.

"He does. He asks about you when you're with one of the others. Wants to know whether you'll be popping in on him."

I feel a pang of guilt.

"There you are!" She snatches the keys from under a folder, then turns to me. "Same time next week?"

Somehow I hear myself offering to take care of it. As I head to the cleaning cupboard to fetch rubber gloves and a bin liner, it occurs to me that I find the prospect of cleaning up Neville's urine-soaked bin more appealing than a night in the park. Not something to tell my mum.

THURSDAY 22nd OCTOBER

HANNAH

Shit. Not any old shit. The real kind that's about to hit the fan. I found two tampons at the bottom of my school bag whilst I was looking for my favourite pen this evening. Forget the pen, now I'm standing looking at the kitchen calendar trying to remember when my last period was.

I can't remember.

In films everyone seems to know when their periods are due – they have them marked in red in their diaries or whatever.

I don't have a diary.

I stand there for a moment longer and try to think. The tampons in my school bag came from the machine in the toilets by the science labs. It's the only one that still works and has "Mr Dhupam is a rabbit shagger" written in marker pen on the side. I had to make an emergency purchase after Year 11 assembly, which was the first one after term started…

I count forward past Jay's party, Mum's birthday, Lola's dentist appointment. Four weeks – it should have been then, right? – but I count another week then one, two, three, four, five, six days.

My finger rests on today's box:

Mum book club 7 p.m. – Life of Pi

That can't be right. About the date, not the book club

… although really it should be called film club, since Mum only ever reads the first few chapters before streaming the movie on Robert's laptop.

Focus, Hannah.

I count again. I'm nearly two weeks late – or is my period standing me up? Is it a no-show rather than a late show?

It can't be like that. In the movies everyone's always sick for a few days before they take the test. They think it's those dodgy prawns or a bad hangover, but no: baby.

But no: it can't be like that.

Really. It can't.

Robert's coming down the hall and I leave the kitchen, dodging past him on my way towards the stairs, then I'm in my room and at the computer. It's a very shiny new one, a present from Mum and Robert for my birthday in July. They hope it'll help with school work, but I like to think of it as an extension of my phone – email, iTunes, Facebook… I wonder if anyone's commented on my status…

Focus, Hannah.

I type so quickly that it takes a second attempt before Google asks me if I mean "pregnancy symptoms".

I suppose I do.

FRIDAY 23RD OCTOBER

HANNAH

It's the last day before half-term and it's raining when I walk out of the school gates and up the road. Katie is steaming because I've told her she can't come round to mine straight from school, that I'll come over to hers later. I've told her there's somewhere else I've got to be.

I hurry past the cemetery and try to forget it's where I pulled Mark Grey. He trod on my foot so hard as he grappled with my bra that I thought he'd broken it (my foot, not the bra). It kind of brought home to me that maybe he wasn't my type. Too chunky. And sweaty. You should see him during PE – gross. I wasn't joking when I said I can't forgive Katie for her bad taste.

By the time I get to Cedarfields and sign the visitors' book, water is running off my chin and it blurs my signature. I head to the end of the corridor, where I knock on the door and wait, listening to the shuffling and kerfuffling on the other side. Then the door opens.

"Hannah?"

"Gran." I step in and give her a hug, resting my nose on her tiny, bony shoulder and smelling her lily-of-the-valley perfume. I close my eyes, trying to remember what it was like when I was smaller than her and she was the one who had to be careful not to squeeze too tight. Tiny, bird-like body or not, she's the strongest person I know. The steadiest. The least judgmental.

"You're soaked." She steps back and eyes me suspiciously. "Don't sit down until you've dried yourself – there's clean towels in the bathroom. This place ain't no hotel, but they do have plenty of fresh linen."

I like the way she says "hotel" – as if there's no "o" in it. I spend a long time in the bathroom, towelling my hair dry, looking at my reflection, going to the loo just in case…

Gran watches me carefully when I come out and sit in the chair opposite. "What's up, pet?"

That's when the tears come and I reach out, knotting her fingers with mine. When my eyes clear I see there's a tissue on my knee that wasn't there before. It's rumpled and very, very soft and I know it's come from Gran's sleeve.

I open my mouth, but I can't form the words. Instead I just shake my head and start crying again, snuffling into the tissue until it's soggy with snot.

"Come on, now, Hannah, you're scaring me." I look through my tears to see her fix me with a stern glare. "What's the matter?"

"I think I'm pregnant."

The word seems to hang in the air for an impossibly long moment. Everything has stopped and the room holds its breath, waiting for the meaning to sink in. *Pregnant*. My insides are hollow and I can hear the word echo through me. Except I'm the opposite of hollow, aren't I? That's the problem.

Gran blinks once, then a couple of times, her lids fluttering over her eyes.

"Oh. Really?"

I nod and take a deep breath that wavers in my lungs like it's not sure it should be there.

"Oh," she says again, blinking some more. "Are you sure?"

"I looked up the symptoms on the Internet." She huffs at that. I'm always telling her stuff I've read on the Internet and every time she says that if everyone was meant to know everything, then God would have made us all much cleverer. "I've not been sick, but I've got the other symptoms – my boobs are tender, I'm tired…"

"You've not had your monthly visitor?"

I shake my head. "It should've been and gone by now."

I look up to see Gran looking at me with wise eyes, twinkly with the moisture that always seems to be trapped there. I can't tell what she's thinking. Is she disappointed in me? She must be. The thought makes me start to cry again, silent, sad tears spilling off my face and onto my school shirt.

"Hey, pet, shh." She pulls me to her. "You don't know anything for sure until you take a test. Have you?"

I shake my head into her cardigan. Gran gently pushes me upright and creaks out of her chair and takes a twenty out of her handbag. I get up, intending to wave it away, but she presses it into my hand and gives me a look that means business.

"There's a chemist round the corner by the parade. Get two tests and come back here." She strokes the back of my hand with soft, cool fingers. "You don't need to do this alone."

Rex is having a house party. Depending on who you ask, he's either celebrating the end of the half-term, or the end of his relationship with the invisible girlfriend. Either way, he plans to get wasted and get laid – in that order. He's invited half the school to his house tonight and it's all the guys have been talking about. Tyrone is grumbling because Marcy's got some modelling job that means she can't come. I say, "grumbling"; I mean, boasting.

I cut my visit to the old folks' home short so I could come early and hang out with Rex. I don't really know why he asked me over, but it's nice of him and since there's a certain weight of expectation from Mum that her son will socialize on Fridays, I accepted.

I'm starting to regret my decision.

"What do you reckon?" This is the fourth shirt he's tried on and it doesn't look that different from the last three.

"Fine," I say, looking at my phone and wondering when the others will get here.

"Come on, man. I need your help."

"Why?" I know nothing about clothes, nor why Rex cares. It's just a house party.

"You always dress cool. I want to look good."

"In that case I should have brought my mum over. She's the one who buys my clothes," I say, letting my guard down.

Rex laughs and I do too. It feels like we're mates.

"Seriously, though. I need to look good." He crashes back onto his bed and looks at me.

"Why?"

"Have you ever fallen for someone you shouldn't?"

I shrug, but Rex isn't really asking me – for which I am grateful.

"That's totally happening to me." He sits up and looks at me seriously. "Don't tell anyone this, but I'm, like, obsessed with Katie Coleman."

"Really?" I have no idea how he's found anything in her to obsess over. There's no depth there that I can see.

"I know, I know…" He doesn't. He thinks I'm puzzled because of her reputation. Actually that's the one thing I can understand Rex would find enticing, since he seems unbelievably desperate to get his end off. "But I just think she's got levels, y'know? She's such a tease, but half of it's just front."

There's an obvious joke there about the cup size of Katie's front, but I don't go for it.

"I thought you pulled her the other week?" The night I left the park with Hannah.

"Nah." Rex shrugs. "Was in a relationship, wasn't I?"

I hope that question is rhetorical, because if I had to answer, I'd tell him that it doesn't count if the person you're seeing doesn't exist.

"So … now you're single, you'll shag Katie?" I ask, without actually wanting to know.

"Might not be that easy, mate."

"Yeah, right." My disbelief is palpable.

"Just because you went there with Hannah doesn't mean Katie's the same…" I should remind him that Katie gave one of his friends a hand job behind the toilets in the park, but he's still talking. "Besides, you've seen how Tyrone is about Hannah – can't stand her."

There's no arguing with that. I could count on one hand the words he's spoken to me since the Hannah incident.

"You can't let Tyrone tell you who to fancy," I hear myself saying.

"I know, but he's my best mate and Hannah's *Katie's* best mate … I don't want it to be difficult if I start seeing her."

He wants to *go out* with her? I thought we were just talking about tonight.

I'd like to say that Tyrone's big enough to let his friends do whatever – whoever – they want, but that's a lie. Tyrone is someone who likes to control everyone – especially his friends.

HANNAH

Oh God. Oh God. Oh God. The last thing I want to do is go to a party, but if I bail on Katie she will literally kill me.

I guess that would solve my problem.

I'm late getting to hers and she's already fully made-up and wearing a bra that's two sizes too small in order to give her extra lift.

"You look like shit!" is the greeting I get and I swallow, my throat too dry to function.

Katie Im pregnant.

But one of her little brothers has come running into the hallway with a water pistol and she's too busy screaming at him not to ruin her skirt for me to get a word in. Silently, I go upstairs and empty the contents of my bag onto her bed. I packed in a hurry and I've forgotten to bring a pair of going-out pants. I'll just have to wear the ones I've got, even if they aren't all that sexy.

My heart stops beating – a second for every boy I can remember who's taken my pants off.

Then it starts up again and I go through the motions of getting ready, my brain on pause as I brush mascara deep into the roots of my lashes and dab gloss onto my lips, before I wriggle into the dress I brought. Katie's still downstairs and I can hear shouting. The walls are thin in her house and there isn't enough room for all the people that live here. Turning her iPod up, I stand side on to the mirror and pull my dress straight, staring at my reflected tummy as if I'll somehow see something there that I didn't notice before. It looks the same as ever to me. The door swings open and I jump back guiltily.

"You bring anything?" She means alcohol and I shake my head. "Why not? We can't turn up empty-handed."

"Why don't you sort it out for a change?" I snap and she looks at me, shocked for a second as she balances on the brink of being hurt before she teeters over into anger.

"What is *wrong* with you? You haven't been the same since you shagged that stuck-up Satan spawn." She's talking about Aaron Tyler. They aren't getting on too well after he told her to stop calling him Emo Boy during English today.

Katie doesn't like being told what to do.

"Sorry." Tell her now, Hannah.

But I can't.

"Whatevs. You should stop stressing over him. He's not even that good-looking." Katie then launches into a full-blown character assassination, as she adds some last-minute touches to her make-up. I get bored after the millionth time she slags off his clothes.

"I like the way he dresses," I say. I don't especially, but I can't stand hearing this any more. It's too much noise when all I want is quiet.

"You would," she says, tracing another line of black across her eyelid. "He dresses like Jay and his mates."

She's right – he does.

"It's probably because he came from that posh school," she carries on, switching to the other eye. "He's got more money than the rest of us."

"What posh school?" No one knows much about where Aaron came from. Still. Katie shrugs and I decide she's making it up. Besides, his family can't be *that* rich. I mean, Mr Tyler's only a teacher, so he can't earn much. Not like Robert, who shits Rolexes. Besides, although our school's not posh, it's hardly as if the people that go there are poor – you only need to clock how many of them wear new trainers each term.

Katie gets annoyed with me on the way to the party because I won't have a smoke or go halves on the gallon of vodka she wants to buy. I don't know what I'm doing about … It … but I can't help totting up all the drinks and cigarettes

I've had in the last month and the thought makes me feel panicky. Turns out me refusing to chip in doesn't matter since every offy we enter tells us to leave before we even get to the shelves. I'm kind of relieved, TBH, since there's no way they'd've fallen for Katie's blatantly fake ID anyway.

I apologize for forgetting to bring anything and Katie forgives me enough to link her arm in mine, although she slips it out the second we get to Rex's front door. It's Mark Grey that answers and he's so drunk he doesn't bother talking to our faces, just our tits.

"Rex is here," Katie whispers, as we walk in.

I stare at her. "Yes. Rex is here. It's his house. Where did you think he'd be?"

Katie scowls. "What is it with you? Did you down some bitch pills with your tea? You don't have to take the piss all the time, you know."

"Katie, I—" But she's already huffed off and I think better of shouting, "I'm pregnant!" across a crowded room. All I can see are people I don't want to talk to and boys I've either shagged or who've turned me down. I see Tyrone in the other room, surrounded by girls like he's the star in his own rap video and I see Aaron Tyler standing in a doorway talking to Anj. Although I sit with her and Gideon in French I don't see as much of Anj as I used to – we go way back – and for the first time in a while I wish things were different. Anj was always easier to talk to than Katie.

Oh *God*. I can't do this – *any* of this. I want to scream, I want to cry, I want to escape, but there's someone else at the front door and I hurry upstairs instead. Maybe there's somewhere I can be alone, get my head around things, work out what to do next. Why the *fuck* did I come here? I listen at a couple of the doors, hear the grunts, groans and arguments you'd expect and walk in on Fletch, sprawled, T-shirt rucked up and baring his belly as he snores on the floor. I can't believe I let him have sex with me.

It can't be his.

The thought floods through me turning my blood to ice and I feel faint with fear.

The next room I try is a connecting wardrobe you can get into from either the hall or what must be Rex's parents' room, proving my point that the kids at Kingsway aren't exactly poor. There's someone in the bedroom, on the phone by the sound of it, but I feel safe as I slide my back down the far wall until I'm sitting on the floor.

Maybe I can just sit in here for a bit. No one will notice.

AARON

Gideon comes back from the kitchen carrying three plastic cups filled with something pink.

"Really? Punch? I'm never sending you for drinks again, gay boy," Anj says.

"It was this or very vintage Martini Rosso. Take your pick, straight girl." Gideon hands over the drinks as I watch Hannah Sheppard jog up the stairs. The contents of my cup smells like paint stripper. No way am I drinking that.

"So how come you moved schools?" Anj thinks she's making small talk, but the reason I moved schools is far from small. I say something about needing a change of scenery and ignore the glance she exchanges with Gideon. There's a bit of a pause.

"Not acting as your bestie's wingman now he's flying solo tonight?" Gideon asks.

It takes a second for me to catch up. "Rex and I aren't best mates."

"I was talking about God's Gift." Gideon nods towards the crowd of girls that have accumulated around Tyrone's spot on the sofa.

I laugh. "I am definitely *not* Tyrone's mate. Best or otherwise."

They look surprised – Tyrone's friendship is something I'm supposed to want.

"I pulled Tyrone once," Anj says, wistfully, and Gideon and I stare at her. "Don't look so shocked – I'm a good catch for a boy who likes a bit of cream in his coffee."

"Of course you are," Gideon says, grinning. "I just would have expected to *know* you pulled such a hottie. When did that happen?"

"Ages ago. The Easter you abandoned me to go to South America." Gideon rolls his eyes and I get the impression this is an old argument. "It was before Marcy made him cool."

"What?" I say. I thought it was the other way around.

"It's all because of his girlfriend that Tyrone became King of Kingsway. Before then he was just some guy who was quite good at basketball."

"Not even that good. Rex is way better." Gideon takes

up the story. "But Tyrone got taller and toned-er last term and fooled everyone into thinking he was better than he really is. Rex is happy to go along with it. Those two have been mates for ever, so little old Rex is just pleased that he's not been left behind."

"It's Marcy that rules the school." Anj nods, dark eyes wide and earnest. "Her and that coven of bitches she surrounds herself with. Don't get on the wrong side of her, or you'll get cut from everything. You may as well stop existing."

They must have seen my face. Sceptical is an under-statement.

"Seriously! There was a girl who left our school last year because Marcy teased her every single second until it became too much."

I want to ask what happened, but this topic of conversation is making me uncomfortable. I don't like speculating on why people leave schools.

"Have you seen Katie Coleman's here?" Gideon asks Anj. "Word is that she's after Rex."

"Poor guy." Anj laughs, then looks around. "Where's Hannah, then?"

My eyes slide towards the stairs, and I notice that Tyrone has left his spot on the sofa and is walking up them.

HANNAH

The carpet in here is so deep that the door carves an arc across the pile as it opens. I wipe the tears from my face and wait to tell whoever it is that they'll have to find somewhere else to shag.

"Hey, kitten." Tyrone comes in, shuts the door and sits down next to me. I never noticed how creepy it is that he thinks calling me "kitten" is sexy. Kittens are about as sexy as granny pants.

"Hey." My left leg is buzzing where his thigh touches mine and I wonder if I could lose myself in this feeling.

"You're looking pretty gorgeous tonight." He brushes his fingers gently up my bare leg and under my hem. I breathe in deeply, focusing on his touch. "Is this for me?"

I nod. It's not – Tyrone didn't exactly factor in to my thoughts when I grabbed this dress off the back of my chair. More on my mind.

I'm pregnant.

I stamp down on that thought so hard my head hurts with the effort and I concentrate on Tyrone as he twists round and leans over. His eyes are closed as he leans in and kisses me. It starts slow, but it soon gets more exciting, more promising. I remember how easy it is to turn him on and I slide under him, legs opening so our bodies fit together better in this cramped little space. I don't even realize that my hands have worked their way under his T-shirt until I'm scratching my nails gently along his spine.

He kisses my neck and I sigh at the feel of his lips on my skin.

What am I doing?

This is such a stupid idea.

His hands run up my body straight to my breasts.

"Ow." I wince, surprised at how bruised they feel.

"Sorry," he murmurs then slides his face down into my cleavage. "They just look amazing."

He nudges aside the top of my bra and that's when I freak out.

"Get off!" I buck and twist under him, suddenly claustrophobic with this boy's body on top of me in this closet in someone else's house.

Tyrone sits away from me. "What's wrong?"

"I can't…" I'm breathing fast and shallow and I feel faint. I can't do this. I can't have sex with Tyrone. I can't.

"Hannah, are you all right?"

"No!" I shriek. I'm shivering. Tyrone reaches out but I shuffle away from him, only there's not much room to move and I press my hands to my face, wishing him away.

I hear the *swoosh* of the door on the carpet.

AARON

Tyrone is crouching on the floor of what appears to be a wardrobe talking to a girl who's pressed herself right into the corner, dress ridden up far enough that I can see her pants. She looks up. It's Hannah.

"Get out!" Tyrone's voice is squeaky with fear.

"I think it's you that should get out." My voice is cold and hard and the sound of it scares me even more than it does him. That voice does not come from a good place. It comes from a part of me that I'm supposed to have left behind. Before I know it, I've pulled Tyrone up and out of

75

the door, his face so close to mine I can almost taste the sweat standing out on his skin.

I'm trying to reel it back in and my silence gives him a chance to speak. "I don't know what you think you saw…"

"I think I saw you behind a door with a girl who I just heard yell 'no' at you." My grip on myself is distinctly less steady than the one I've got on the boy in front of me.

"You what?" Puzzled then horrified. "No, it's not like that. I wasn't … shit, man, you think I'd do that?"

He takes my silence to mean that I do.

"Aaron! There's no way I'd force myself on a girl. I swear. We were fooling around and it was all fine then she just went mental. I swear. We wasn't even doing anything yet. I swear on my *life*, man. Swear it."

I walk past him and shut the door. He might be telling the truth, but I'll wait and hear Hannah's side. Although she's pulled her dress down, she's still shaking, so I take off my jumper and give it to her.

"Thanks," she says as she wraps it around her. "You must think I'm such a head case."

"I don't really think anything."

"I heard what you said to Tyrone. Don't worry, no one can make me do anything I don't want to do. Least of all him. Least of all that." She smiles as she says it, fleeting and small.

"I'm glad to hear it," I say. "I didn't want to have to fight him."

It sounds like a joke and Hannah smiles again, a little bigger.

"That doesn't surprise me." Then she sighs and she seems faded, deflated, miserable. "I just want to go home."

HANNAH

Aaron walked me home. We didn't talk much, but it was nice to have the company.

All I can think about is how this happened. I use condoms, FFS, and I know they were all on properly because I'm the one doing it. Tyrone put up a bit of a fight, but if he's refusing to wear one for me... I know I've got a reputation – ask Katie who I lost it to and she'll say it was the summer-jobber at Lola's playgroup, ask anyone at school and they'll say whatever name they saw scratched in a park bench or heard whispered in the corridor – but whatever, whoever, whenever they say, I'm not a skank. There are times when it's not been, like, full-on sex, but has there been a tiny possibility of something ending up where it shouldn't...? No. There is definitely no chance that I got pregnant from not wearing knickers in a nightclub and straddling that guy's lap while we pulled. That's the kind of question you read in problem pages and the agony aunt calls you out for being incredibly stupid on more than one level.

But I am being stupid, because I know exactly when this happened, don't I?

Yeah, I use condoms. Except for that one time, with that one person...

I open up the text conversation we had afterwards and

skim down the threads until I reach the last one I sent:

Just a 1 nite thing? thats it? srsly?!

And I make myself read his reply, no matter how much I know it will hurt:

What did u think was going to happen?

Not this, that's for sure.

SATURDAY 24TH OCTOBER

HALF-TERM

HANNAH

There's an angry voicemail from Katie. She must have been drunk when she left it because all her words are slurred together and she repeats herself a few times. There's something about being worried. (Which meant she hadn't checked her texts before calling me. As if I'd leave without telling her.) Then she tells me that Tyrone was looking for me. And something that's so garbled I only catch Rex's name after the second listen. Basically, I'm a bad friend.

I stare at the text I'm about to send.

Im pregnant…

Then I delete it and ask if she'd like to hang out in town later.

HANNAH

Since Katie's decided she's in a mood with me, I've been concentrating on how to tell my mum. I've tried, I really have. But I can't work out when to do it:

* over dinner: *This casserole is lovely. The beans look like tiny little foetuses. FYI, I'm growing one of those. Foetuses, not beans.*

* in the car with Lola singing in the back: *Hey, Lolly, shush a minute. So, Mum, did I mention I'm pregnant? Please don't drive into that wheelie bin. Or that postman. Or the side of that house.*

* in the middle of a homework/school work/too-much-time-going-out argument: *NONE OF THAT SHIT MATTERS, MOTHER! I'M PREGNANT, ALL RIGHT?*

I know it sounds spineless, but I'm scared of how she'll react.

You see, Mum's a nurse.

At the Family Planning Clinic.

Yeah. I know.

We had the chat about the birds and the bees ages ago, with regular refreshers on the occasional car journey. I'm better educated about sex than on any subject I'm taking for GCSE, but then it's not like I have History books lying on my kitchen table with key facts written in teen-speak the way Mum's leaflets shout "Rubber is kinky – get dressed before you get down" and "Nothing cool about chlamydia" at me whilst I eat breakfast. It would be very hard not to have a clue in this house.

But it's always – *always* – been a case of "As soon as you're sixteen, we'll get you an appointment." There's not a single part of Mum's brain that suspects it might be a bit late by then. And the thought of *me* being the one to bring it up... It's one thing talking about fictional sex, but a whole conversation of cringe if she knew I was *actually* doing it. A thought that's enough to keep me away from the Clinic even on her days off – the girls on the reception gossip so badly, Mum'd know about it before I even got home.

So condoms are the only option I've got. You can buy them at Boots.

And there's always the morning-after pill. Not that *that* went to plan.

In the back of my mind I always thought I'd go and get an abortion. Simples.

The reality? Not so simples.

This is life and death we're talking about. I mean, I don't think you exist until you're born, not properly, but there is something in there and it's something that matters. If babies in the womb didn't count until they came out then no one would give pregnant people who smoke funny looks, or tut too loudly when they have a drink. There wouldn't be all these rules and guidelines about what's good for the baby if the baby didn't matter at all.

But is it *alive*? Would I be *killing* it?

You hear about people changing their mind outside clinics because they find out that their foetus has already got fingernails or genitals or a tattoo saying "Mum" on its arse or whatever. But it's not like fingernails = soul. They don't qualify you for anything other than a manicure.

I'm all for choice, but what happens when you *really* don't want to choose?

AARON

Mum has taken the day off work to go shopping with me for some new clothes. She finally noticed that each of my five T-shirts is on the cusp of disintegrating, although I think the last straw was discovering a hole in the crotch of my only jeans.

After three shops Mum decides that it's time for lunch. There's a brief squabble when she tries to make me decide where to eat. I don't care where we eat so long as it's not sushi, but Mum seems to take it personally when I say this. It's like I have to care about *everything* these days and today there's a lot of things to care about. Grey socks or black? Baggy, skinny or straight leg? For some reason she wanted my opinion on where to park the car. When she pushed me on the lunch issue, I snapped that it was up to her.

We aren't on the best of terms when our food arrives.

"They've given you a baked potato when you asked for chips," she says and turns to call back the waitress.

"Mum, don't – it's fine," I hiss and she turns back to me.

"I knew that girl wasn't listening." She starts trying to shuffle some of her chips onto my plate.

"What are you doing?" I move my plate away and some chips tumble to the floor. "Stop it. I'm fine with a baked potato."

"Fine, Aaron." She slams down her plate so some more chips escape. "I'm just trying to have a nice day with my son. Is it too much to ask that our waitress gets the order right?"

This isn't about chips.

"Mum, we *are* having a nice day." She looks at me dubiously. "You know I don't have to have everything my own way to enjoy myself."

"You should have your order your own way," she says, but she's smiling and I smile back.

"Whatever, I just mean stop trying to please me all the time. If I say I don't care about something, it doesn't mean I don't care about *anything*. It just means I want you to choose."

"OK." Mum nods, then adds, "But, Aaron, you're my son, and what I want is to make sure you're happy, so don't bite my head off for trying."

"No, Mum," I say. "I'll try to remember that."

She never used to worry about making me happy.

But they found a new school, new jobs, new house – new life.

My happiness means more than it should to my parents.

HANNAH

It's late but Mum's in the sitting room finishing a coffee – I don't see another mug, which means Robert's having his in his study. Now is the perfect time. I psych myself up in the doorway: just do it, just do it, just do it—

"What is it, Hannah?" Mum hasn't even looked up from her magazine. All I can see from here are upside-down pictures of soap stars in bikinis. I walk round until they're the right way up and sit on the arm of the chair.

"She's put on a lot of weight," I say, pointing to one of them.

"She's skinnier than me," Mum says, pursing her lips.

"Not really." I'm lying because I want to get into her good books.

Mum gives me a sideways glance and an eyebrow-raise. "Smaller than a size-six midget, am I?" She shakes her head. "Whatever it is you want, the answer's no. You've been out ever since school broke up and I've not seen you so much as look at that fancy new computer you made such a fuss about getting to help you with school work."

The words stall between my brain and my mouth.

Mum turns the page and the banner reads, "Grandmother at thirty – and pregnant!" There's a picture of an impossibly-young-looking woman and her daughter both posing with their giant bellies touching so it looks like a Maths diagram.

Mum tuts and turns the page. "I get enough of that at work."

This is not the right time.

WEDNESDAY 28ᵀᴴ OCTOBER

HALF-TERM

HANNAH

I have failed to tell my best friend.

I have failed to tell my mother.

Who else is there?

My thumb shakes as I scroll through my phone looking for an answer. I make it to the bottom before I scroll back up, mentally crossing out each entry as I go. For a moment I pause when I get to his number and before I know what I'm doing I'm holding the phone up to my ear, not sure whether I actually want him to answer.

"Hello?"

"It's me." My voice is so quiet that I clear my throat ready for whatever I'm going to say next.

"Of course it is."

Is that a sigh in his voice? I can't help but react to it. "You didn't have to answer if you didn't want to talk to me."

"What? Where's that coming from?" He's annoyed now.

"It's not like you've made an effort…"

"We talked about this."

"No, actually, we didn't. We texted about this. Texting isn't talking."

"Whatever, Han, this isn't a good time."

"It's never a good time!" I snap, thinking about all the

times I have tried to tell the people that matter that I'm pregnant.

"Was there a reason you called? Or did you just want a fight?"

I close my eyes and think about him, the way he looked at me that night, the way he touched me – as if he wanted me more than anything in the world. There's a murmur in the background and I wonder what he was doing before he saw my number flash up on his phone. The possibilities that come to mind make me sick with jealousy.

"You still there?" he says, but I end the call before he can hear that I'm crying as hard as I did the day after I got pregnant.

I have failed to tell the father.

My phone rings, but I let it go to voicemail, knowing he won't leave a message. He doesn't try again. Through my tears I carry on scrolling up until I reach Anj. Once upon a time she'd be the first person I'd call – now she's just the first person in my phone book.

I throw my phone across the room and press my face into my pillows and cry so much that it feels like I'm turning inside out.

This is it. Decision time. I know what all the people I've tried to tell would say. Who, out of my mum, my best friend and the absent father-to-be, would tell me to keep it?

Maybe that's what's stopping me: I don't know what I want, except that I want to be the one who decides.

THURSDAY 29TH OCTOBER
HALF-TERM

HANNAH

I went to see Gran today. She managed to get me a doctor's appointment tomorrow morning – I was too upset to book it myself. She held me tightly and let me sob on her, stroked my hair and told me she understood when I explained why I couldn't tell Mum.

When I left, she kissed my cheek.

"Paula will love you no matter what you decide. Just like I will."

Neither of us mentioned my dad. Her son.

FRIDAY 30TH OCTOBER
HALF-TERM

HANNAH

I had my answer planned, but the doctor asked the wrong question. She didn't ask what I was going to do next. She asked me what I wanted. And that question had a different answer.

And I told the truth. I want to keep it.

Shit.

What now?

MONDAY 2ND NOVEMBER

HANNAH

Katie and I are pulling a sickie for PE. She's forged a doctor's note saying that she's got back problems and I told Prendergast that I'm on my period – something that couldn't be further from the truth. He'd taken some convincing because he's learned to be suspicious whenever me and Katie back out of team sports, but I played a blinder and cried at him. Works every time.

There's only two of us on the sick bench, which is exactly how we like it. Our books are open on our laps and from across the other side of the hall it looks like we might be working. I'm sure Prendergast isn't so stupid as to fall for it, although he *does* teach PE…

After a week of sulking, it seems Katie's finally forgiven me for Friday. Whilst I'd simply like to write a note in the margin of her Physics worksheet telling her that I'm preggers, I choose an easier starter for ten, planning on working my way up to the harder category of Life-Changing News.

"So," I say, glancing sideways at Katie. "Rex, huh?"

"What about him?" She does a better blank face than me, I'll give her that.

"Spoken to him since his party?"

"No."

"Text?"

"No."

I roll my eyes. "Guys are such dicks."

But Katie's looking at me strangely. "What do you mean?"

"The whole avoiding you after he's got what he wanted. Lame."

"Who said he's avoiding me?" Katie says, scowling. "For that matter, who says he got what he wanted?"

"I just th—" This is not going according to plan.

"What? That I'd shagged him?" Katie's doodling some angry circles in the corner of her worksheet – one of them has teeth and a little frowny face.

"Sorry, Katie. I didn't realize…" Because this is something that *never* happens. When Katie wants a guy, she gets him. Immediately. I know she wants Rex – and he's *desperate* for her – so what's she playing at?

"No. Well. Unlike some of us, I'd tell you if that was what happened."

"What's that supposed to mean?"

"Nothing."

"Is this about Aaron?"

Katie draws another circle – this time she gives it a pair of horns and a pointy tail. "First you're all mopey about it and then you're all pally with him. I heard he took you home after the party."

I look away guiltily. I hadn't told her about that.

"What are you doing, Han? The boy's bad news."

"Oh, really?" I say, sharply. "And you know because…?"

"He just is."

"You're wrong. And it doesn't matter anyway because

there's nothing going on there."

She snorts her disbelief.

"Charming. Now you're showing a little willpower around Rex you think you can judge me?" I'm pissed off that she won't believe me. "Let's see how long *that* lasts. I give it a week, tops, before you do the dirty and you never speak to him again."

Katie looks at me face-on so that I get the full effect of her lip curl. "You think that's all I'm good for? One shag and he'll fuck off?"

I frown. That isn't actually what I think at all – I think it's the other way round – but everything I'm saying is coming out wrong and I decide to shut up before I do some lasting damage. We sit there in silence, Katie drawing increasingly disturbing faces in her circles and me watching as Rex and Aaron stand in the corner of the hall together, laughing about something.

Katie and Rex and me and Aaron. Worst. Double-date. Ever.

AARON

"How was your first day back?"

"Fine," I say, twisting round to throw my bag on the back seat as Dad pulls out of the car park to join the queue of traffic edging up the hill. A few seconds pass before I realize he's waiting for more information. "It was fine, Dad. Really."

"What does that mean?"

"Fine as in OK, as in all right, as in satisfactory."

"When I write 'fine' in an assessment I mean 'fine as in could be better'."

"When I say 'fine', I mean fine as in…" I think about lying and decide against it. "As in nothing special."

"But not…?"

"No. Nothing awful, either." Because for that to happen I'd have to care about something, and I don't. I lean to turn the stereo on, but Dad turns it back off using the remote on the steering column. I switch it on again. He turns it off. On. Off.

"For God's sake, Aaron!" he snaps and I sit back in my seat, Dad looking over at me, huffing. He's angry and sad and frustrated. Everything my father feels shows on his face – it's what makes him a good teacher. He loves his job, loves his subject and his passion is infectious. The flipside is that he can't hide anything, even the things he'd rather no one could see.

"Dad—"

"You're not trying."

I say nothing.

"You can fool your mother, but I can see that all this park business is a charade. Tyrone, Rex, Mark Grey … they're not your type."

"And who is?" I say, but there's no substance to my sarcasm.

"Let's not get into this again. I know it's not my place to choose your friends." Dad looks over at me. "Which leaves it up to you."

I was worried he might say that.

THURSDAY 5TH NOVEMBER

BONFIRE NIGHT

AARON

Dad does not like this time of year. He does not like Diwali;
he does not like Bonfire Night. We should keep him
indoors with The Kaiser, although I reckon the cat has fewer
issues with fireworks than my father. I've already lost count
of the number of times he's used the words "pyromaniac"
and "explosives" as he catalogues how many pupils he's
caught trying to bring fireworks in today. I'm relieved it's
only a short journey to Cedarfields. The staff asked if I'd
help out tonight instead of tomorrow. I get a sparkler, a
jacket potato and an excuse not to listen to Dad.

"I'm cold," Neville complains once we're out on the
balcony.

"Here," I say, handing him a second coat. He eyes
it suspiciously, but cold trumps taste and he puts it on.
It's my mum's and he wrinkles his nose at the smell of
her perfume. Some of the residents are in wheelchairs,
covered up with fleecey blankets and for a moment I'm
hit with a nightmare image of the lot of them bursting
into flames from a stray spark. But the wind's blowing
the other way and we're miles from anything even faintly
flame-like. I can see Neville's got the same idea because
he makes a joke about fire extinguishers and glares at
his nemesis, Donald Morton, who ignores him but makes

a comment about how nice it is to smell an expensive scent these days. It's all I can do to stop Neville shedding Mum's coat and bolting back inside.

"Shouldn't you be out with your boyfriend tonight?" Neville's still convinced I'm gay. It's because I'm clean. Neville is not clean and is as heterosexual as they come. He is the walking definition of a dirty old man.

"I am," I say and wink at him.

"Aye, well you could do worse."

"You too." I give him a cheeky grin.

"Don't push your luck," he grumbles, but he's smiling.

The fireworks start up on the lawn, prompting a few half-hearted "ooh"s and a good deal of "used to be better in my day" murmurings but the naysayers soon fade to silence as the rockets are fired up, squealing from the lawn to burst shattered shards of light against the night sky.

The home is at the top of the valley and, as our fireworks start thinning out, we can see others blooming over the rest of the county. It's beautiful and even Neville, whose default setting is curmudgeonly, mumbles something about it being "bonny up here". The staff hand out sparklers to those who present a low fire risk and I'm surprised when Neville takes one, but he waggles it around enthusiastically, boyish glee on his face as echoes of zigzags and loops fire in our retinas. I wonder who he really is – who he was – before he became such a cantankerous old bastard.

"What're you staring at?" Neville's voice snaps me out of it.

HANNAH

As always, Gran came to ours for Bonfire Night. It doesn't matter that she's from Dad's side of the family, not tonight, when she and I sit on the bench by the back door having the same conversation as last year, tracing over old memories to keep them fresh, remembering Grampa's favourite night of the year. Remember, remember, the fifth of November.

There's less talk this year with the weight of responsibility sitting between us – the knowledge that I'm pregnant and that I've not told my mum. Gran can't understand what's stopping me now the decision's been made, but she's old, she's forgotten what the future looks like when you're fifteen. Who she is depends on things that have already happened. Who I am depends on what lies ahead. All the things I thought would happen have vanished – just like that – and without them I'm not so sure who I am any more. I need to get a bit more *me* going on before I face my family.

Mum drops us back at Cedarfields before going to get some petrol, so I have time to have a cup of tea with Gran before I say goodbye. I'm paying zero attention to my surroundings as I walk along the corridor to reception.

"Hannah?" There's a tap on my shoulder and I turn around. Aaron Tyler. What's he doing here?

"Hey, Ty," I say, tucking a strand of hair behind my ear. There are lots of stray bits of hair since I was chasing Lolly around the garden and had to burrow under a hedge to catch her. Why did I have to bump into someone here?

Why him? We haven't spoken since Rex's party.

"Could you maybe just call me Aaron?"

Crap. I've been calling him by the wrong name. I just assumed he was a surname-nickname guy.

"Yeah," I say and sort of edge sideways, hoping he'll get the hint. I don't want to talk – I look a mess in this skanky old hoodie and I bet Mum's already filled up and got back to the car park.

"How come you're here?" he asks, walking along the corridor so that I can't escape him. I keep the pace up.

"Visiting my gran."

"Yeah?"

"You?"

"Same. Visiting." He looks like he doesn't want to talk about it.

God, this is a rubbish conversation. Why did he even stop to talk to me? We walk in silence until we reach the doors.

"Hey, look," he says, almost touching my arm.

"My mum'll be waiting," I say, hoping he'll hurry up.

"I just wanted to tell you something. About the other night…"

"Can you forget what you saw? It was all a big mistake."

He looks confused and then nods. "The Tyrone thing. Right."

It's my turn not to understand. Wasn't that what he was talking about?

"I meant you and me."

Great. So this is why he stopped me – to embarrass me on every level possible.

"I told you before. It. Doesn't. Matter." I start to open the door, but he holds it shut against me. I don't like him doing that, but the action puzzles me. It doesn't seem very Aaron-Tyler-teacher's-son-ish.

"Listen to me, please," he says, in a very serious voice. It's not threatening or anything ... but it makes you listen.

I cross my arms and wait.

"I wanted to explain something." He sighs, sort of to himself. "Look, it's not that I wouldn't ... you're really pretty..."

I snort.

"Less so when you do that."

I'm so surprised that I almost snort again. *Almost*. I stop myself because even though I'm pregnant, and even though I *know* he's not interested, I still care what he thinks.

"I really like you. Not a jump-your-bones variety of liking. I just think you're interesting."

Huh?

"I mean ... wow, I'm not doing this very well, am I?"

"No." I am officially lost.

"I'm not up for anything romantic right now – with girls, or boys, either, for the record."

"Glad we got that cleared up," I say. Gideon will be disappointed – he's convinced Aaron's a closet. He hasn't shut up about him since Rex's party. In French he declared that shagging me was all part of being in denial. I didn't correct him on the facts.

"But I do want to know you better, Hannah. You seem..." He's lost for a moment, then finds what he's looking for.

On cue my mum runs out of patience and beeps the horn.

Mum is full of questions on the drive home. All of them are about "that good-looking boy" she saw me talking to.

"If I'd realized you were talking to him, I wouldn't have sounded the horn. I thought you were gossiping with one of the nurses."

"He's just a boy from school, Mum," I say, bored of this conversation.

"He's cute," she says.

"You think?"

"You're telling me that you don't?" She obviously doesn't believe a word I'm saying so I stay silent. Instead I think about what he said as he opened the door for me, the cold wind ruffling his hair as he looked at me.

You seem worth knowing.

If he'd said that to me at school, or in the park I'd have come out with something sarky in response. But standing at the entrance to Cedarfields, I hadn't felt like being that person.

I wonder if the person Aaron saw just now is the person he sees at school.

AARON

Neville is unhappy with the state of play because, for the first time in two months, it looks like I might actually win.

"We'll have to learn another game," he grunts as he sweeps the cards off the table and starts shuffling them. His knuckles might be the size of golf balls and his skin mottled and knotted with veins, but the cards dance in his fingers like a black and red lightshow. "Here," he hands me the pack, "you shuffle."

I stack it so badly that half the cards splash to the floor. Once I've collected them I sit up to see Neville failing to hide a satisfied smile. He holds out his hand and waggles his fingers, taking the deck back and showing me how to shuffle them properly.

It's long after dinner, but we're sitting in the dining-room with the lights off, apart from the lamp by our table, and we're all alone. The door's open and I can hear the television in the opposite room, can see the echo of coloured light on the doorframe.

I look up as someone walks past. It's Hannah.

She usually visits on Sundays. After Bonfire night I got a call from Neville – the first ever – asking me to come visit him on Sunday. He didn't say why and when I got there, I got the usual underwhelming welcome and all we did was play cards next to this window and argue about stuff on the news. No different to usual. Hannah and her gran were walking in the grounds and Neville pointed her out to me, asking me if I liked the look of her. I told him we went to the same school and he told me that her gran was one of *the better ones*. Praise indeed.

I watch Neville's hands as he cuts the pack.

I'm the only person who visits him. Even so, when I started popping in on my round of tea-time chats, he didn't seem to want me around. He still doesn't. But after a grunted "You again?" we hang out. We talk. Not about much in particular, but he starts to relax and tells me things, teaches me.

"You paying attention?" he says, snapping me back out of it.

"No," I confess.

"Too busy thinking about your girlfriend?" He looks at me beneath bushy white brows. There's nothing wrong with his eyesight, particularly where girls are concerned, so I'm not surprised he noticed Hannah walk past.

"I've told you before, she's not my girlfriend."

"You're an idiot not to try. She's got that look to her." I don't say anything because I don't want to encourage him but he carries on anyway. "You can tell she knows what she's doing."

"You know she's only fifteen?" I say. Hannah's one of the youngest in our year.

"So? I lost my virginity when I was thirteen."

"Thanks for that," I say and concentrate on trying to

thumb the cards together.

"Sandy Dixon – two years older than me. I thought I'd hit the jackpot, I'll tell you. She were a corker, had a tiny waist but hips you could hang a coat off." He's gazing off into the middle distance, remembering. "Fantastic arse."

I smile. Swapping sex stories is definitely not why Mum got me this placement.

"Mine was a girl I met on holiday this summer," I say.

"A girl?"

"Yes, Neville, a girl."

"Short hair, tiny tits and a moustache?"

"No. Long hair. Medium breasts. No moustache that I could see." I look at him levelly and he grins.

"Does she have a name?"

"Kerry," I say, remembering sneaking away to the beach and finding a discarded sun lounger, hands getting into places easily because she was only wearing a sundress and a bikini and I wasn't wearing anything under my shorts. We were both utterly rubbish, but it hadn't been unpleasant. The next night had been better.

"Did you see her again?"

I shake my head. I left her behind in Australia along with the pain I'd taken with me.

I watch as Neville lifts up the corners of the cards I've dealt. It feels good to share my history with someone. I can't do this at school – there'd be too many questions. The past isn't something to be cut and pasted into the present; I'd have to unfold the whole thing like a newspaper, showing every column just to point to one caption. I don't want anyone to see the headlines in my past. All Neville and I know about each other are our names. No context, no politics, no preconceptions. Knowing absolutely nothing about each other makes it easier to share the most private of memories.

Neville might not be the type of friend my dad had in mind, but he's good enough for me.

HANNAH

I'm knackered. Bone-tired. I think it's to do with the pregnancy. And I've been drinking loads of water, so I need the loo every five seconds. I squeeze in another pee before I leave and it's when I come out that I see Aaron leave the dining room with Neville. At least, I assume that's him.

When the old coot sees me he winks at me.

Must be Neville. Gran told me that the guy Aaron comes to visit is a perv. Well, she used better language than that, but that's what she meant. Apparently the nurses call him Randy Robson – which I guess is his surname. Grandad on Aaron's mum's side? Although I find it hard to believe he'd be related to anyone so dodgy.

Aaron sees me and waves.

"Aren't you going to introduce me?" the old man says.

"Hadn't planned on it," Aaron says, but he's grinning. He's got a good smile, that boy. Not that you see it enough. "Hannah, this is Neville. Neville – Hannah."

"Charmed," Neville says, taking my hand and kissing it with dry lips.

"The pleasure's all mine," I say and wink at him the way he did just now.

Neville just looks at me and nods, then looks at Aaron. "Told you," he says. "I'll leave you babies to see yerselves out."

Neville shuffles off down the hall.

"He told you what?" I ask, but Aaron just shakes his head.

"How come you're here tonight?" he asks, as we walk to the glass doors.

"Jay's visiting this weekend," I say. "I don't want to miss Sunday dinner if he's going to stick around for it."

"Jay?"

"Stepbrother. He's doing Psychology at Warwick uni." Even I can hear the slight swell of pride in my voice. I sound like Robert.

"His dad your little sister's dad?"

I nod.

"She looking forward to seeing him?"

"Yup. He's stronger than me so he can chuck her about a bit more, which she loves. Until she bumps something and then she cries and comes running to me for a cuddle. Lola's not quite as tough as she thinks she is."

He's holding the door for me and when I glance up I see him looking at me closely.

SATURDAY 14TH NOVEMBER

HANNAH

I'm standing by my bedroom window. I'm clean, dressed and waiting for Jay to arrive. The window's wide open and I've stuck my head out like a dog in a car. It rained last night, so everything has that damp, fresh sheen to it, like the world's been given a once-over with a polishing cloth. It's weird. There's a whole world outside carrying on no matter what and I'm just here, standing in my bedroom, growing another little human inside me.

I put my hand on my tummy and wonder how big it is right now. Baked bean? Broad bean? Butternut squash?

Seriously. What's with my baby/vegetable obsession?

I look at my watch. He's late, which is hardly a surprise. I've decided I'm going to tell Jay about the baby – family hasn't exactly been his number one priority recently, but something like this trumps all-night drinking sessions and falling asleep in lectures. This is Jay: someone I can trust to stand by me while I tell everyone else.

Decision made, I feel almost calm, although God knows I shouldn't be. So much of this baby's life has already been decided, like whether it's a boy or a girl. If it'll have curly hair or straight. Right- or left-handed. Good at Maths or sucky at Science. Sporty or lazy. A life mapped out before it's even started living.

It's only my role that's left up to chance.

I feel a familiar rising panic and tap my tummy to distract myself.

"You OK in there?" I say. This is the first time I've spoken to it and it sounds like I'm a loony. Surprisingly enough the foetus has nothing to say back. I'll have to look up when they start kicking and stuff – not for a long while yet, I know, but I figure if I'm not sure what to look out for I might miss it.

A car pulls into our road. A red hatchback with a missing hub cap on the front wheel. Jay's car.

AARON

I close my book. I'm bored.

This is an epiphany. I haven't been bored in my own company for months.

I don't really know what to do with this information though. Who do I think I'd rather be hanging out with? There's only so much of Neville's company I can take and it's not as if I have many other options. I think about Hannah, but she gave me her number under very different pretences. Besides, it's not like she'd welcome a call whilst the anointed Jay is there.

I go and get a different book instead.

HANNAH

I don't like her. At. All.

She's too skinny. Too posh. Too blonde. Too loud. Too

snooty. WAY too patronizing.

I don't like the way she says Lola's name. "LO-la" – really stressing the "o", as if it's a sweet she can't quite fit in her too-perfect mouth. And she's one of those people who's all "don't mind me" when you can't help but mind her because she is UNBELIEVABLY ANNOYING.

I tear a strip off my naan with a vengeance.

Lola begged for Chinese, but this one says she can't eat Chinese, something about MSG. Then she said how much she loves Indian food. Lola's five years old – what's she going to find to eat at a curry house? But no, we've got to do what Jay wants and he'd rather make this angel-faced bitch happy than the little sister he hasn't seen for two months.

I helped Lola find something she could eat, but poppadums are no replacement for prawn crackers and she's sulking. She's knackered too – you can tell because she keeps rubbing her eyes every other forkful. Only no one seems to be paying attention to her because they're all too busy listening to Bitchbag tell us how amazing the curry in India is. She spent her gap year there, teaching blind/deaf/disabled children how to open up to love or some such shit. That's where she got her nose pierced and where she bought the thousand and one bangles that she's wearing round her wrist. It's like sitting at the table with Santa's reindeer trotting round you.

She tried to tell me what curry to order because Jay said I liked spicy food.

"You don't want a korma, Han." "Han" is not an

acceptable thing for her to call me. That is the name that only my family and close friends use. She will never be either. "Order a rogan josh. Or a biryani – ooh, look, they've got prawns. Do you like prawns? I love them."

"No. I don't like prawns."

"Oh, Hannah, of course you like prawns." Mum patted my hand as if I was no older than Lola. "She likes prawns, Imogen."

It doesn't matter whether I like prawns or not. I'm not meant to eat them and I was having a hard enough time trying to work out whether anything too spicy would give me the shits.

In the end I settled for a tikka and a naan – should be safe with the same thing as Lolly, surely?

Jay's looking at me funny across the table. When no one's looking he mouths, *"Are you OK?"* at me. I just look at him, then look at *her* and back at him.

Why hadn't he said he was bringing home his new girlfriend?

AARON

I finish my book and look at the clock beside my bed. It's late – nearly midnight. All of a sudden I feel entirely exhausted. Not because I've been awake too long, or exerted myself too much by reading *Catch-22* in one afternoon, although that's no mean feat.

It is living that exhausts me. Sometimes it's all I can do to get through a day and today has been especially hard.

Perhaps because for the first time in six months I didn't want to spend it alone.

HANNAH

So much for my plan. Jay went straight to his room with Imogen when we got back – he didn't even come down to say goodnight to Lolly properly.

But when I come out of the bathroom he's there, waiting.

"What's up?" he says.

I just look at him. "It's the first time you come home and you bring your girlfriend with you. Could you not tear yourself away from her for one night to spend some time with your family?"

Jay folds his arms across his chest, hiding the familiar faded lettering of his ancient *Family Guy* T-shirt. "Harsh, much?"

"Is it?" I say and I walk past him to my room angry with him, with his girlfriend, with myself. That's the only chance I'll have to tell him face-to-face and I bottled it.

MONDAY 23RD NOVEMBER

AARON

Today I'm sitting the first of my mocks. In one hand I have a clear zip-lock pencil case containing a pencil loaded with new lead, three black fine-liner pens, a short ruler and enough geometry gadgets to shake a perfectly perpendicular stick at. In my other hand I'm holding a calculator that has more functions than a Smartphone and a "lucky" coin – a quarter stamped flat in front of my eyes in Disneyland when I was ten years old. I've taken it to every exam since and my results have been pretty good. I doubt this has anything to do with the coin, but it's small, it's something to play with between questions and, what the hell, it might be lucky.

It's Prendergast, whose lesson we're missing, who opens the doors, not bothering to *shush* us properly when we file in and murmur to one another as we work out where to sit. It takes me a while to find my seat but when I do, I see I'm sitting across the aisle from Hannah.

Sheppard. Tyler. Makes sense.

She smiles at me as she pulls her chair out. She's got a litre bottle of water with her.

"Thirsty?" I ask, looking at the bottle.

"Uh-huh," she says and takes a sip straightaway.

"Pace yourself. You might run out."

"Ha, ha," Hannah says. "You're just jealous."

I smile. Then I realize everyone else has settled in and is watching the clock at the front of the hall.

"Good luck!" I give Hannah a cheesy thumbs up and she rolls her eyes.

"*You too,*" she mouths around another swig from her bottle. Then Prendergast is walking past, handing out spare paper and I start to get a little bit nervous, a little bit excited and my throat dries up.

I wish I'd brought a bottle of water.

HANNAH

It's a bad sign when you don't understand the first question. Even worse if you don't understand the first fucking page.

I close my eyes and wonder if this is just another exam-based nightmare. Then I try turning the page.

AARON

Hannah's on to the next page already? I know the first lot of questions are pretty straightforward but...

Hang on. She's turning the next page. And the next.

My heart goes out to her. If she can't answer the first question then she's screwed.

Whatever's going on with Hannah mustn't distract me. One of the concerns about moving was that my grades might slide. I've got to get at least a *B* in Maths or Dad will kill me – Mum will hand him the knife.

I finish the first page and move on to the next. Harder questions and I get quite involved in one of them, so much so that I don't realize it's taken me fifteen minutes to get an answer and I'm not entirely convinced it's the right one. I'll check it later.

I glance over to Hannah, wondering how she's doing, hoping she's found something to answer. It's all about getting started. Once she answers one question she'll get in the zone, get calmer and the things that floored her at first won't seem so daunting.

She's not looking at the paper, which is pushed to one corner of her desk and threatening to slide off the edge. She's simply staring straight ahead.

As I look, I see a tear trickle down her cheek. She sniffs, really quietly and presses the sleeve of her shirt to her nose. She can probably feel me looking, so I turn away, back to my paper. It's not as if there's anything I can do to help her.

FRIDAY 11TH DECEMBER

HANNAH

It is 11 a.m. I have an appointment for my first scan in fifteen minutes' time.

My life is such a mess. The only person on this planet who knows I'm pregnant, apart from the doctor and the midwives who're always sucking the blood out of me and then checking the pressure to see if I've actually got any left, is my gran. My eighty-three-year-old gran, who lives in a semi-residential home and has to book trips out two days in advance, who is on so much medication I'm surprised that hugs from her aren't on the list of banned substances for pregnant people.

The thought of telling Mum proper terrifies me now that I've left it so long – it's like a rock at the bottom of my stomach. Last week I heard her talking to Robert whilst they watched the news. I was sitting in the dining room trying to jam something useful about Citizenship into my head, but the door was open and Mum talks loudly when she's off on one.

"These politicians should come down to the clinic – see what it's like on the frontline. Kids get no sex education any more – no wonder they're all at it like rampant rabbits without a thought about the consequences. They need educating, by the system, by their parents. So what if the teen pregnancy rate is falling? It's still the highest in Europe."

"At least it's going in the right direction."

But Mum carried on like Robert hadn't even said anything. "Do you know that some of them treat abortion as back-up birth control?"

"Rather that than there be no choice."

"*Of course.*" I could almost hear the shudder in her voice. "If everyone who got themselves in a fix went through with the pregnancy…"

My ears started ringing, the blood rushing to my head in horror. But Robert was saying something and Mum's rant changed direction.

"… no thought about what happens next. All they know is what they see on the Internet. Porn directors have taken on the role of parents, who just dodge the issue completely."

Robert laughed and I only caught the last part of what he said. "… so hard trying to tell Jay."

"Same with Hannah. Thank God those two have their heads screwed on."

I cried myself to sleep that night.

Of course, there is also the issue of the Father. But whilst we're on the subject of dads, there's always mine lurking in the background to add a little turd to the icing on my fucked-up cake of awfulness. I got an email from him part-way through the exams.

Dear Hannah, here's wishing you the best of luck in your exams. I know you'll nail them. Luv, Dad.

And there was an e-card with a four-leaf clover where the leaves peeled away to reveal a leprechaun dancing a jig with

"All the luck o' the Irish" in a speech bubble over his head.

Seriously. WTF?

"I know you'll nail them" – really? Have you spoken to Mum recently? Have you seen my reports? Nail them in the sense of literally taking in a hammer and pounding the sheets to the desk with a nail?

"Luv" is a word used by boys when they're too chicken to come out with the real thing on a Valentine's card. It is not OK to use it to express fatherly affection at the end of an email.

The card. There are no words.

From where I'm sitting I can see the seconds ticking away and watch as the minute hand jerks forwards towards fifteen-minutes past the hour. I stare at the hand as it edges round until it's nearly reached twenty past.

That's when I look down from the far end of the hall to the English paper on my desk, a half-started sentence about *Macbeth* scrawled on the top of my sheet of paper. I have failed these exams and now I've failed my baby.

SECOND

AARON

"So are you coming out tonight or what?" Tyrone clamps a hand on my shoulder so hard that I have to suppress a wince. He has been uncomfortably nice to me since Rex's party. I mean this in the most literal sense. I've endured nearly two months of regularly having his arm thrown round my shoulders, my back slapped, arm punched... Tyrone's love hurts – and it's earning me envious looks from the people who wish they had it. If only I could tell them that he's doing this because he *doesn't* like me, then the basketball lot could stop giving me death stares and go back to ignoring me... And then what would I do? Read books in my lunch hour and hang out with Neville until he falls asleep on his cards?

I don't know. That sounds like a slippery slope to me. Better to have fake school friends than none at all.

It seems the way that everyone celebrates the end of term around here is much the same as they celebrate the end of a week. By going to the park. Joy. I pitch up late, having helped Neville seal and stamp his Christmas cards. There were more than I expected and I asked who they were for.

"Family," was the gruff response, but after a little coaxing – and some of the Jack Daniel's I'd planned on

117

taking to the park – he warmed up and told me more.

"This one's my brother. Greville." I bit my lip and he nodded. "I know. Long story – and a boring one. You don't need to worry about these two." Both a "Mrs", both in Scottish cities. "This one's for my niece, Bea and her husband. Nice couple. This one's for her ex-husband. Not a good husband, but a great nephew-in-law. He married the woman he was banging the day his kid was born."

I looked suitably scandalized and Neville gave me every detail as if it was a lead story in today's tabloids. The way his memory works is fascinating. I thought the elderly became vague about everything when they hit the seventy mark, but Neville is sharp as a razor on things like this and he's pushing ninety. Knowing the difference between his dressing gown and his mac on the other hand…

"And this lot are all my favourite students."

That brought me up short.

"You know I used to lecture History, don't you?" And he filled in an answer in the empty crossword of his past. It explains why he's such a pain to watch films with – in future I'll bring ones set in a period he's not an expert on. Like the future.

The park is freezing. This is not a surprise because it is, after all, December, traditionally a time when people congregate around log fires and sip mulled wine whilst wearing knitted jumpers with reindeer on the front. But we are teens and we throw snowballs in the face of frostbite. Or we would if it ever snowed.

Rex and Katie are together on the swings. The two of them kissed at his party and a few weeks ago Rex copped a feel in the bushes, but since then they appear to be locked in some kind of holding pattern – neither of them pulling anyone else, but not taking things further with each other. It's driving Rex crazy – and in turn, me, as I'm the one he wants to talk to about it. I pointed out that Katie hates me and he should probably find someone else to help him, but he thought I was joking. The curse of Tyrone's "funny" tag lives on.

Tonight it's too cold for the pair to change the status quo and I get summoned over right away by the ever-clueless Rex. Hannah's sitting on the swing next to them looking bored.

"Drink?" I wave my bottle at her and she shakes her head. I pull a Thermos out of my bag and wave that at her. She laughs and nods and I pour her a hot chocolate, ignoring the revolted expression on Katie's face.

Hannah wraps her fingers around the plastic cup and breathes in the plumes of steam rising from the surface. She's wearing a woolly beanie pulled low to cover her ears and it's pushing the tip of her fringe across her face like a bird's wing. She catches me looking and gives a little frown.

"I like your hat," I say and sip from my own non-alcoholic cup, having handed Rex the whisky that Neville didn't get through.

Hannah and I swing back and forth slightly out of time, but my swing slows as I scuff the toes of my trainers on the ground and we end up swinging in unison before the movement subsides. I enjoy the silence between us and the feel of the hot chocolate in my hands, the gentle sway of the swings. Simple pleasures that aren't so simple to come by.

"I don't know why he's here."

"He's my mate, Katie," Rex replies in a murmur that I only hear because I'm listening for the answer.

"'S'freak." I look up at exactly the right moment to catch her looking at me. "What are you looking at, Emo Boy?"

"He's probably looking at that massive mascara smudge halfway down your cheek," Hannah says immediately, not giving me a chance to say something foolish.

Katie scowls, but she rubs a finger pink with cold under each eye. I have no idea whether there was a mascara smudge there in the first place, but there is now. I smile at Hannah, who grins back.

"Get a room," Katie says, petulantly.

"Oh, fuck off, Katie," Hannah says with a surprising amount of venom and stands up. "You coming? Leave these two to suck face instead of trying to make witty conversation."

From the benches where we end up I can see a flicker of fire in one of the wire bins by the toilets. A small crowd has gathered around it and I recognize Marcy and Tyrone standing together throwing scrunched up paper on the flames. Hannah notices the direction of my gaze.

"Tyrone thought it would be a good idea to burn revision notes."

"Because he's never going to need them again…?"

"Yeah. If it's an idea of Tyrone's, it's probably a bad one." Hannah looks at me. "Thanks for keeping quiet about what happened at Rex's party."

"No one to tell." I shrug, half-joking, half-truthful.

"Thanks anyway. I could do without the trouble right now."

I hear the "right now", but I don't really know if I should question it, so I don't. Hannah reaches out and puts her hand on mine, sliding her fingers between my gloved ones and squeezing. I'm not sure what this is about, but I squeeze back, although it's hard to tell how much through the inch-thick material.

"I can't work you out, Aaron Tyler, but you do seem to have a knack for doing the right thing at the right time."

"I haven't done anything," I say, mystified.

"That's the point," she says and takes her hand away.

HANNAH

"Hannah, I need you to take Lola shopping with you." My mum never asks favours, she commands them.

Only I cannot accept this command. I. Really. Cannot. When Gran asked to see a picture of the scan I was forced to tell her I hadn't gone. *That is not what I expected of you, Hannah.* The depth of her disappointment brought me to tears in seconds – even thinking about the look in her eyes is enough to cause my chest to burn with guilt. She stood over me as I rang to book in a new scan with my very angry midwife, and Gran's arranged to come with me, in case I fail her – and the baby – again.

Christmas Eve isn't exactly the best time to get out of family duties, but I've got to try. If Jay hadn't deserted us to go on a last-minute ski trip with the other half of his family, I could have palmed this off on him. As it is, all I'm left with is: "I can't take Lola with me. I'm buying her presents."

Mum rolls her eyes. "I knew you'd leave it late. Look. I've bought her everything on her Christmas list…"

Everything?! I saw that list – it was, like, three pages long.

"I'll say some are from you. I'm already doing that for Jay. You don't even have to pay for them."

I just stare at Mum. I'm having trouble processing my

irrational rage at her for buying Lola everything she wants and for suggesting she'll decide which ones I can give to my sister, as if I'm as thoughtless as Jay, who couldn't even be bothered to come home, and… I think my brain just timed out. Shit. Come on, brain, get it together, or the second person you end up telling about the baby will be Lola.

AARON

This year I bought one Christmas card. I open the cellophane, take out the card and open it.

Blank, like my mind.

I stare at the white space so long that I lose sight of everything around me, something I've been known to do. There are no words for what I want to say.

I fold the card shut and close my eyes.

I see my nightmare.

Eyes open, Aaron. Card open, Aaron.

Dear Mr and Mrs Lam,
There are no words.
Thinking of you – always thinking of Chris. I think you should know this.
    Ty

HANNAH

"What are we doing at the hospickal?"

"Hospital," I correct Lola gently and pat her hand. On

my other side, Gran squeezes my shoulder as she uses me to balance on the paving. It's been salted, but none of us want her to slip – although I guess there are worse places to do it than right outside A&E. Once inside, the three of us head to the maternity unit.

"Name?" says the woman at the desk.

"Hannah Sheppard."

"What's going on, Hannah?" Lola is tugging insistently at my jacket.

"I'll tell you in a minute."

"You said that ages ago."

"… down there." The woman is pointing to a partly occupied row of chairs.

"Sorry? I didn't catch that."

"If you take a seat down there, someone will call you."

"Thanks."

"White book, please."

"What?"

"She asked for your white book, love," Gran says, in a way that isn't actually helpful.

"Yes, I know!"

"No need to shout at Granny Ivy!" Lola starts to cry.

I look desperately at Gran and at the woman at reception, who hasn't quite lost it on the patience front. Yet. I flounder around in my bag, knowing that I've got the stupid thing with me because I have to take it with me all the time in case I get hit by a falling piano or something and whoever treats me needs to know how pregnant I am. I taped the cover of a magazine over it so it wouldn't look so suss – there it is!

"This is a copy of *Cosmopolitan*," the woman says.

"No, my white book's inside," I explain. Only she flaps the cover open and she's right: it *is* a copy of *Cosmo*, and I start to panic that I've left my white book on the kitchen table…

I close my eyes and try to ignore Lola's wails and Gran's helpful *"hormones"* stage whisper to the woman at the desk.

"Gran. Can you take Lola to sit in the chairs, please?" I say. And just like that they're gone and I breathe another slow breath and put my bag on the desk and dig around until I find my white book with the massive headline that announces that this is THE SEX ISSUE, which makes me smile. It makes the woman at the desk smile too.

"Why are we here? Is something wrong with Granny Ivy?" Lola is still hiccupping a little when I join them.

"Come here, Lolly." I pull her up onto my knee, exchanging a glance with Gran, who wanted me to tell Lola before we got here. "There's nothing wrong with Granny Ivy."

"You promise?"

"Promise."

"Is there something wrong with you?"

"No." I've got to be quick because I can see the idea terrifies her.

"Good." She throws her arms around me and I can feel her patting Gran's hair.

"I've just got to have a test for something," I lie, because what else am I supposed to do? The second person to find out my news cannot be Lola. It just can't.

"Hannah Sheppard?" A woman in a shapeless blue top and trousers steps out into the corridor and I stand up.

Then I sit right back down again.

"I can't do this." I'm shaking and I can see Lola's getting worried, but I can't help it. "Gran, can you come in with me?"

She looks at Lola and back at me. It wasn't supposed to happen like this.

AARON

The hall is packed with towers of suitcases and presents when I open the door. Mum is looking frantic because she can't find the spare key to give to Next Door so they can come and feed The Kaiser whilst we're away. Dad is looking in the bowl by the door.

"Where've you been?" he asks, not looking up from the change he's sifting through in his quest for the key.

"Nowhere," I say. That causes him to look up. I'm usually more forthcoming about such things.

"Your mother wants to know if you've packed your thermal underwear."

We're going to see Gran – Dad's mother – for Christmas. In Yorkshire. I would be *insane* not to pack my thermals after last year's "surprise" hill walk. I answer with a nod and pick up the cat, who's trying to chew the corner off one of the presents. He gives in with bad grace and lets me hold him close, lets me feel the solidity of his fat furry body.

I drop him gently back to the floor and think of the days when holding the cat and smelling his fur was the only thing that brought me comfort. I wish we could take him with us.

HANNAH

It doesn't look much like a baby to me, but according to the woman who actually knows what she's talking about, it's perfectly healthy – although I lose count of how many times I'm told off for leaving it so late, since it makes it impossible to date accurately. I don't tell her she doesn't need to. She keeps trying to chat to me, thinking I'm worried about what I'm seeing and the fact that I'll need to have a different test for Down's, but the thing that's worrying me the most is that I've left Lola on her own in the corridor outside.

Gran asks if we can have an extra picture, but you have to pay and I didn't come with any cash.

"I'll get one for you, love…" But Gran doesn't have anything smaller than a twenty on her. The nurse tells her there's a tea counter down the corridor and Gran toddles off to get some change whilst I nip out to check that Lola's where we left her.

She is.

"Is everything all right?" she asks, looking up from the game she's playing on my phone.

"Yup," I say, noticing a bit of ultrasound jelly is soaking through my top.

"Is that a Smartphone?" The nurse is standing at the door, looking over at us.

"Uh-huh." I'm distracted, trying to rub off the excess jelly without anyone noticing.

"So it can take pictures?"

I nod, still not paying attention.

"Bring it here. We can use it to take a photo of the baby."

There's a moment of silence in which I pray the nurse did not just say that.

Then Lola gets up and hands over the phone.

"What baby?" she says.

AARON

The first thing my grandmother does is hug me with a desperation that nearly throttles me. This is the first time she has seen me since my "dark period". It entertains me how the family shorthand makes me sound less like Aaron Tyler and more like Pablo Picasso.

"So good to see you, Aaron." Gran clamps my head between her palms and looks at me intently, eyes searching mine, looking to see whether I'm the same boy she saw this time last year.

She's going to be disappointed.

HANNAH

It's one minute to midnight. One minute to Christmas and I'm snuggled up in bed, curled around my almost-bump.

Baby.

I press the light on my phone and look at the screen.

Baby.

The nurse labelled the image *bottom* and *head,* which is helpful because I'm not sure I'd be able to tell too easily.

Baby.

I thought it would feel different knowing what it looked like, but I still can't believe it's inside me.

Baby.

Maybe I do feel different.

My baby.

FRIDAY 25TH DECEMBER
CHRISTMAS DAY

HANNAH

I'm dozing on the sofa, listening to Lola play with her second favourite present, a doll she's named Kooky. Her first favourite present (her words, not mine) is the little black rabbit that Mum and Robert managed to keep a secret even from me. It turns out he's the reason I was kicked out of the house yesterday, the little bastard.

Lola didn't know what to call him and she asked Robert to choose, so the rabbit's called Fiver. He's now sleeping in his hutch in the utility room, which I know because I just went to check on him. I always wanted a rabbit and, if I'm honest, I'm a bit jealous – although give it a week and I'll be the one checking his water and changing his straw anyway. Still. If he was my rabbit, I wouldn't have named him after his price tag.

What will I call the baby? I guess it's a bit early to start thinking about it – seems like it's bad luck or something. I don't want any of that. Seeing it on the screen yesterday made me realize just how much I want everything to be OK. With the baby, I mean. I'm not so stupid to think that everything's going to be OK with my family.

I watch Lola reach over and take Robert's new mobile off the coffee table, bored of Kooky already. I shut my eyes again and snuggle further into the cushions. I want this for my baby: cosy fireside family Christmases and big dinners, a pretty twinkly glowy tree and Disney movies…

I think I drifted off.

"… Hannah's asleep," I hear Robert say and Mum sighs. I suspect I am about to be summoned for dishes so I keep my eyes tight shut and breathe quietly. *So* not in the mood for dishes right now.

"Careful with that, Lolly – it's not a toy," Mum says.

"I am being careful," comes the reply.

There's a pause and I can imagine that Mum's still there, watching Lola to make sure she's not about to break something.

"What are you doing?"

"I'm using Daddy's phone to take a picture," Lola says.

"What of?"

"Kooky's baby."

It takes every little bit of control I have to stop my eyes from snapping open. Instead I lift my lids, just a crack, to see that Lola is holding Robert's phone over Kooky's tummy as the doll lies back on a cushion.

I shut my eyes and pray for a Christmas miracle.

"How's Daddy's phone going to help?" I hear Mum step further into the room.

"It's going to take a picture of Kooky's baby inside her tummy." I kind of glossed over the details on how the nurse got a picture of my baby and Lola definitely thinks mobile phones have something to do with it.

"You are?" Mum asks.

"So we know the baby's OK," Lola explains.

Please shut up, Lola…

"And is her baby OK?"

"Yes."

There's a short silence, then, "Lola, where did you learn about this?"

"Hannah."

I pretend my hardest to be asleep, like a little kid hiding under a bath towel thinking no one can see me if I can't see them.

"Hannah told you?" Robert chimes in, disapproval ringing in his voice.

"No. She said not to say…" Lola's not sounding so certain now and I can imagine she's looking over at me.

"Hannah?" Mum says my name in a way that's meant to wake me up.

Keep your eyes closed.

"I know you're awake."

I open my eyes. They're both looking at me: Mum curious; Robert cross.

"You were telling Lola about making babies?" Mum obviously thinks this is her area of expertise, not mine.

"I—"

"You shouldn't be talking about it with her. She's too young." Robert weighs in a bit louder than he means to because he's had a little too much wine.

"Robert. Volume," Mum says sharply, as she has been doing all evening.

"Stop shouting!" Lola interrupts. "You'll scare her baby."

Oh, Lola…

"What?" Robert and Mum don't seem to realize what's going on; they're looking at Kooky still.

"Hannah's baby. You don't want to scare it by shouting."

AARON

I'm sitting on the stone bench that overlooks the sloping front garden. It's cold, but my cheeks are still burning hot from being shut inside close to a log fire and too many relatives, and there's a white heat in my mind that's so intense it's almost consuming me.

I breathe, watching a little of it disappear in the air.

One breath at a time, little by little, heat out, cold in, until I'm there.

Uncles Matt and Dave were talking to Zoë, Matt's wife, about me. About how pale I looked. About how my parents hadn't come to them to talk about the problem. About how they shut out the Family. That was no way to deal with these things – we're family, we share our problems, we share the *burden* of our children's woes. We don't hide and pretend everything is all right.

But did you hear? They sent him to counselling.

Counselling? Well, of course, he would need that after—

I heard Gran walk in, sensible clops of sensible shoes on the flagstones.

It didn't stop them.

He only went to three sessions. (Wrong, Uncle Dave. I went to four.)

Well.

Well.

Well.

Stephanie told me she'd set him up with visiting.

Visiting? Who?

At one of the old folks' homes her company do the supplies for. (Gran does not put herself in the category of old folks because her back's still straight and her mind sharp.)

How's that supposed to help?

No answer. I imagine there was a lot of shrugging. (Mum's logic was that I need some perspective – a bit of purpose. Which is true.)

Little Lynette told me he's very withdrawn. (Of course, I forgot, brattish seven-year-olds are experts in psychoanalysis – I should have gone to Zoë's daughter for counselling.)

It's the quiet ones you've got to watch.

Mm.

Mm.

Mm.

Goes to show.

I walked past the door. You could almost see the shared thought bubble:

How long has he been there? Did he hear us?!

"We're leaving on Monday," I said, looking back. "Best to finish the conversation then."

Then I came out here.

There's a swell in the volume of voices as someone

opens the back door and crunches down the path towards me. Dad sits down and holds his hand out flat then grunts.

"Snowing."

It's winter. We're in Yorkshire. I am not entirely blown away by this turn of events.

"Your mum is currently tearing strips out of Zoë and the uncles."

I say nothing.

"They feel pretty bad about it."

Still have nothing to say.

"Talk to me, Aaron." He pauses. "Please."

I turn and look at him. He's staring at me, eyes a little bleary from the smoke and the alcohol and yesterday's four-hour drive.

"There's nothing to say." I watch him watching me, looking for signs of mental instability. "I think they're unwise to talk about me whilst I'm in the house. And rude. But then, y'know, your family…"

I crack a smile to show I'm joking but Dad's echo of the same is weak. Our timing's all wrong these days.

"Come back to us, son."

I stare at the ground between my feet and focus on the fuzz of frost on the blades of grass.

"It's hard. I'm trying."

But I wonder whether I really am.

Dad puts his arm around me, pressing his face into my hair. "I just wish I knew what was going on in here."

"Guilt, Dad."

There's a silence between us. This is old ground.

"We're all guilty of something," he says and I know he's thinking that there was something he could have done to help. That my parents' love is so strong they'd rather see a flaw in their parenting than a flaw in their son is overwhelming.

It's too much to be forgiven when all you want is to be blamed.

HANNAH

"I can't tell you who the father is" sounds a lot like "I don't know who the father is" to an already hysterical parent.

"How many have there *been?*" The look that crosses my mother's face shames me more than anything I've ever done with a boy – and yet it's still easier to let her think I've been knocked up by a nameless random than tell her the truth. I think that would be one truth too many after learning that not only am I over three months pregnant, but that I turned to Gran for help.

Robert tells me to leave the room. We will talk in the morning. As I turn to shut the door, I see Mum burrow into his big broad shoulder, pressing her face into the cheesey Christmas jumper he wears every year. I watch as her shoulders shake and he wraps his arms around her, protecting her from the hurt I've caused.

I shut the door and slide down the other side. Mum has Robert. I have no one.

And it's all my fault.

AARON

Sleep is dangerous country. You relinquish control of body and mind, hand over everything and leave yourself vulnerable for those unwaking hours.

I never used to have problems sleeping. Not before. Now sleep and I are uncomfortable bed companions, with me lying frigid beneath the sheets waiting to feel its arms slip around me, then giving in to the inevitable. Sleep cannot be trusted. Sometimes it takes you away for what feels like a lifetime to deposit you awake and alert mere minutes after it claimed you. Sometimes it snatches seconds and gives hours in return. And when you slip behind that black curtain there's no telling what waits on the other side…

Sometimes I'm living my dreams, sometimes I'm aware that I'm dreaming, but there's a special kind of dream that is a living nightmare. I know what's coming, I'm aware of what I'm being dragged inexorably towards, but I'm also living it, like it's something I've never experienced before, so I get to feel the horror and the dread every time, as if it's the first. How does my brain allow this to happen? What stupid short circuit has been set up so that I get to experience apprehension and surprise at the same time?

And why is it that this dream can strike at any time, turning innocuous fun, or satisfying sexy time, or even calming blankness into something that erases every bit of good feeling I've ever had and forces me to face the worst of myself?

It starts with the rain.

In my dreams I get 3D, surround sound, smell-o-vision... I also get wet. IMAX has nothing on me.

First I feel the drops splatting one by one. But it's just me – no one else around me is getting wet. Every time I ask them, I point to the sky and to the wet drops on my arms – *Look, I'm wet* – but after I've shown a couple of people I start to notice that it's not water that's falling on me. It's blood.

That's usually when the sky darkens and the rain starts to fall properly. Whoever else is in the dream starts to melt away, they get lost in the torrents of rain falling from the sky, because it's rainwater falling from the sky – it only turns to blood when it lands on me. I'm getting wet, and cold and scared. *Where is everyone?*

Then I hear a voice calling me.

Ty!

This has been confusing me recently, because I'm getting used to being called Aaron now but, still, my dream self recognizes my name and starts to follow the sound. It's not easy, the rain is loud and there's thunder in the air.

Ty!

Only when I'm already walking towards the silhouette of the person calling my name do I start to wonder who it is, but I never guess. I both know, and don't know.

It's Chris.

I point to my bloodstained clothes. "It's raining blood, dude."

"It's not raining," he says. "It's me."

There's silence. Everything stops: the rain, the thunder. A perfect moment of stillness.

Then he's ripped open from the inside out, blood spraying over me and there's this noise. A *whumph* and a crunch and a sound that I only ever heard once, but I've listened to again and again and again…

And I'm listening to it now, watching him fall to the floor in front of me as I stand there in the rain, covered in blood – his blood – watching my best friend hit the floor and he's screaming in pain and writhing around and I'm sobbing but there's nothing I can do because I can't move towards him – every time I try I'm moving further away.

But no matter how far away I get, I can hear him screaming and sobbing as if he's right there inside my own head.

Because he is. That screaming and sobbing? That's me.

SATURDAY 26TH DECEMBER

BOXING DAY

HANNAH

"Ivy."

"Paula."

I give Gran a kiss on the cheek and go through to her kitchen to put the kettle on, passing the tiny fake Christmas tree in the corner. There are some presents under it waiting for me to share the fun in opening them. There's one for me from Dad. At least I hope there is – there wasn't one under our tree.

Something tells me there won't be any present-opening today or, if there is, it won't be joyful.

I take the teapot over to the table in Gran's dining area where Mum and Gran are sitting awkwardly upright like two people on a stage, set to start a performance they haven't rehearsed properly. There are two more chairs: one near Gran; one near Mum. I sit on the bed.

"You know why I'm here," my mum says.

Gran nods and gives me a sad look. I called her this morning to tell her what happened, but Mum caught me, took the phone off me and invited herself to Cedarfields.

"I understand that you've been helping Hannah through all this?"

Gran nods again and pours the milk in the cups then adds the tea. "You don't take sugar." More a statement than a question, but Mum still waves it away.

"Ivy, I don't know where to start…" Mum stalls, revs up and tries again. "You should have come to me right away."

"Paula, dear, you know I shouldn't."

Mum has no reply to this. I'm not surprised. I don't either.

"Hannah's the one who's to make these decisions, not me." She flickers a piercing gaze up at Mum. "Not you."

"She's only *fifteen*! What were you thinking? She needs help and support for a decision like this. This is something that changes not just her life, but the lives of everyone around her."

I feel like asking Mum not to talk about me as if I'm not here, but perhaps it's better this way.

"Hannah didn't make this decision lightly, did you, love?"

I shake my head and stare at the floor.

141

"I can't believe I'm hearing this. Do you know how irresponsible it was to let her do this?"

"Do what, exactly?" Gran's voice is sharp and it stops Mum short. They look at each other and I glance from one familiar face to the other, looking for something that seems obvious to everyone but me.

"You know what," Mum mutters.

I'm confused. "Er, Mum?" I say. "*I* don't…?"

Mum turns to me as if she really had forgotten I was there and the look she gives me isn't one she's practised a thousand times on a thousand troubled teenagers. It's a look that seems to come from the saddest part of her soul.

"Hannah. I don't think you should have decided to keep it."

There's a stillness in the room. Of course, I know that this is what she thinks. I've known it all along. But I never thought she'd *say* it. Not now. Not once I'd decided.

I stare hard at the floor, forcing back the tears that loom. A hand rests on mine and I turn my palm up to close my fingers around Gran's. I hear a creak of a chair, feel the mattress bounce as Mum sits next to me and tries to put a comforting arm around me. The arm is there, but it brings no comfort.

"I'm sorry, Hannah," she whispers. "I will never say this again. But please, are you sure this is what you want? Are you sure you want to keep the baby?"

I feel Gran's hand in mine, feel a little squeeze of the fingers. She has never asked me this, never doubted that I know my own mind. She knows me so much better than my own mother does.

Then I nod, just once, before finding out what it feels like to have my mother sob on me instead of Robert.

SUNDAY 27TH DECEMBER

HANNAH

When Dad rings off after I call to thank him for my Christmas cheque, the handset informs me our conversation lasted three minutes and twenty-three seconds. Mum, who is standing over me, shakes her head.

"Let me guess, he's working?"

I nod and she lets out an angry huff.

"Is he coming over soon?"

I nod again. He's got a meeting with some producers later this month. Or early next month. I know how it is when pitching a script to the bigger players. Which I don't. I'm fifteen. I know about handing in your homework on time and worrying about your bra size. But Dad doesn't know how it is with me.

"Tell him when you see him. It'll be easier face-to-face and another few weeks won't make a difference."

I try not to notice the little dig she got in there.

FRIDAY 1ˢᵗ JANUARY

NEW YEAR'S DAY

AARON

"I got you something," I say to Neville as we sit down, the harsh winter light glinting on the frosted lawns outside the dining-room window. Hannah and her gran are out there walking arm in arm, careful steps across the salted paving.

I put a book on the table. It's tied with brown string around the cover and there's a piece of paper tucked under the string that says, *Time to learn some new tricks, old ~~dog~~ MAN.*

Neville pulls the string off, grunts at the note then looks at the cover of the book.

Chambers Card Games

He looks at the note again and laughs.

HANNAH

We sat with Aaron and Neville at lunch. It was nice. Things at home are worse than awful – Mum can barely look at me, Lola's throwing proper epic tantrums that even I can't charm her out of and Robert's fuming. Jay should have come home after his ski trip, but his mum dropped him at Imogen's instead. Robert blew up at Jay about it and now they're not speaking. The pair of them are so stubborn I'll be surprised if we see Jay before *next* Christmas. Robert hasn't told him what's going on with me. I guess he wanted to do it in person and that's why he went postal over the Imogen thing. Yet another problem I've caused.

Visiting Gran was a break from all that, or it was until Aaron asked me what I did for New Year.

"Did you have fun with Katie and the others when you went out last night?"

I told him I stayed at home with Lola, which is true. When I last called Katie she said she'd let me know if anything exciting came up, which totally opened it out for a joke about her and Rex. After end of term at the park they went back to hers, but she'd just started her period so nothing happened. On the plus side, it finally pushed Rex into manning up and actually asking her out. Katie's enjoyed making me eat my words – going on about dates at the cinema and dinner at Nando's. I'm pleased for her. Really. And it makes a nice change from hearing her boast how fast her Katie Coleman Special works, not that she's had much chance to try it out with her brothers crowding out her house and Rex's parents being more than a bit weird about him having girls over. Ten weeks. That's got to be a personal best for Katie – I'm surprised it hasn't grown over.

When I didn't hear from her I assumed she'd had the chance to celebrate New Year with a different kind of bang.

But Katie didn't stay in with Rex. They went out, Aaron said. *With the others*.

So the question is, why didn't Katie ask me along too?

AARON

I watch Neville slide his present onto his bookshelf amongst the history books I used to think were for show. When he limps over to the wardrobe I think about asking how his leg is – it looks stiffer than it did two weeks ago – but he's riffling amongst his clothes, muttering to himself, then he's grumbling at the hanger he's trying to get hold of, until he finally pulls something out.

"Try this."

"What is it?"

"What does it look like? It's a leather jacket." Neville shakes the garment at me. The dark leather is soft as I take it and look at it, running a thumb over the sleeve. I've always liked the smell of leather, there's something warm and organic about it, appetizing for senses other than taste; for touch and smell. I pull it on and shrug my shoulders into it, reaching out to see where the cuffs fall on my wrists.

It's a perfect fit.

Neville makes a "turn around" gesture and when I turn back to face him, he's nodding. "Thought so."

I don't want to assume anything – it seems impudent to think Neville is going to let me borrow a jacket that makes me feel much cooler than I really am.

"Merry Christmas," Neville says with a nod. "It's yours if you like it."

"What?" I look up from posing in the mirror. "Mine? I thought maybe you'd let me borrow it..."

"Nah. It's a gift. I bought that jacket when I was your age. Wore it all the time, even after I settled down to be a lecturer and I was supposed to be dressing respectable. My wife liked me in it."

Wife? I look up sharply, but that's not where this conversation is going.

"Neville…"

"It looks good on you, kid." He gives me a wicked smile. "And, to be honest, you could do with a few fashion tips."

HANNAH

On the way home I check every folder I've got in my phone, trying to convince myself that Aaron's got it wrong, or that somehow I missed a message. Who am I kidding? It was New Year. My phone was on *all night* – there's no way I missed anything.

The scrape of the handbrake nudges me out of my head and back to reality. It's starting to snow and once I'm standing on the drive I stick out my tongue to see if I can catch a falling flake, promising myself a wish the way I did when I was little. Back then I wished for my parents to stop arguing, for a new bike with pink handlebars and white tyres, for a rabbit or a hamster or even a goldfish to care for.

These days I'm the one causing the arguments, I couldn't ride a bike even if I had one and my sister's the one with the rabbit.

"Hannah?" Mum's standing by the front door. "Come on, it's freezing."

Robert's in the sitting room with his laptop and Lola's sprawled on the floor concentrating on copying a rabbit from her *How To Draw Animals* book. I mean, I say "rabbit" but, to be honest, what she's drawing looks more like a donkey.

"Did you speak to him?" Mum asks, but Robert shakes his head. "For goodness' sake, Robert, you've got to tell him sooner or later."

"Don't tell me what to do with my own son, Paula."

For a second I think she's going to say something, but Mum just turns and walks out. As she passes me in the doorway I can see she's crying.

"Mum—"

"Don't, Hannah. Just … don't."

My family is falling to pieces. It'll take more than a snowflake wish to put it back together.

AARON

Rex and Katie are official. This means that instead of reserving their lust for the privacy of their houses or the dark of the park on a Friday, they're comfortable with multiple *very* public displays of affection. It's against school rules, but anyone doing it out of view of the staffroom gets away with it.

"Gross."

Someone verbalizes my thoughts. I turn to see Anj next to me, looking, yet trying not to, at Katie and Rex. She bites her lips together when she realizes I've caught her out.

"Sorry, didn't mean to say it out loud."

"You only said what we're all thinking," I say, as I notice someone standing in the doorway. It's Hannah. She's glancing at the happy couple over her shoulder as if there's somewhere she's meant to be. Presumably with Katie.

Anj asks if I'd like to sit with her in Maths.

"Can I do that?"

She shrugs. "New term, new desk buddies."

"Choose wisely, Miss Ojo," I say with a smile. "You may live to regret your decision."

"No more than I regret the one I made at the start of

last term." She rolls her eyes. "Seriously. The girl I sit with at the moment keeps copying my answers, *without even hiding it.*"

"I promise you won't know I'm copying." As I grab my bag, I see Katie walking on ahead of us. She's talking to Marcy and one of her friends – Nicole – and the three of them start laughing about something as they walk through the door. Right past Hannah.

HANNAH

I stay in the toilets. No one'll notice I'm missing. I've skipped lessons before and only once have I got into proper trouble.

No one'll notice.

Not even my best friend.

The way she looked at me…

Like I wasn't even there.

Like I'm not the person who's held her hair while she's puked up in my bathroom. Like I'm not the person who lied to her parents when she was out all night with some guy she met at a club so that I got into trouble instead. Like I'm not the person who's shared her secrets and my secrets until they became *our* secrets. Like I'm not the person who's always there when she needs me.

I think about the fight we had on the phone at the weekend. The one where I found out that she'd gone out with Rex and his friends – and his friends' girlfriends.

"You mean Marcy was there?"

Silence.

"You went out with Marcy without telling me?"

"Because I'd knew you'd be like this about it."

"Only because she's such a bitch!"

"Come on, Han. It's not like you haven't given her a reason…"

My turn to be silent. I couldn't believe she'd said that. It doesn't matter what excuse your worst enemy has to hate you, your best mate should *always* take your side. Shouldn't she?

My mascara's all over the place and I have to dab at my eyes with toilet paper to try and sort it out. I don't want Katie to know I've been crying because she'll know why. I don't want to be the weak one. The bell goes for the end of first period and I hear a group come in. If I was in a movie this would be the point that I'd hear them bitching about me across the cubicles without realizing I was here. I hold my breath and listen, but my life isn't a movie and they're not talking about me. They're talking about boys. As if they'd be talking about anything else.

Katie avoids me during morning break, arriving late for Citizenship stinking so strongly of smoke that I can still smell it, even once she's shuffled to the far corner of the table. I try to catch her after, but I get picked on to collect the stupid textbooks and by the time I'm back at our form room, Katie's gone. Determined to be strong, I refuse to ring her to find out where she's gone and head to the canteen instead.

I hardly ever come here so I have no one to eat with. I think about chickening out, but I'm starving and at least the food is hot and cheap. I get a tray load of chicken, "chipped potatoes" and beans, then look for a seat.

There's an empty table at the back that I practically sprint for. I slam my tray down at exactly the same time as some half-height kid in the year below.

"Hey! I got here first," he says, annoyed at me as I sit down.

"And? There's five other seats." I sweep my fork around at them.

"Billy no mates, are you?" he sneers. "I'm here with FIVE friends, so we need your seat."

"You're not getting it," I say, taking my anger out on a piece of chicken. He opens his mouth to say something else when someone slides into the seat opposite me. I look up to see Gideon, who gives me a wink. Anj and Aaron slide in from the other side and the kid looks like he's about to have a fit.

"Hey, gorgeous. You joining us for lunch?" Gideon says in the campest voice I've ever heard him use and the kid makes a bolt for it.

Aaron looks over at me and smiles, just a tug on the corners of his mouth, as Gideon starts quizzing me about a PSHE project I didn't know I was supposed to have done. When I look back at Aaron, he's still looking at me. He's noticed, hasn't he? I wish he hadn't.

The day passes slowly, silently, since the person I usually talk to is ignoring me. The theme continues when I come home to an empty house. Mum's at work and Robert and Lola are at his parents'. It's too long to wait to dinner so I head straight to the kitchen for a glass of milk and some biscuits and crisps. It's only once I've put the milk back in the fridge that I notice the Post-it note that's fallen off the door:

I spoke to Jay.
Please call him – he'd like to hear from you.
R

I fold the note carefully in half once, twice, and put the square of paper in the bin.

Not tonight.

THURSDAY 7ᵀᴴ JANUARY

HANNAH

Katie and I still aren't talking and it's killing me. Not that she'd know. I've had plenty of practice hiding my feelings recently.

Only maybe, just maybe, I shouldn't have hidden them from my best mate. That was what kept me awake last night and I realized that the reason I'm so angry with Katie for going off with Marcy is because I'm finally ready to tell her the truth.

Yesterday I found out that she'd gone with Marcy to Nicole's the night before to dye her hair. It looks good. Red suits Katie better than the blonde she's always been, but it hurt to be seeing it for the first time at registration when I should have been the one rinsing the dye out of her hair and screaming in excitement once it was dry. Not Nicole. Certainly not Marcy. There's a bitter little part of me that wonders whether Marcy's making a move on Katie as payback for what she suspects went down with me and her boyfriend. And then I swallow that pill, because I need to face up to the fact that, like Tyrone, Katie is happy to be tempted.

It's time I let her know how important she is to me.

I catch her during the last part of the basketball game that's on after school. She's sitting on the bench just outside the fire exit and I sit down as she lights up, so she can't make an excuse and walk off the way she's been doing all week.

My hands are shaking and I jam them into my pockets.

So I do it. I tell her.

"Four months?"

"Thereabouts."

Katie takes a drag of her cigarette and I see that she's upset with me. But then, "You've still got time to get rid of it." She blows smoke out of the side of her mouth and away from my face. "I'll come with, if you want."

I'm not sure what disappoints me the most: the fact that she's saying this, or the fact that I'm not surprised.

I'm too sad to even cry. I just hand over my phone with the ultrasound image opened.

"Abortion not something you're considering, then?" she asks, mildly.

"Not exactly."

"You're telling me all this now." Her finger taps close to the tip of her fag. Katie fidgets when she's angry. "And…?"

And I'm growing a *person* inside me.

And I'm still at school.

And I'm not with the father.

And I'm lonely.

And I'm scared.

"Nothing," I say as I stand.

Katie squints up at me, her face twisted slightly as she studies me. Maybe she realizes what a cow she's being, but this is Katie we're talking about, so I'm not over-hopeful. Having three brothers teaches you how to be stubborn.

"Why didn't you say something before?" she asks.

"Didn't know how." That sounds so weak.

"I'm your best mate, Han. You should have said something." Katie gets up and grinds out the stub of the cigarette. My heart does a double bounce – *I'm your best mate, Han*.

I wait for something more.

So does she.

"You're not even going to say sorry?" she says.

"You what?"

"About not telling me until now."

"Er, fuck off!" I say, thinking she must be joking, but, even as I say it, I realize I couldn't be more wrong.

"You should have come to me sooner, talked things through before you did anything stupid."

I can't believe I'm hearing this. "Like?"

"Like keeping the baby. You're fifteen. Do you even know who the dad is?" She doesn't leave me enough of a gap to respond. "Doesn't really matter. You're on your own now."

"I know," I say in a pathetic little voice that I wish wasn't mine.

"Look, I'm sorry." Katie steps closer and I think she's going to hug me. She doesn't. "I'm not trying to make you cry."

Am I crying? I hadn't realized.

"You've been pushing me away and now it's … it's just a lot to take in."

Finally, when I'd stopped hoping, Katie pulls me in for a hug so that I have to hold my breath against the smell of stale smoke. Then I feel her slipping her phone out of her pocket and there's a whispered, *"Bollocks."*

When I step back she looks set to sprint. "Late for Rex?"

"The game finishes in ten minutes and I was going to go and change…"

"Going somewhere nice?"

She looks shifty. "Just out."

"Who with?"

"Come on, Han. You don't want to come out with us lot, do you? Not in your condition." And she nudges me, giving me a smile that's all teeth and no heart.

I wave her off, pretending I haven't noticed that she has become part of "us lot" and I have become "you". It's been a seamless re-invention of Katie, Hannah's BFF, to Katie, B-ball WAG and Marcy-clone. As she walks away I notice that her fingernails are painted, not bitten, and the foundation tidemark has been subbed-out for a more subtle fake-tan fade. The hair was just the Cherry Crimson Tide on the cake.

I've been so caught up in my own problems that I hadn't noticed she was drifting away.

FRIDAY 8ᵀᴴ JANUARY

HANNAH

My day starts with a text:

Hey Hannah, u might want 2 check FB. Hope ur OK, Anj

A text from Anj that does not contain a question about French homework is big news.

It takes me about ten seconds to log in to Facebook.

Fifteen minutes later I'm still there. I don't think I can move, let alone put my clothes on. It's like my body's in shock or something. Even my brain seems to be broken – I actually can't believe what I'm seeing. I keep hoping that I'm having one of those dreams where you think you've got up but you haven't.

It took me a while to work out that a lot of the comments on my newsfeed were about me. Then I clocked the posts on my wall – some nice, some not so. I've got a few messages too. I don't read them.

There's another text on my phone. It's Gideon.

Not sure if congrats is what ur after, but JIC – yay! Gx

My throat catches as I read it, but I grind my teeth together and tell myself to focus. I need to know how this happened. I only told … and she … she couldn't? She *wouldn't*…

I open Katie's profile. She's changed her picture – it's now a close-up of her cleavage with faces drawn on each boob winking at each other. It used to be a photo of me and her dressed up for Jay's party. I check out her status, but it's the same as when I last checked:

No longer an airplane blonde ☺

Comments are split between people who get the joke and people who don't. I notice that Marcy has liked Rex's comment – about having *first-hand experience [pun intended]* – and I go through to her page. Marcy hasn't bothered sorting out her privacy settings so it doesn't matter that we aren't friends.

And it means that the whole world can read her status:

OMG. Hannah Sheppard is 4 months pregnant. Hands up who saw that one coming!

AARON

There's something in the air. I missed registration because the car wouldn't start, and the people I share a bench with in Chemistry wouldn't know what was on the grapevine unless someone plucked the information off and turned it into a smokable substance. I hurry to Geography, hoping to catch Anj before the lesson starts.

As I turn the corner I see that she's standing with Gideon, who should be the other side of the school in my dad's class.

"I always thought she was exaggerating…" Gideon is saying when he sees me coming and shoots me a grin.

"She was. You only have to sleep with one guy to get pregnant." Anj has her back to me, but I heard her loud and clear.

"Who's pregnant?" I say, breathing a little too heavily after my semi-sprint from the Science block.

It's Anj who tells me.

"Hannah's pregnant."

"Hannah who?" says my mouth because it's not actually connected to my brain.

"Sheppard." But I knew that.

"How?" I say. Which isn't what I mean. I wish my mouth and brain could communicate. Gideon gives me a cheeky smirk and says something about a "special cuddle", but Anj elbows him.

"It's all over Facebook," Anj says.

"He's not on Facebook," Gideon tells her before I can. It's the first time I've heard someone's looked for me and I feel awkward. Best to focus on Hannah.

"Is that how she told everyone?" I can't believe this is true.

"Not exactly…" Anj looks uncomfortable.

Gideon fills me in. "Apparently Katie told Marcy whilst they were out last night. I'm pretty sure it wasn't meant to be a global announcement, but then Marcy put it as her status and now everyone's talking about who the father is." He slides a glance through the open door at Fletch, who's at his desk, head in hands, but it's me that Anj is looking at.

"Anyone tried asking her?" I say.

"No one's seen her," Anj says, getting out her phone. "I texted this morning…"

"I think she might be lying low. There's loads of people

posting on her wall and saying some pretty harsh stuff," Gideon says.

I wish I found this hard to believe.

Anj taps on her phone, breaking school protocol, before emitting a shocked, "Oh my God!" We look at her and she turns the phone towards us so we can see the screen.

It's a Facebook page called "Whos the Daddy? Yous the Daddy?" Normally I'd be appalled by the terrible English, but for now I'm more horrified by the content.

There's a picture of Hannah in her school uniform and someone's drawn a cartoon bump over the top with a question mark inside. There's loads of members – presumably all from our school – and people have already started posting suggestions as to who might be the father. One of the posts near the top catches my eye.

Whoever suggested Mr Tyler is way off – his son's deffo the daddy!

I don't know the kid who wrote it, but he looks about ten in his profile pic. Nice.

Anj clicks on the pictures page and I glimpse a few familiar faces badly Photoshopped onto some less familiar bodies doing ... well, doing the nasty. Why would anyone do that?

HANNAH

I'm all cried out for the moment and I feel sick. Mum offered to miss her hair appointment and stay home with me, but what's the point? It's not like her being here will change anything. I'll still be pregnant. I'll still have a giant knife wound where my best friend stabbed me in the back. No need for Mum to have crap hair as well. This is the first time Mum's ever let me stay off school without taking my temperature. She's beside herself with rage about Katie telling Marcy – I'm guessing that's what happened, anyway; I can't imagine it was anyone in my family.

The doorbell rings.

"Go away," I whisper.

It rings again after a while. I risk peering out of my bedroom window and see Aaron at the front door, fiddling with his phone. If he's ringing me, he'll be disappointed. I turned my phone off an hour ago. I head down and open the door though.

"Hi."

"Hi."

I open the door wider and he steps inside. He smells nice, safe.

Then he does something unexpected – he hugs me. As I lean into him and rest my head on a shoulder broader than Mum's, I think how strange this is. We've not hugged before today, we've not really even talked *that* much, but Aaron's the only person who's hugged me during all this without being pushed.

"Shouldn't you be at school?" I say into his blazer.

"Shouldn't you?"

"Point taken." I let go and walk towards the kitchen. "How'd you know where I live?"

"Anj. And Fletch asked me to send his love. Well, something like that. I think he's convinced himself that he's about to become a dad."

"Oh God," I mutter and shake my head as I offer Aaron a drink from the fridge.

"How are you?" Aaron asks, as he cracks open his can of choice. (Diet Coke – huh.)

"Pregnant," I say. This is so weird. I feel like I'm having tea with the queen or something.

"So I hear. How's that working out for you?"

I look at him. He's a funny one. I can't figure him out. He's so direct about stuff but at the same time it's as if he's far away from it all, not a part of things.

"Pregnancy's fine – it's just my friend that's a bitch." I sip a glass of milk. MILK. I used to hate milk, but these last few days I can't get enough of it.

"You know most people are just curious, they're not actually hating you or anything." He looks away, embarrassed almost. "I guess you've seen the Facebook page?"

"What Facebook page?"

AARON

I show her on her laptop upstairs, hating myself for it, figuring it's worse *not* to know something like this ... but I've seen more expression on my dad's face when he's checking the BBC weather page.

She clicks off the page and shrugs.

"You OK?" I'm the epitome of lame.

"Not really."

"As I said, most people …"

"… are just curious," she finishes. "Well, it's none of their fucking business, is it?"

Hannah gets up and kicks the chair out of the way before storming downstairs and, since I don't know what else to do, I follow her. She's opening the back door and rushing outside, then she's standing in the middle of the lawn and screaming so loud I think her voice will break.

"*I'm pregnant. All right?*" She spins round to look at the neighbours' twitching curtains. "ALL RIGHT? And I'm fifteen! Fuck off!"

"Hannah…" I say, edging closer, not sure if now's the right time to point out that she's still in her pyjamas and slippers.

"FUCK OFF!" She screams right in my face before collapsing forward so fast I nearly drop her, and she's kneeling in the cold, wet grass, sobbing and screaming and growling – actually growling. We stay like that a while, me crouching awkwardly, treading the corner of my blazer into the grass, Hannah contorted into my arms, crying herself into silence. I wonder what the neighbours are making of this and I look up to see an old lady and her husband staring out of one of the windows. I give them the finger and enjoy their outraged reaction. They shouldn't be looking. This is private.

"I'm wet," Hannah mumbles and staggers to her feet. "Got to shower."

I follow her indoors and stand in the hallway, where she

turns, halfway up the stairs, and asks me if I'll stay, apologizes for being mental. I tell her not to worry and that I'll wait in the kitchen. There's a book in my blazer pocket, one I've read before, but since I don't have anything better to do I start at the beginning once more. Maybe it was a mistake to come here – it's not as if I was invited. But Hannah needs someone and that someone may as well be me...

"Hi."

I jump.

"I didn't hear you," I say, putting my book down.

Hannah smiles, picks up the book to look at the cover and wrinkles her nose. "Never heard of it," she says before pouring herself another glass of milk and digging out a pack of ginger nuts. I decline the offer as she sits down next to me – she smells of coconut and her hair's still wet. When I look at her, I see someone I recognize: myself, I think. Not in a literal sense. I don't wash my hair with coconut shampoo and I have certainly never worn a Little Miss Naughty T-shirt. But she looks soul-weary and I know about that.

"Thanks," she says and meets my eyes. "I mean it. It takes guts to tell a person something they don't want to hear. Most people would be too scared to face up to it.'

"You're not," I say.

"Wrong. Facing up would have been telling Mum sooner, or my best friend."

"You didn't tell anyone?" I say, surprised.

Hannah smiles. "I told Gran."

I smile too, but hers has turned into a sigh and she

slumps forwards, her forehead resting on the tabletop.

"Fletch isn't the dad," she tells the table.

"Thank God for the baby. Anybody would make a better dad than him." It's meant to be a joke, but something tells me she's a long way from finding it funny.

"You think I don't know who it is, don't you?"

"I never—"

"That's what my mum thinks." Hannah lifts her head to look at me, the imprint of the tablecloth on her forehead.

"I don't think anything." I should leave it there. "Except—"

"Except what?"

"Whoever it is has a right to know."

Hannah winces at this. "He will not want to know. Trust me."

So she *does* know who it is. "I would," I say.

"Well, he's not you." She looks at me with such intense sorrow that any suspicion we were talking about Tyrone dissipates. "Can we just leave it?"

"OK." Hannah obviously has her reasons. "Consider it left."

She looks at me for a moment longer, her face softening before she puts her head back on the table. "Thank you."

"Don't mention it." I finish my can and look for a change of topic. "Can I have a ginger nut?"

She pushes the packet towards me and then waggles her fingers for one, still face down on the table cloth.

"Anything else?" I ask, wondering if she needs a top-up of milk.

"A dad for my baby?" she says with a laugh.

HANNAH

My joke wasn't exactly funny, so I don't think his silence is rude as I sit up and down the dregs of my milk. It's only when I start to stand, turning to offer him another drink, that I realize he's watching me.

"Me," he says.

"You what?" I say, caught somewhere between sitting and standing.

"I could do it, if you wanted."

I sit down with a thump.

"You could say I was the father."

AARON

My parents have had a lot to deal with in the last year. One thing I must do is be straight with them.

"No. No. Don't do this. Don't do this to us, Aaron…" Dad is shaking his head as he backs out of the door, as if leaving the room will save him from what I'm asking. I look at Mum sitting on the sofa, hands pressed together between her knees, staring at me as if I'm something she hallucinated.

I don't know how to make them understand.

Dad fetches two glasses of whisky from the kitchen and hands the largest to Mum, who snaps out of her trance and takes a swig so large a little of it spills on her jeans.

"Let me get this straight." She holds up a hand as I open my mouth to explain. "This Hannah girl is pregnant and doesn't know who the father is, so you have volunteered your services as … what exactly?"

"The father. For now." I look at Dad, who's seen the Facebook page. "You've seen what they're saying about her."

Mum hasn't. I can see she finds it hard to believe it's that bad. "Just because she doesn't know who the father is?"

The way Dad's looking at me, I know he's thinking about a list of names that includes mine.

"I *know* it's not me," I say, just to be clear.

"Have you even asked her who it is?"

"Not exactly." Mum opens her mouth. "Look, shush—"

"You are not in a position to be shushing anyone," Dad snaps and I shut up. I feel a flare of frustration in my chest and imagine myself pressing it back down, folding it forcibly back into the box it belongs in. This is not the time for me to turn.

I need them to see that this is not about Hannah. This is about me.

"I can't keep on like this."

There's an immediate shift in mood.

"Like what?" Mum murmurs and I notice they're now holding hands. It's a subtle movement, because they're already sitting so close, but I see the way their fingers slide together, each drawing strength from the other.

"You think it's working. That I've got new friends." I look at Mum. "That I'm moving on." Dad. "But I'm not. And I can't."

The rage that threatened to rise has subsided and I'm close to tears.

Mum stands up and puts her arm around me. "Aaron. We have done everything we can to help you. Everything. What else is there we can possibly do?"

They have moved house. Moved job. Moved mountains. And I'm still stuck in the same place I started. I need Hannah to help me out.

"I know it's a lot to ask. But let me do this. Let me matter. Let me make up for it…" And I'm crying now, my mother holding me in both arms and kissing my head.

Dad walks out of the French windows and through my tears I see him punch the back fence until it splinters, then kick the panel until his foot makes it through to the other side. Then he walks back in and puts his arms around us, the blood from his hand smearing on my shirt, and he sobs so hard I think it might break him.

HANNAH

This time I don't reject the call when his number comes up. How much worse could it possibly get?

"Four months?" His voice is not unkind and it makes me want to cry. "You said that you'd take the morning-after pill."

I say nothing. He's done the maths – arithmetic and probability – and he's come to the right answer.

"You didn't, did you?"

"No," I say, very small, very quiet.

"Hannah—"

"Don't. Don't say it. I know. All right? I know." My voice isn't going to hold up to a full sentence so I stop. The silence that follows is filled with conversations we haven't had because I didn't try hard enough to tell him the truth when it mattered.

"Shit." He whispers it. I can picture his face and my heart hurts so much it's as if someone's crushing it in their fist. "Does anyone know?"

"You mean apart from everyone at school, the whole of Facebook—"

But he's not in the mood for my jokes. "I meant about me."

This is my chance. I could ask him to do this – I don't have to have a stand-in, I could have the real thing...

"I think we should keep it that way for now," he says.

Which is exactly what I knew he'd say.

SATURDAY 9ᵀᴴ JANUARY

HANNAH

My sister is upstairs. Mum and Robert are in the sitting room. Aaron and I are in the hall. He isn't holding my hand or anything cheesy like that, but he's standing close and it's nice to have someone standing shoulder to shoulder with me for once.

Before we go in he says, "We can do this."

We.

AARON

Well, that was fun. Not the all-night discussion I had with my parents last night about how to pretend to be the parents of a boy who got an under-age girl pregnant. Not the epic planning session Hannah and I had whilst sitting on a bench near her house in the ever-darkening dusk. Not the tears and the recriminations that we went through in her front room; Hannah's mother's relief and anger resulted in some ugly blame-throwing that her daughter had to scream to stop – *"I just wanted to tell him FIRST!"* Not the moment when Lola, Hannah's kid sister who I've never met, came down crying because she'd heard all the noise and was frightened.

No: the journey home.

"Hannah is my daughter," Robert said, looking straight ahead at the traffic, his expression prompting my pulse into a drum roll. "I love her like I love Lola, like I love Jason."

Robert flicked the indicator and we turned down the back road. The darker, lonelier back road...

"I haven't forgotten what it was like being young and in" – he paused, squinted slightly – "lust. And I know that, in the heat of the moment, things happen. What's done is done."

He stopped speaking and I listened to the engine rumble as he went down a gear for a particularly tight corner. I tried not to worry about how fast we were going. It was an expensive car – if we crashed, we'd survive. Probably.

"I know that when this happened, you weren't thinking about anyone other than yourself."

I didn't correct him on the technicality.

"Only now, there's someone who you actually have to think about. You have to put that person first and make decisions that aren't easy, ones that you wouldn't make if you only had yourself to think about. Do you understand?"

"I think—"

"You don't." He swerved the car into a lay-by and stopped. He turned to face me and looked at me with terrifying gravity. "You have no idea what I'm talking about. You don't know what it's like to put another human being before yourself. You don't know the lengths that parents will go to to protect their children."

"I suppose not," I said carefully.

"Parents will *die* for their children."

For a second I honestly thought he might try and kill me to see whether I would die for Hannah's baby. Robert eased back into his seat a little and looked at me carefully, studied my face.

"When I say Hannah's my daughter, it means I'd die for her, and anything else in between – even if it meant she hated me – so long as I felt it was the right thing to do. So I'm doing one of those things right now." Robert met my eyes. "If you aren't serious about Hannah, if you aren't serious about being there for her baby – for *your* baby – then when you get out of this car, I never expect to see you again."

He turned back to the front.

"You have the rest of the journey to consider what I just said."

We drove the rest of the way back in silence. When he pulled up, we both sat staring forwards for a few moments. I unclicked my belt and got out of the car. Leaning back in, I met his eyes and nodded, just once.

"I'll see you tomorrow."

HANNAH

It's late. Robert's not come back from dropping Aaron off and I'm about to sneak across the landing to Lola's room for a cuddle when I hear a murmur from the hallway. I step over to the banister and look down. The sitting-room light's still on, but the murmur I can hear isn't the TV, it's Mum talking to someone on the phone. I can just see the side of her face as she sits on the chair by the door. I'm about to leave her to it when I hear his name.

"Be reasonable, Geoffrey…"

Dad. I guess family gossip has worked its way over to him. There are lots of cousins on Facebook.

"… It's not as simple as you're making out…" Mum sounds knackered – this evening has taken it out of everyone. "Please don't use that tone with me. I am not one of your assistants. I am your ex-wife and the mother of your daughter – the one you haven't seen in over six months."

I wait, imagining the indignation coming down the phone line all the way from Ireland. Dublin. It's not even like he lives in Australia or somewhere properly far away. It costs less than a pair of new shoes to fly here. Takes less time than it does to watch *The Incredibles*.

"Shouting about it won't get you anywhere – she's made up her mind – and there's the father…" It seems Aaron's timing has been perfect. "Of course I've talked to her about her options!"

Flashback to Gran's on Boxing Day. I blink away the memory.

"Don't you *dare*."

I wonder what Dad could have said to make her use the Voice.

"Her father? Is that what you think you are? Since when? Since you asked me to lie to her on her birthday when you missed your plane because you were too busy working to notice her turning ten? Since you refused to allow her to have a private education because you couldn't stand the thought of Robert paying for her when you wouldn't? Since you needed reminding that she was taking her mocks just over a month ago?"

I close my eyes. I didn't want to hear this, but now I can't walk away.

"You listen to me" – the Voice has changed; it's in its killer phase now – "you come over here and you talk to her face-to-face. If I hear you have sent an email I will stop you from ever seeing her again."

A pause.

"If that's the way you want it to be."

I hear the phone crashing down on the base unit then toppling out, and Mum swearing as she pushes it back in place.

SUNDAY 10TH JANUARY

HANNAH

So. He's cutting me out. Not properly – it's not as if Robert's about to sign the papers and adopt me (although since I took his name when Mum did, I'm halfway there already, right?). It's just that my father has a new project on that means he's going to be away on set for the next eight months and he really doesn't have time to deal with this right now. The meeting with the producer was brought forward, things kicked off really quickly. No time to come over and tell me in person that he's not ready to become a grandfather yet.

He phoned his mother to tell her. He emailed mine. But he left it up to them to tell me. I knew something was wrong when Mum parked the car and came into the home with me. She's sitting on the other side from Gran, who's glowing with anger. Frail as she is, I'd worry for Dad's safety if there wasn't the Irish Sea between the two of them. Both Mum and Gran are watching me as if I'm about to break down into floods of tears.

But I don't.

It's exactly what I thought would happen and, in a weird way, I'm just relieved that I was right. I've spent a lifetime assuming the worst of him and if I'd discovered he was capable of anything else… Then I would have been the villain, not him. I'd rather it wasn't that way round. I've had enough of getting it wrong.

So. No crying over this one.

You can't lose someone who was never there in the first place.

FRIDAY 15TH JANUARY

AARON

On Monday I walked up to Rex and told him Hannah's baby was mine. It seemed the most efficient way to get it out there and it worked. By lunchtime the whole school was talking about it – even the teachers. The look Dad gave me as we passed in the corridor was martyred to say the least. By the end of the day, three boys were suspended for the Facebook thing. Apparently the Kingsway administration takes cyber-bullying seriously – although Anj said that Marcy deleted her status before she got caught.

The next day it became very clear that I'd been dropped from the basketball crowd, but almost immediately Anj and Gideon picked me up. Hannah too. Something tells me I'm safer down here than I ever was at the top of the food chain. Not least because, for the first time since October, no one has asked whether I'm going to the park tonight. I'm spending it with my mum, compensating by watching a rom com with her on the sofa. Definitely preferable to the park.

In amongst all this, we got our results back. Mine aren't too bad – a haul of Bs, As and a couple of A*s is enough to reassure my parents. But Hannah's haven't exactly been good news. I found her kicking a bin outside the gym when she was meant to be meeting me for lunch. It was tanking down and her uniform was soaked through. She pulled the scrumpled bit of paper out of the bin and showed me before she started kicking the bin again.

I can't say I blame her.

SATURDAY 16TH JANUARY

HANNAH

Mum's back. She's rustling about in the kitchen and I think about sneaking upstairs—

"Hannah?"

I stay quiet, but I can't mute the TV in time and Mum comes in.

"I've made you a cup of hot chocolate, love."

"Can't have too much caffeine," I mumble and she sighs.

"There's not enough caffeine to keep a flea awake in the mug I've made you." Tiniest of pauses. "The baby will be fine. Come and drink it in the kitchen."

When I go into the kitchen there's some magazines on the table which give me The Fear. They are magazines I have only started noticing in the last few months, magazines I didn't even know existed until I became an under-age member of the MTB club. Don't know what MTB means? I didn't either. It means Mum To Be.

On the front are pictures of women with terrifyingly white smiles and tanned skin – presumably exuding that glow I have yet to give off – hands proudly resting on bumps that look more like beach balls than bellies. On one of them you can see the woman's belly button – only you can't because IT'S NOT EVEN THERE. Gross. On others the women are holding babies whose faces must have been

Photoshopped because no babies I've ever seen look so fresh-faced and happy. Nor mums for that matter.

I look at mine as she walks past and sits at the table next to two gently steaming mugs and the landslide of glossy magazines.

"I'm not looking at those," I say warily.

"Just come and sit down with me, Hannah." Mum sounds tired, but she doesn't look cross or anything, which is new. I sit down and pull the hot chocolate towards me. She's used my favourite mug with the extra thick rim and the giant smiley and I wrap my fingers around it, an echo of the night Aaron offered me hot chocolate from a Thermos in the park. Who knew how much more he'd be offering me now? The boy's a lifesaver – well, a reputation saver.

Mum sips her drink and looks at me.

"I've not handled this very well," she says. Which is an understatement. "I never thought you'd get pregnant so young, but, even so, I see girls in your situation every day, terrified of what their parents will say when they find out they're pregnant. I tell them that their parents will love them no matter what and I reassure them that it's their body and they have a right to make their own decisions and not to let other people pressure them into anything…"

She trails off and sighs. "But all that goes out of the window when it's your own daughter."

I say nothing and concentrate on not thinking about Boxing Day. Or the way she flew off the handle at Aaron for taking advantage of me. If she knew the truth… So. Much. Worse.

"We all make mistakes, Hannah." She puts her hand over mine, around the mug. "Me included. I should have said this right away, but I love you. You are my precious little girl, and you always will be, no matter what. I'm not saying that I'm not hurt by some of the decisions you've made, but perhaps they were made for the right reasons. Perhaps you were right to confide in your gran before me. Perhaps you knew me better than I knew myself." Her fingers brush my skin. "But I'm your mother and I love you and I would walk through fire for you – you won't understand until you become one yourself. But I'll be with you through this."

Her eyes are filling up and my mouth and throat feel run through with sandpaper at the effort of not crying. Then, for what feels like the first time in months, Mum pulls me into a proper hug and squeezes me so hard that the tears are forced out of me. I rest my head on her shoulder and smell her perfume and close my eyes and let the weight of worry lift off me. It's not all gone, but still … having Mum hold me like this makes things seem a little more do-able.

"But we're going to have to do something about those exam results."

Bollocks. I knew this was too good to last.

HANNAH

Gideon holds the door open for me and I walk out into the corridor and straight into Marcy. I back off quickly, not wanting the hassle, but she turns the second she sees me, her posse surrounding me like a shoal of piranhas.

"Watch who you galumph into, pregna-slut."

"Get over yourself, Marcy," I say, trying to squeeze past her, but there isn't room. This shouldn't be rumbling on, not after Aaron's announcement last week. I'm not sure I've the energy to do this now.

"She probably couldn't see you over her belly," one of the others says with a snigger and I find myself running a hand over my stomach, protecting the bump. They can't possibly see it in this baggy old school jumper – it's hard enough to tell without it.

It's only then that I notice Katie's with them, at the back. She's not even looking my way and something inside me snaps.

"Shame I can't see who said that – Marcy's ego's in the way," I say loudly, pretending to try and look round her.

Gideon puts his hand on my arm and tries to pull me away.

"You don't want to get in a slanging match with me, Spanner," Marcy says. "I've got way more ammunition."

"I can't help being more interesting than you. You try

hard, I'll give you that – but even taking your clothes off for a living doesn't make you interesting."

Her lips tighten angrily and the posse look puzzled. The only reason I know she's done a topless shoot is because Tyrone told me – he'd been jealous of someone else seeing her tits. Ironic, given he had his hands on mine at the time.

"You're just jealous—"

"Of you?" I laugh, but it's not a nice noise. "No thanks. I'd rather be a statistic on teen pregnancy than a stuck-up bitch who sells her body for pocket money."

She spits in my face and everything's quiet as I hurry to wipe it off. I can't help myself: "At least your boyfriend had the decency to aim a little lower last time I sucked him off," I say in a voice that reaches everyone's ears.

Her hand lashes out and slaps me.

184

"What are you going to do now, Marcy? Pull my hair?" My cheek feels hot where her palm caught me and she might have scratched me a little with her freaky long fingernails. We stare at each other. She's simmering with rage and embarrassment. That her precious Tyrone might so much as *look* at someone as far down the ladder as me is enough to be ashamed of, but to suggest that he would actually *go* there…?

But we both know he has, because we've both seen the fear in his eyes when he looks at me these days.

I smile a little smile that's meant to look secretive, but obviously it's not secret, because I'm smiling so that the person in front of me gets the message loud and clear.

"Bitch!" Marcy flies at me with her talons and fists and

even her feet as she digs a heel into the top of my foot. I shove her back as hard as I can because I don't trust her not to go for the bump. She staggers back in a comedy manner and her friends catch her and push her back towards me, circling round us, preventing me from getting away. It's not so comedy any more and I'm scared by the look on everyone's faces as I shrink back into Gideon, who's as much use as wet bog roll. My arms are held low, defending the only thing I care about and I tense as Marcy lashes out—

"Get off her!"

Marcy's swipe whiskers past my eyes and then there's a body in front of me, guarding me, protecting me, protecting the baby.

Aaron.

"How do you even know it's yours?" Marcy yells at him, trying to push him away, but he's solid in front of me. "She'll shag anyone who looks at her."

"Marcy—"

"She's just a filthy little slut that got what she deserved."

"Stop it."

"You're just another number, only you're so stupid you actually think she's telling the truth about that little parasite—"

The tirade is cut short as Aaron steps so far into her space that Marcy's forced to back up.

"I said *stop*." Aaron's voice isn't exactly raised, but it's sharp and scary and it silences all of us.

Marcy stares at him as he stands in front of me and I wonder what she's seeing. Whatever it is, it scares her.

"Exactly what part of attacking a pregnant girl do you think is acceptable?"

"She st—"

"Pathetic excuse. Like you. Just go."

Marcy's struck dumb.

"Go. You just attacked my friend and started insulting the baby she's carrying – I can't possibly imagine why you think you're welcome here any more." He looks around at the crowd that's gathered. I see Katie at the back, see her look away as Aaron's gaze lasers into her. "Any of you."

Everyone starts muttering to one another and slouching off to the next class as Marcy strops off with a comet trail of friends following her, whispering, glancing back at me in disgust.

Whatever. I have the only friends I need.

I catch Katie looking over her shoulder as she whispers something in Marcy's ear.

Repeat after me: I have the only friends I need.

AARON

Hannah's waiting for me outside the staffroom after lessons.

"Thought you'd gone home," I say. After this morning I wouldn't blame her.

"I don't run away." She runs a hand up through her hair and I realize she's wearing less make-up, her nails are free of varnish and she looks ... fresh. "I wanted to say thanks. For this morning. With Marcy."

I shrug. She doesn't need to thank me.

"One day I'll be the one coming to your rescue, you know," she says with a smile.

HANNAH

"You already are," he says and he ducks his head away as if he doesn't want me to look too closely. As if he doesn't want me to see him properly. I think about how many times I've laughed at something he's said – the way I'm tempted to right now – and I wonder if he's ever really joking at all.

FRIDAY 22ND JANUARY

HANNAH

Mum said that Dad called to speak to me last night before he leaves today, but she followed my instructions to the letter and told him where to go. Apparently he wanted to clear the air. Newsflash, Dad: not happening. The worse things get with everyone else – with Marcy, with Katie, with Dad – the more I realize that it doesn't matter that Mum isn't perfect, she's still my mum and she's still doing the best she can.

I look down at my tummy. I guess I can identify with that.

Mum isn't the only one, either. Anj and Gideon are being really nice to me, sitting with me whenever they can (although that still leaves a lot of lessons on my own). Aaron's amazing too. Always there, just quietly, whenever I need him. I have no idea how this boy ended up in my life, but there will never be a time when I am not grateful for it.

"Hannah Sheppard?" The midwife sticks her head out of her office and I get up, conscious of everyone looking at me still in my school uniform, judging me.

And then my mum's hurrying down the corridor – a shuffle-run which is the best she can manage in her sensible work shoes.

"I'm here, I'm here, sorry I'm late. Couldn't find a parking space…"

But it doesn't matter. She's here now and that's all that counts.

AARON

I've only just got there when my phone beeps a text.

"I'm dealing today until I master the riffle," I say as I check my phone, ignoring the tut issued by Neville. He's saying something about manners, but I'm not really listening.

2nd scan all ok – no idea if boy or grl, had its legs Xed! Thought ud like to no. Hx

She's right. I do like to know.

SATURDAY 23ᴿᴰ JANUARY

HANNAH

I'm starting to lose my rag over what to wear tonight. I haven't been out – to the park, to the cinema, to a club, *anywhere* – since the start of the year and it turns out that all my decent clothes now make me look fat. I know, I'm pregnant and my body's got to make space for the other person inside me, blah blah blah, but I don't *look* pregnant. I just look fat. And my best bra's starting to dig in, which isn't improving things.

There's a pile of clothes on the floor and I want to jump up and down on them and scream, only I'm worried Mum'll hear and I don't want her to know. Her answer will be to look at those stupid magazines and suggest I try some of the frumpy bump-friendly fashion that I would only wear if I had a brain transplant. I feel like there's something wrong with me – I'm supposed to want to be a different person now that I've been sperminated, but I *don't*. I want to be Hannah, just pregnanter. What's so wrong with still wanting to look good? With wanting to show off my new improved pregnancy curves in push-up bras and clothes that look teen not tragic? I want people to think *Hannah* before they think *pregnant*.

I don't even know why I'm bothering. It's only a trip to the cinema with Gideon, Anj and Aaron. Those guys don't care if I turn up in leggings and a hoodie.

Somehow that thought depresses me even more.

I don't want to be the only one who cares what I look like.

AARON

Inevitably, I'm the first there. This comes from my father's innate love of punctuality – which also means that instead of letting me wait for the others in the warm car, he ushers me out as fast as possible so that he can get back home on schedule. He is unsympathetic to the fact that his son has come out without a coat and may well die from hypothermia.

"Your mother and I thought you were capable of dressing responsibly by now."

And with that, he raises his eyebrows and makes a "hurry up" gesture.

This is the first time I've been to the cinema since we moved and I peer into the foyer, wondering whether they sell hot drinks in addition to unseasonable ice cream and slushies. There's a rush of footsteps behind me and I half turn, ready for trouble, but it's only an exuberant Gideon, who slams gloved hands on my shoulders and delivers an unnecessary "Boo!"

Anj walks up behind him, looking at her phone.

"She just got a text," Gideon explains.

"Hannah?" I ask, wondering if Anj got the same text I did about her running late.

"Someone *far* more exciting…" Gideon snatches the phone, handing it to me as he shouts, "Translate it!"

before clamping his arms round a frantic Anj.

It's in Spanish and I catch the gist before Anj breaks free with a scream and grabs it back, blushing furiously.

"How much did you get?" she says, not meeting my eye as she deletes the message.

"Not much," I lie. The text contained some distinctly extra-curricular phrases from someone called Felipe. Gideon looks disappointed and I stage-whisper that I'll tell him later, which causes a bit of a slapping storm between the three of us until it suddenly loses wind. Anj avoids our stares when we turn to look at her.

"So I got a bit carried away with my Spanish penpal." She glances up and blushes even more. "What?! He's totally hot. *You* would." She nods at Gideon.

"I demand evidence."

Sighing, Anj opens up Facebook, scrolls down her friends list to Felipe Montes and clicks on his profile. I try unsuccessfully to ignore Gideon as he makes gagging gestures behind Anj's back, for which he receives a flick on the forehead. When Anj clicks back to her friends list I see a Jason Sheppard listed there.

"Is that Hannah's stepbrother?" I point, curious.

"Mmm … Jay," Gideon says, dreamily.

Anj nods. "I'll second that. In fact, I'll call shotgun."

"You mean dibs."

"That too." Anj turns to me to explain. "Jay is the most gorgeous person in the whole of this town."

His profile picture doesn't look anything out of the ordinary to me.

"I demand evidence."

The pair of them smile as Anj opens up a page of his photos and Gideon says, "Hottest guy in town. Fact."

"I thought I was number one?" I joke.

Gideon feigns thought before delivering a dismissive pat on my arm. "You come a close second."

"For the purposes of reining in your ego, Aaron Tyler, I feel I should inform you that you most certainly do *not* rank second on my list of hotties," Anj says as she jabs at the screen, trying to find a suitably pleasing picture of Jay. "No offence."

Which makes me laugh.

I look at the picture she's found, but I'm not sure I see what these two can.

"Man, he is fit," Gideon mutters.

"He is a fit man all right." And Anj lets out a lovelorn sigh.

"Really?" I shake my head. Outraged into action, Gideon grabs the phone to hunt for a more convincing picture. He's flicking through when I see something. "Hang on a sec, go back."

The girl on the screen looks beautiful, dark hair swishing around her shoulders as she raises a bottle to the person behind the camera. She's standing next to Katie Coleman, who does not look anything approaching beautiful.

"Hannah looks stunning!" Anj says and we all lean a touch closer to see if we're seeing it right. Normally Hannah wears very little clothing and a lot of make-up when she goes out, but in this photo she's wearing a good amount of both. I scroll through a couple more photos taken on the same night – "A proper send off" the album's called – and find one with Hannah and Jay. The two of them aren't looking at the camera – it's an action shot of them dancing and they're completely natural. They look good together. Put him next to hot Hannah and I can suddenly see what Anj and Gideon mean about Jason Sheppard.

"Hello?" A hand swooshes in front of the screen and we all look up.

HANNAH

Aaron, Anj and Gideon all give me equally blank looks and for a second I panic that I was never really invited out in the first place. Until I remember that I was the one that did the inviting.

"What?" They're still looking at me. Maybe I've overdone it on the eyeshadow…

"I was just showing Aaron photos of your fit stepbrother," Anj says with a grin. "You know, the one I've crushed on since for ever. His leaving party looks like a night to remember."

"It was," I say and summon up a smile.

AARON

We move inside and I hold the door open, letting Gideon and Anj through, followed by Hannah. There's a distant look in her eyes as if her mind is in a different time and place and I wonder what she's thinking about. I think we creeped her out with how odd we were about Jay's Facebook photos. It's hard to explain that we acted like that because we'd just been re-evaluating Hannah's hotness.

Whilst Gideon and Anj get snacks I wait for Hannah by the ticket machine, subtly checking her out as she frowns at the screen. Whatever effort she put into this outfit – a lot given the way it hides her middle yet shows off the shape of her bum and legs – it's less try-hard than anything she ever wore to the park.

It looks good.

HANNAH

When I turn away from the machine I catch Aaron looking at me.

"What?" I'm sick of this. What is it with these guys tonight?

Aaron smiles – the nicest of his smiles, one where there's nothing more than a secretive curve to his lips. "I like your outfit."

Oh. Well. He's forgiven, then.

I fall into step beside him to join the others and I smile at the ground.

Aaron cares what I look like.

MONDAY 25TH JANUARY

HANNAH

For the first time in *ever* I'm looking forward to school today. Which is not like me. At. All.

It's because I want to see my friends. Actual more-than-one-who-I-see-*all*-the-time friends. Plural. It's not like I wasn't friendly with Anj and Gideon before now, but I don't know if I'd have said we were mates or anything. Not like with Katie.

The stupid thing is that if I'd never started hanging out with Katie, then I'd have probably been mates with Anj and Gideon instead. Anj is the only one here who went to my primary – she lived on the same road as me and we were regular trick-or-treat partners. On hot weekends Anj would come and play in my paddling pool – she still came over even once we moved in with Robert on the other side of town. The summer before we moved up to Kingsway, the summer after Lola was born, Anj and I spent most of our time running in and out of the sprinkler system on the back lawn. Once we ran out of breath, we'd go inside to get drinks, wearing T-shirts over our swimsuits in case Jay had his friends round – then act more mature if he did. None of them ever noticed.

My first day at Kingsway was terrifying. There are thousands of kids and the buildings are massive. I don't think I've ever felt smaller – but at least Anj was there being small with me.

It wasn't until halfway through the first term that I started hanging around Katie. She was really gobby and I'd been a bit scared of her, but we eventually bonded over a hatred of PE. Anj has always been sporty and she got picked first for everything, even by the boys. I was always one of the last to be chosen because I was so short and skinny; Katie because she'd decided it was better to give off CBA vibes than try something and fail. We'd end up sitting on the subs bench together and friendship followed from there.

One of the other reasons Katie was never picked was because she isn't a team player and that attitude goes for everything, including friends. As we became mates she began edging Anj out. She'd invite me somewhere and never mention Anj. I'd sit next to Anj in a lesson and Katie would come right up to the desk and ask me to sit with her at lunch. When she invited me to her birthday party, I assumed that everyone in the class had been invited. They had – everyone except Anj. Stupidly, I'd felt special. When we started at Kingsway, out of the two of us, Anj was the one people talked to. I was just "Anj's friend". No one even knew my name. For someone to pick me instead felt good.

It didn't take long before Katie was the only one coming to my house and the person Anj spent the most time with wasn't me, but Gideon. It wasn't a big deal when it happened – it wasn't as if we'd started school with matching friendship bracelets – but I wish it had been. If Anj had ever asked me what I was doing, I might have actually *thought* about the choice I was making.

That summer I invited Katie round to our house on one of the hottest days of the year. I got my costume out and I started early in the sprinkler so that when Katie arrived I was already slick from the spray. She'd eyed me up and down when I answered the door.

"That's what you wear in the garden?"

"Yeah. What's wrong with it?" I'd looked down at the swimming costume I'd got to go on holiday with Dad at Easter. It was purple with a sporty white swash across my very flat tummy.

"Nothing." Katie had shrugged and walked in, then she'd taken off her clothes to reveal a bikini so small that it barely hid her early developments in the boob department.

We'd gone outside and I'd stood like a useless purple lump as Katie pulled out a sun lounger and lay down on it, stretching herself out like a cat. Ten minutes later, Jay came and sat on the end of the lounger to talk to her. I sat on the grass and watched them.

The next day I begged Mum to take me shopping for a bikini.

WEDNESDAY 3RD FEBRUARY

AARON

It's cold, it's windy and tiny droplets of drizzle lash what little of my face is exposed to the elements. How I ended up being roped into going to the corner shop to buy Hannah an ice cream is beyond me. I'm even more bewildered that I've been tasked to bring back treats for Anj and Gideon as well.

The bell on the door is broken, which suits me fine when I see who's browsing the magazines as I walk in the shop. Katie's hair is plastered to her head and there's a distinct shiver to her stance. Thankfully, she's too distracted to notice me walk to the freezer. By the time I've collected everything, Katie's moved on to arguing with the shopkeeper about serving her cigarettes. There's a stash of gossip magazines and various diet drinks on the counter in front of her. I guess as bottom feeder of the WAG hierarchy it's her job to brave the rain and fetch supplies. I could be accused of hypocrisy here, since Katie's going to get more enjoyment out of those magazines than I will out of this Feast, Gideon's banana milkshake or Anj's disgusting prawn-cocktail crisps, but at the end of the day I'm aware of the difference between buying refreshments and buying friendship.

"Thanks for nothing," Katie hisses at the shopkeeper,

turning so violently that she's propelled the metre it takes to bump into me. For a second her glance slides over me as if I'm nothing but an obstruction, then her eyes narrow.

I step past and pay for my haul, aware that Katie hasn't moved. As I head for the door, she falls into step beside me.

"News flash, Emo Boy, it's *winter.*" She snatches Hannah's ice cream from my hands and flicks it against my shoulder hard enough for it to snap before handing it back as we reach the exit.

I jam my toe under the edge of the door.

"Buy another one," I say, quietly.

"Fuck off!" Katie tries to yank the door open, but I lean my weight on it. "Get out the fucking way!"

I wait, impassive.

"Aaron!"

"So you do know my name."

"Just move."

"Don't want to keep your friends waiting, do you?"

She shoots me a murderous glare. "As if you're going to stand there all day." But I can tell by the way she looks at me that she's not sure I won't. "What do you want?"

I look at her and wait some more until she storms off in a cloud of swear words, returning with a new ice cream.

"Thank you," I say, holding the door open for her.

"I hope you choke on it."

"Unlikely. It's for Hannah." Katie's three paces ahead, but she still hears me and I see her half turn, her face relaxed enough for me to see something there – a sadness so profound that for a fleeting moment I think that maybe—

"Well, Hannah can fucking choke on it, then, can't she?" She marches ahead of me, arms crossed against the wind, magazines tucked under her blazer. Katie knows she made a mistake, but she'll die before she admits it. She traded everything she had for the chance to be Marcy's lapdog. There's no going back now.

TUESDAY 9ᵀᴴ FEBRUARY

AARON

Hannah fidgets during English. It's distracting.

Could you maybe sit still for more than thirty seconds at a time? Some of us are trying to work here.

I turn my notebook towards her and tap the page.

Cd u mayb stop bein such a suck up? Some of us r tryin 2 bum here.

She adds a little smiley face with the tongue sticking out. I find it entertaining the way Hannah writes as if she's texting.

What's up?

Because something is. Emoticon aside, Hannah isn't smiling.

Wot u doin @ wknd?

The question unnerves me. It's Valentine's Day on Sunday.

Seeing Neville on Sunday.

I make a mental note to switch my date with Neville, which should amuse him.

Come 4 family dinner on Sat? There's a pause in her writing as Mrs English looks up from marking a stack of essays to check we're all dutifully reading our texts. *J up 4 wknd.*

Jay's home? This is interesting.

SATURDAY 13TH FEBRUARY

HALF-TERM

AARON

"Hi," I say and hold out my hand.

"Hi." Jason takes my hand and sizes me up as he shakes. "So you're Hannah's boyfriend."

Hannah and I give him what must be identical stares. Whatever he's been told, I'm sure no one's told him we're actually dating. That has *never* been the story.

"Sorry, I'm not sure what the appropriate title is…" he starts to say, but Hannah shoots him down.

"How about 'friend' – you've heard of those, right?"

Immediately I reassess the situation. Hannah's been subdued this week, something I'd put down to hormones, which is the excuse she gives for absolutely everything. But I was wrong. Whatever this is, it has less to do with hormones and more to do with Jay. Whatever it is, I'm on Hannah's side. As if I'd be anywhere else.

"Aaron!" Lola flies out of the front room and cannons into me for a hug.

Robert comes out of his office and claps his son on the shoulder. "So you two have met, then?"

"Just now, Dad. We exchanged maybe a sentence before Lolly came in and stole Aaron from me." He playfully prods his little sister in the cheek, but she presses closer to me instead of him. It's nice to be the favourite, but there's something in the way Jay looks at me that tells me I'll regret it.

Dinner is a Chinese takeaway that Hannah and Jay go to collect in his car. Paula and Robert are busy in the kitchen, leaving me and Lola to play Mario Kart in the front room. This suits me fine – although, being more of an RPG player, I endure a relentless drubbing from the nearly-six-year-old girl next to me. Lola doesn't seem to mind that I'm a far from worthy opponent and when she hears her brother and sister come in, she pulls me into the kitchen and sits me next to her.

"And Mummy on the other side." Lola pats the chair to her left.

"What about Jason, Lolly? You haven't seen him in a while. I'm sure he'd like a chance to spend some time with you." Only parents do this – presume it's OK to speak for you even when it's obviously inviting trouble.

Lola looks at Jason with wide eyes as he puts the bags on the table then she leans into me a little as she looks up at her mum and beckons her closer.

"I don't want to sit next to Jay. He's not been very nice to Hannah," she whispers into her mother's ear so quietly that I only just catch it and I'm sitting right next to her.

Hannah's mum frowns and leans in to whisper back.

"I'm sure they made up when they went to get the takeaway." She catches me looking and I turn away. "Please, poppet, ask to sit with Jay – he's missed you."

Lola glances at me and after I give the slightest of nods, she announces that she's changed her mind.

Disaster averted, we settle down and I watch as Jay tries to engage Lolly in conversation, then I watch Hannah watching him. It's not as if I believed Paula before – about her stepson and her daughter making up – but it looks like they've been arguing some more. Hannah's jaw is locked in attack mode and she's snapping prawn crackers like a piranha. Jay on the other hand won't look at her. At all. Not even when she asks him to pass her the soy sauce.

The conversation takes a dangerous turn at the unwrapping of the duck pancakes when Jay asks me whether I'd like to come and see what Warwick is like in case I fancy applying. He's just being polite (or smug) but it draws attention to the fact that in two and a half years' time I should be in a position to go to university.

"I thought I might go somewhere close by," I say, smearing plum sauce on my pancake. Hannah and I haven't really got an exit strategy for our fabricated relationship so I'm forced to ad lib.

"There's not many good places that near. I checked." Jay looks at me and I swear his expression is challenging. Under the table, Hannah presses her foot gently on mine. I ignore Jay and eat my pancake.

The subject comes up again at the fourth tub of rice. This time from Robert.

"Seriously, Aaron, what are your plans for the future now that" – he trails off and looks at Hannah – "you've others to think about?"

"I was thinking of seeing how it goes. Making plans

seems a bit premature." Good answer – well done, me.

"Mm. It never hurts to be prepared." And that appears to be all Robert has to say on the matter.

But not Jay. "Still, gotta think about your options now, haven't you? Work out which subjects to concentrate on when you're revising – no point worrying about Biology if you're going to study English, is there?"

"Aaron's pretty smart, Jay." Hannah steps in before I finish my mouthful. "I don't think he needs to worry about his revision the way you did."

Ouch.

Robert frowns at his stepdaughter, opens his mouth to say something, then sees his wife glaring him into silence.

"Keen, huh?" Jay sticks his lip out and nods in what can only be described as a patronizing manner. "What're you doing hanging out with Hannah?"

It's meant to be a joke but no one – not even Lola – cracks a smile.

I've had enough of this.

"Being a friend. Obviously a subject you missed out of your revision."

In any other company that might have been chalked up as a point to me but Robert stares at me in a way that makes me feel smaller than a grain of egg fried rice. There's no chance to rectify the situation in the flurry of activity as empty containers are stacked and leftovers touted about and I regret what I said. Robert is someone I want to think well of me.

After dinner we go to the front room and provide a

dutiful audience whilst Lola acts out a scene from *The Lion King*. I've seen it before. Actually, I think I helped her learn the lines. It's late, though, and Lola can't stop yawning, so Paula takes her upstairs for a bath, and just as Robert gets up to drive me home, his phone rings.

"Aaron, I'm sorry, but I've got to take this call and I could be a while…"

"That's OK." After my transgression at the dinner table the last thing I want to be is an inconvenience.

"I can run you home," Jay says with a smile so forced that I'm sure he's only doing it to impress his father. It works and as Robert rubs a hand over his son's head on his way past, I can almost see the thought bubble appear above his head: my son is the *best*. Or something more eloquent.

Hannah comes out with me as I fetch my coat.

"Sorry about Jay," she says with a sigh.

"I thought he was meant to be a nice guy?" I say.

"He was." Hannah shrugs. "University is turning him into an arse."

But Jay is golden. He is fanciable no matter what he looks like. He's nice however he behaves. For guys like him, there will always be an excuse.

"Break it up, snuggle puppies." Jay radiates irritation as he stalks out of the door. "Hannah, are you coming too?"

She is, which means I'm in the back because Hannah gets carsick. Jay makes a joke about evening sickness and I get a kick out of informing him that pregnancy hasn't made Hannah ill. I know he was only joking, but it's fun to be arsey to an arse. Obviously Hannah doesn't think so since her shoulders are creeping up with every bit of one-upmanship Jay and I engage in. I'll stop.

It isn't long before I discover that Jay drives like a maniac. After he drives straight over the middle of one those painted roundabouts, I hear Hannah hiss at him to slow down. He drops to a petulant ten miles an hour below the speed limit.

The journey passes in silence before Hannah starts directing Jay to my house, until he pulls up outside, a squeal of the tyre scraping the kerb.

"Thanks for the ride," I say.

"You talking to me or Hannah?" Jay laughs as I get out. I stop for a moment as the door shuts. I try to walk away, but I find myself opening Jay's door, leaning in until my face is close to his ear and I can see my knuckles are white as I grip the doorframe so hard that I lose the feeling in my fingertips.

"I don't know if you're being a twat because it comes naturally" – my voice is quiet and precise – "or because you've been studying it, but that's your stepsister you're talking about." I take a breath and tighten my grip on the door. I must not let go. Of the door. Of my temper. "Show some fucking respect."

I swing the door with the full force of my outrage and turn away. There's no clunk as it shuts – instead I catch Hannah's voice issue a warning "Jay..." at the same time as a shove from behind sends me sprawling onto the bonnet with a squeak and a *thunk*.

Scrabbling upright, I swing round to find Jay right in my face. "I don't know what you *think* you know about me. But you don't get to talk to me like that."

My hands squeeze up between my chest and his so I can push him out of my space. Bad idea. He pushes me back harder. I don't mean to grab his shoulder to stop myself from toppling backwards, but there you go. All of a sudden I am in a fight. There's a sting on my jaw where his knuckles catch me, but I know exactly how much it hurts to throw a punch so I yank a fistful of his top and twist so he falls face first onto the bonnet.

How can I stop this? I need to shut things down. I can't be here, I can't do this…

But Jay's back up and swinging at me. I jump back and pain blossoms as his fist catches me full in the nose, then that's it – I'm lunging for him with my hands balled up, aiming for his head. I catch a hit somewhere and we're grappling and shoving. I kick out and at the same time I see a splatter of blood fly across his jeans. Jay's thumb is digging painfully into my jaw as he pushes my face away and I reach up and clamp my hand around his wrist as I ball my fist up, ready to—

"STOP IT!"

The scream is right in my ear and it rings in my hearing along with the blood pounding in my head.

"Just fucking stop it!" Hannah is shouting at Jay now and she's between us, pointing a very straight finger at his face, daring him to disobey. Jay says nothing, licking his split lip and shaking his hand out, reminding me of the pain in my own. My nails are digging into my palms and my whole arm feels jarred. The ache I feel in fingers I once broke reminds me why this was such a bad idea.

"Get back in the car, Jay."

He doesn't move.

"Just do as I say – all right?" Hannah looks weary and Jay switches his gaze from me to her before doing as she says.

He shoulders his way past me, forcing me to stamp down a burning need to pull him back and lay into him once again.

Instead I walk towards my front door, Hannah following me up the path.

"OK, so now we're even," I say with a thin smile. "I save you from Marcy and you save me from Jason."

"It's not funny, Ty."

I close my eyes. I wish she wouldn't call me that.

"I know. I'm sorry. I just…" I bump my head gently onto the window in the door and rest it there. "He was being such a tool."

Hannah says nothing. A car turns into the road and in the sweep of its headlights I catch the glisten of tears in her eyes.

"Don't say that."

"It's the truth. Your stepbrother is a class A—"

"He's the father." The whispered words are so quiet I could have imagined them. I *want* to have imagined them. "Jay's the father of my baby."

There must be a right thing to do, but I don't know what it is and I can feel the distance stretching between us with every second that passes. By the time I realize that anything is better than nothing it's too late and she steps back from the hug I reach in for.

"I can't…" She waves me away.

"Hannah—"

"I'll call you tomorrow." With that she runs away down the pavement. I step after her, but the hall light clicks on and, just as I pause, I see Jay get out of the car and run after her. And I stop dead, because even if I run after her, even if I beat Jay to it, what am I going to do when I get there?

HANNAH

I don't know where I'm running. I don't know this part of town too well. I stop at the first bench I see and sit down. Running is probably a bad idea in my condition.

Stupid baby. I wish—

That almost-thought makes me cry even harder. I hadn't meant it. I've never even slightly wished that, but…

Tears keep coming and I'm nearly choking on my misery. Only I can't seem to stop.

Someone sits down next to me and rests a hand on my back. I look up to see Jay.

A little part of me was hoping it was Aaron. That part is disappointed. The rest of me? Jury's out. I'm still very angry with Jay.

"Hannah, I'm sorry."

"You–should–be," I manage to say between hiccupy sobs. I breathe deeply and try to get a little control here. "You're such a … tool."

My voice catches on the last word and I think about what just happened with Aaron – not when I told him the truth, but the fight beforehand. Aaron. In a fight. One I think he might have won. That's not the Aaron I thought I knew.

"Come here, Han." Jay moves closer, his arm sliding all the way around me until I'm nestled into him and I can almost hear his heart through his jacket. "I'm so sorry."

What is it that he's saying sorry for? For fighting with one of the best friends I've ever had? For asking me if I'm really sure that he's the father? For it never being the right time to tell people? For saying he doesn't need a picture of the scan? For everything that's happened between us?

I don't want him to be sorry for that.

Because I'm not.

AARON

I watch at the window, lights off, waiting for them to come back, worried about Hannah. When they finally do I see that Jay has his arm around her and she's leaning into his shoulder.

"Hannah…" I whisper, a wave of disappointment washing over me. When they get to his car, Jay opens the door for her. Neither of them makes a move to get in.

I turn away, not wanting to know what happens next.

The last time Jay looked at me like this was the night I got pregnant.

"What are we doing?" he whispers, eyes searching mine, one hand on the door, the other on the roof of his car, circling me in the space between. I take him in, concentrating on every little detail of his face – the stubble on his jaw; his nose and eyebrows; his lips and the way his tongue moves behind his teeth as he speaks. "It wasn't meant to be like this."

He turns away and I sink into the car, my body charged with wanting. As Jay slides into the driver's seat, he puts the key in the ignition, but he doesn't turn it. Instead he turns to look at me. "I don't know what to do."

"You've been driving for over a year now," I say, smiling, and he smiles back at me in such a way that my pulse hammers in my throat.

"Strangely enough I didn't mean about that." He rests the side of his head on the headrest, the same way I'm doing, eyes not leaving mine.

I want him to kiss me. I want it so much that I could almost confuse imagining it with doing it. Is he thinking the same? And then, as if I've wished it into happening, Jay bridges the gap between us and tilts his head until his mouth is on mine, trying to own me just as I'm trying to own him, our breath rushing together, noses pressing into each other's cheeks… My body isn't mine, my brain is a mess and I can't stop one hand from reaching up and curling around the collar of his jacket, pulling him closer to me as I lift away a little, catching my breath as I meet his gaze.

"Han…" He doesn't finish the thought before he's leaning in closer and we're kissing once more and I'm thinking that the unthinkable, unhopeable, has happened. Jay has changed his mind.

AARON

When Mum comes in asking if I've seen The Kaiser anywhere, I'm still sitting in the dark, in silence, waiting for the sound of Jay's car driving off. If I'm honest, I know this behaviour is a bit disturbing, but they've been sitting in his car ten minutes now and every second that passes, my mood darkens. Tonight's events and the way I'm responding to them is scaring me.

Mum asks me why I'm sitting with the light off and I shrug, ears straining as I think I hear an engine firing up.

"Aaron, you know it's this kind of behaviour that worries a mother." She sits on the bed and I hear a car pull away, the engine rattling. They've gone.

I look at Mum. I can't tell her the whole story, but… "I found out who the father is."

HANNAH

It was always going to be a night to remember. Robert's cash plus Jay's mates equals a pretty awesome party: a marquee in the garden and a ton of pre-uni hotness in our house? Yes, please. It took a bit of persuading to be allowed to stay whilst the rest of them went to Robert's parents for the night, but Jay's promise to keep an eye on me sealed the deal.

Jay had said Katie could come too and she arrived early that afternoon. We spent far too long messing about getting ready so that by the time we came downstairs loads of Jay's mates had arrived. I'm not going to lie. I was on the prowl. A summer of flirting with Tyrone and learning how to make a guy lose control had given me confidence. There was this boy, Dion, from Jay's year that I had a massive crush on, but I was willing to wait and spent an hour or so with Katie, playing the field – well, the sitting room – before I left her to it and headed for the kitchen.

Dion was there. I knew he'd clocked me already since there'd been some good glances going on, and it was easy to flirt with him once I got him alone. Until someone came into the kitchen.

"Han?"

I look up from the counter where I'm leaning on strategically folded arms. Jay does not look happy.

"Jay! Dude!" Dion swings round in one of those power whole-arm-handshake gestures, but as Jay shakes his hand he's staring at me. I stop leaning on the counter and hug my bottle instead.

"Chatting up my little sister, are you, Dion?" he asks, all innocent. I want to punch him.

"Little…?" Dion looks at me in horror, then at Jay. "You're Hannah as in…? I didn't recognize her – you…" He has no idea who he should be talking to. "Look. I've got to, um… See you around."

Running would be a pretty accurate description of how he leaves the room.

I do punch Jay. On the arm. Perfect nerve strike.

"Ow." He rubs his arm, but grins at me. "Dion's got a girlfriend, Han. I'm just looking out for you."

Oh.

I huff out, but as I pass I hear Jay say, "Nice outfit." And I smile to myself, forgiving him.

Katie was tongue-deep in some guy's face in the corner of the sitting room and it didn't take long for me to grow bored of eavesdropping on other people's conversations. A change of scene was in order. The marquee was calling and I was in the mood for dancing – and getting noticed. It's all about inhibitions and, let's face it, I don't really have any of those. I slipped in amongst the groups that were already on the dancefloor and it wasn't long before a cute guy started matching my moves. Just as I brought my arms around the boy dancing with me, I felt a pair of hands on my waist pulling me gently back. I didn't mind. Hands on waist is never a bad sign and these hands felt good. They didn't seem shy of touching me.

When the hands spun me round I realized why.

Grinning, Jay leaned in and told me he'd put in a request. As the music changed, I burst out laughing at the opening chords of "our" song, the one we invented a dance to, that we performed at Mum and Robert's wedding after *hours* spent practising in the front room – Jay was convinced he could teach me how to do the "running man", despite not having a clue himself. There and then, without thinking, the pair of us automatically stepped into formation, a circle clearing around us as we put on a step-perfect performance, the pair of us laughing so hard we could barely breathe.

And I felt special. I never feel special. Not really. I don't think many people do. It takes a lot of self-confidence to think that someone you really rate might think you're all right. It takes a leap of faith to *believe* it. But sometimes, someone is awesome enough to take the time to make you feel that way. I knew everyone was laughing as we moved like malfunctioning robots, but the only person who mattered to me was Jay. The same way it's always been, one way or another.

The night passed. I chatted to and danced with a million different people, buzzing so hard that I was one of the last to bed, hunting around for Katie amongst the bodies sprawled on the sofas and in the spare room. But she wasn't anywhere to be seen … until I opened my bedroom door.

No one had bothered to shut the curtains and in the moonlight I saw one guy passed out face down on my bed. But it was the floor show that caught me off guard. I didn't recognize the boy, but he sounded very pleased with what was happening – my best mate bouncing around on him like a space hopper, her back to me. I shut the door as fast as I could, but I couldn't help hearing Katie start to make some weird little squeaking noises. Grim.

I could have knocked on the door, given them a chance to sort themselves out before I went in and reclaimed my room. Instead I went up the stairs to Jay's space in the loft.

"Jay, it's Hannah," I say, opening the door a little bit.

"Hey, Han, you OK?" Waving me in, he sits up, bare chest and bleary beer-drenched eyes.

"Katie's with some guy in my room." I sit on the bed next to him.

"There's a surprise," Jay says. "Want to stay in here?"

"Uh-huh." I get off the bed and curl up on the bean bag, but there's a draft. I wriggle around and pull Jay's T-shirt off the floor and over my feet. I'm aware I'm making a lot of noise. There's a reason for that…

Jay sits up again. "You OK over there?"

"Cold. Got any bedding spare?"

But I know he hasn't and I watch as he shuffles over and lifts up the duvet for me to climb in. "Or you can lie there and run the risk of me killing you for fidgeting too much."

I clamber in, enjoying the warmth of his mattress and the smell of him close by as I snuggle into his duvet. Sleep isn't exactly there waiting for me. I'm hyper-aware of Jay's body on the other side of the bed. It's like I can feel every breath. I half roll over to look at him. His eyes are closed.

I wriggle, trying to get comfortable but I'm not. I feel all tingly and excited. This is stupid. This is Jay. I squeeze my eyes shut and concentrate on the idea of falling asleep.

"Han?"

"Yeah?" I don't look round.

"You're a really heavy breather."

"Thanks!" I smile into the pillow.

There's silence again, but I'm even less sleepy than I was to start with.

Jay shuffles about behind me until I feel his breath on the back of my neck. All I can think about is that whisper of air on my skin. There's movement and I feel an arm reach round to cuddle me. Gently, I lay my hand over his. Jay goes very still, like he's waiting for something. Slowly, uncertainly, I slide my fingers between his and gently guide his hand under my top and onto the skin of my tummy.

I breathe out.

This should be weird. But it really, *really* isn't.

Jay's body is close to mine. I can feel the heat on my back, his legs as they curl into the curve made by mine. Gradually, I find that I'm leaning back, pushing myself into him. The hand under my top strokes very, very gentle fingers over my skin.

The breath on my neck gets warmer and I feel lips on my skin. Feather-light and cool-yet-hot. Jay kisses my neck once, then again, gently around onto my shoulder. He lifts himself up and I turn around to look at him.

We're silent as we look at each other, letting our eyes do the talking. Then we're kissing. I've never been kissed like this. It's the sexiest thing that's ever happened to me. I swell up with need as the kissing swallows me whole.

The hand under my top pulls me round until he's lying on top of me. Somehow, between the kissing on the lips and the neck and the shoulders, he takes off my top and I wriggle out of my skirt until we're there in our underwear, skin on skin, as we stroke and kiss each other. I can feel him pressing against me through his boxers and my hand is sliding down…

As Jay shudders, I can feel it echoing in my own body. He's running the back of his nails down the skin on my tummy, edging up the elastic on my pants as I tense up, knowing what happens next and not knowing all at once. Where is this going? Because this isn't just some guy I've known for a few hours, a few days, a few weeks – this is Jay.

And there are very different rules for Jay. I think.

Our pants come off pretty quickly. As does my bra.

His fingers trace over every inch of my body, over my breasts, my sides and back up to my face. And then he stops and holds my face in his fingertips and looks me in the eye.

"Has anyone ever told you how gorgeous you are?"

I don't say anything.

"You're something special, Hannah." He sweeps forward and kisses me on the forehead. Jay pushes me back on the bed and kisses me, his tongue pushing right into my mouth, before working his way down my body, and down and down and…

Oh. My. God.

I'm in a world of awesome as Jay leans over to get a condom out of his bedside drawer and pulls it on. As he pushes into me there's a hiss of breath from both of us and it's uncomfortable for a second, but then I find I'm trying to burrow into him, pushing back just as hard, kissing whatever bit of skin that comes close, my hands gripping his back, his shoulders, his bum… I'm not thinking about what I'm doing, I'm not trying to be good, not trying to think like he's going to mark me out of ten. I'm just there, in it, feeling it, wanting it so much and then more and more and…

It's over too soon. It wouldn't have lasted long enough if it had lasted all night. I just want more of him than there is.

When he pulls out I deflate.

We curl up on our sides, our foreheads touching, a hand resting on the other's body as we kiss and smile at each other, eyes lit up. There isn't much talking. Mostly smiling, kissing, stroking. I feel a bit stiff – bruised almost, although it lessens as my heartbeat slows to something like normal. After a while, I slide my hand down his body. Then I slide down to join it. Jay doesn't take much persuading when I come back up.

"I'm good to go if you are?" he says, running his hand across my thigh and chuckling as I sigh and roll my eyes back. I did not mean to do that, but it's not like I have much control here. Around him I don't need it.

Jay scrambles over me and opens his drawer.

"Shit." He grabs his wallet open. "Fuck."

"Yeah – that's what I'm waiting for."

"No condoms."

This would be the point where I'd have some in my handbag or my pocket or my bra. Only I don't. Jay climbs back next to me, frowning.

"Never mind," I say. "You don't need condoms to do this." My hand goes straight down and I start again, kissing his neck until he relaxes. Soon we're fooling around, kissing, stroking … and it feels good. This is enough, I tell myself firmly. This is totally enough.

But tomorrow Jay will pack up and leave for university.

There'll be no sneaking off to do this some other time unless I manage to go and visit him, but I can't see that happening. There's always the hope that Jay will come home one weekend but...

It feels so good to be this close to him. Why do I want more than this?

"We could..." I start to say, then stop. Jay stops what he's doing, but I shake my head. "Don't stop."

He starts up again. It feels amazing. I close my eyes and shuffle down until I can feel him hard against me, then I slip up and under and around until he's almost...

"Hannah." Jay pulls away, but I shift so he's trapped and I look him in the eye.

"I'm clean, I promise."

"That's not what I'm worried about," Jay says. "Tell me you're on the pill or something."

I nearly do. I so want that to be the truth.

"You could pull out, or I could take the morning-after pill," I say hopefully, twisting my hips so he can feel me against him. It's killing me, being this close.

"I could..." He edges in, just a little, and I bite my lip in ecstasy. I want this so much. "Or you could..."

Out again.

"We could..."

In again.

"But..."

Out.

"Please, Jay."

In. All the way.

"Have it your way," he mutters, before we stop being able to say anything at all.

The second time is better than the first. Longer, slower, more intense. There is no one I trust more than Jay and, just like I asked, he pulls out.

And so it ended now, him pulling away, his hands warm from holding me. How did a kiss turn into Jay – the first boy that I've loved, that I *still* love – telling me that he can't do this with me, that everything that's happened was a mistake? How did a kiss turn to this? To nothing but silence? I was so stupid to hope things were about to change… The tears I'm crying as I stare out of his car window are no longer for my baby, for my family or for Jay – they're for me.

Because tonight I have learned that Jay is not the boy I thought he was and, as it turns out, Aaron isn't quite the boy I thought he was either.

Two let-downs in one night is more than I think I can handle.

SUNDAY 14TH FEBRUARY

HALF-TERM

AARON

"Are you going to tell me what's going on with you and your missus, or are you just going to sit there and lose at cards?" Neville says. If I hadn't already moved our "date" from Friday, I would have cancelled – but even sitting here with a cracking headache, losing every hand and wondering whether I'll bump into Hannah is better than the wrath of a Neville scorned.

"Hannah's not my missus."

"She's carrying your baby, sunshine. That makes her something more than a friend."

"Whatever," I say and slump back in the chair and gingerly touch the bridge of my nose. My face hurts. So does my hand. "It's not mine."

Did I really just say that? I open my eyes to see whether Neville heard me, but there's nothing wrong with his hearing aid and he's looking at me keenly, waiting.

"You absolutely *cannot* tell *anyone* this. Not the pretty nurse you gossip with when she checks your blood pressure, not the receptionist when you try and charm your way outside." I look at him seriously. "And especially not Hannah's gran."

Neville's looking at me under lowered brows. White wiry hairs emerge from the tangle like antennae and they quiver as he stares at me.

"I know how to keep a secret."

Possibly – provided he remembers it's a secret he's meant to be keeping. I guess it's too late now anyway.

"We've never had sex." Neville frowns, waiting. "I offered to pretend to be the father to help her out – to protect her from everyone at school, to give her support in front of her family." But that's not why I offered. "I offered because I wanted to help her. I wanted to do something meaningful."

Neville slurps his coffee, working his jaw as he thinks over what I've just said. "'Meaningful'. That's a telling word."

"What do you mean?" I expected him to ask about the real father. I didn't expect this.

"You think there's something meaningful in helping out a girl in a way no sensible boy ever would. You two barely knew each other at the start of the year and yet you signed up for this?"

"Hannah needed helping and I need to help – I need to feel like I can do something that matters, like there's a reason—" I stop myself.

"A reason for what?"

I can't tell him. I can't tell anyone.

"Nothing," I say. "I just wanted to help her out. I like Hannah. A lot."

Neville raises his eyebrows and I tut.

"Not like that." Probably not like that. "She's special."

"Not special enough if she don't know the daddy of her babby."

"Stop it." I know he was only joking, and I don't mean for my voice to sound so harsh, but after last night… I'm glad it's half-term. Dad asked if I'd help him fix the fence and there's my cousin's wedding at the weekend. I've enough excuses to avoid Hannah until I can get my head straight and be the person she wants me to be.

Neville stands up, joints popping, his movements stiff. "I don't know what's going on with you, boy." He looks down at me. "But one day you'll realize she's not the only one who needs a friend. And, when you do, you'll know I'm here for you. You might think you're good at hiding whatever it is that's troubling you, but you're not as good as you think."

"There isn—"

"Now get off your arse and help an old man walk to the toilet, will you? I need a piss."

AARON

We get lost on the way there. I'm not surprised since Mum refuses to buy a satnav and Dad gets so carsick he can't read a map. So it's down to me to look up our location on my phone and navigate us to the church.

Cousin Sarah's wedding. Had Dante experienced any of my mum's family get-togethers, I'm sure that he'd have allocated a tenth ring of hell for such occasions. Mum is stressing out so much that the steering wheel is less a tool with which to direct the car and more a prop around which she can curl her shoulders as she snarls at hedgerows and passing pheasants. Dad has wisely reverted to silence after the map debacle. All three of us are aware that we are walking into an afternoon of whispers and "concern", when distant relatives will stare at me as if I'm about to break down on the spot.

It has been agreed that no one needs to know that I'm a pseudo-sire to a school friend's child as well. My parents know that I know who it is, but I've not given them his name.

Jay.

I want to be angry with him. I want to think that he took advantage of Hannah. But this is *Hannah* and I remember very clearly what she said the night I pulled Tyrone off her:

*No one can make me do anything I don't want to do ...
least of all that.*

In all the time I've known her, there hasn't been a single
time when I've questioned that statement. Not even now.

A week after I found out, instead of being angry with
Jay, I find that I'm angry with Hannah.

TUESDAY 23ᴿᴰ FEBRUARY

HANNAH

"Aaron's here!" Robert calls up the stairs.

"Aaron!" Lola screeches from inside the bathroom and comes running out in her bathrobe, all pink from the bath, leaving Mum kneeling by the bathtub, giving me a look as if I was supposed to stop her. I hear Lola launch herself at Aaron and I peer over the banister to see him hugging her before putting her down and shooing her back up the stairs before him.

"… past your bedtime?" I hear as he gets nearer.

"It's story time now," Lola replies, then she turns and grabs his hand. "You can read to me. Two chapters of *Mr Gum*."

"One chapter, Lolly," Mum says and looks at Aaron. If you drew a fat black question mark above her head her thoughts couldn't have been clearer.

"Mum, Aaron's—" I start to say, but Mum cuts me off with a look and Lola wins, as always.

I go and wait in my bedroom, notes spread out on my bed and Post-its ready to be peeled off and stuck in the right pages of my study guide. I shouldn't resent him spending time with Lola, but I do. Aaron was someone who was meant to be mine. He's *my* friend, doing something amazing for *me*, not a stand-in brother for Lola, not another person to help Mum out. By the time he comes in I've worked myself into a pretty dark mood.

"Sorry. She insisted on another chapter. I didn't know what to do so I just carried on for one more and then she was half-asleep anyway."

"Explains why you took so long," I say and turn away.

"Yes, that's why I just said it – I was explaining." He sits down on my swivel chair and looks at my notes scattered everywhere. "Where do you want to start?"

I shrug. Now Aaron's here to help with my revision, all I want to do is strop at him. I want a fight with someone.

Actually, I want a fight with Aaron since he avoided me all last week. When I told him how things were with Jay – and when it all started – it was down the phone. Not exactly ideal. I expected him to say something. I don't know what. Maybe I thought he'd tell me that he was there for me? Or that he understood? That it didn't change things? But he said nothing at all.

Then he went away to some wedding and, now he's back, it's as if we never had that conversation. And he's here for me. He seems to understand. As if nothing's changed at all.

"What have you got so far?" he asks.

When I hand him my latest notes, half of them slide out of my hand so he has to pick them up from the floor and I resist the temptation to scuff them about with my foot. Aaron skim reads what I've done.

"It's a good start, but I think you need to explore the relationship between truth and belief a little bit further." And he's off on one, talking about the book like it's something he really cares about.

I glower at him as he talks. He's really good-looking, which annoys me. I thought he was quite cute when he started, but he's had a haircut since and the more you know him, the better he looks. Some boys are like that, aren't they? I guess personality has a lot to do with attractiveness, which is why when you get to know half of them they instantly become less fit.

"Aaron?" I cut across whatever he's saying.

"Hm?"

"What happened at the wedding you went to?"

He shrugs. "My cousin got married. Mum got a bit drunk. Dad danced. Badly."

"Were there girls there?" I'm not sure what's making me go in this direction, but there's something niggling away at me.

"Uh-huh."

"Pretty ones?"

"I guess." Aaron's looking at the book, deliberately not looking up at me and I see him swallow, just once and I know. I just *know*.

He so pulled someone at the wedding.

AARON

So I pulled someone at the wedding. So what? It's not as if I'm going to see her again.

I don't need to justify it.

Not to myself, not to Hannah.

Least of all to Hannah.

She slept with someone. I know this. I have *always*

known this. It's not as if I thought she had an immaculate conception. But the father is Jay. *Jay.* It's been a lot to take in. And if there's one thing I needed to do, it was to remind myself of where I stand: real friend, fake father. One thing I never have been is Hannah's boyfriend.

So, whatever it feels like, however she is looking at me, I have not cheated.

HANNAH

I cried myself to sleep last night. What did she look like? Who approached who? What did they do together? I let myself think about what I would do if I saw a fit boy at some family thing and I know that it would involve more than a peck on the cheek and a bit of hand-holding. But then, not every girl is like me. Still. All I could think about was Aaron kissing someone. Aaron's hands on someone's skin, undressing them. I picture his eyes closed as he enjoys whatever's going on and it makes me feel sick.

I can't believe I'm jealous.

233

AARON

Hannah asked me to walk to the shop with her at lunchtime. I find her waiting for me outside the school. Her coat won't quite do up any more and she's wearing a thick non-regulation scarf to bridge the gap in her lapels, hands rammed deep into her pockets. The way she's standing, staring so intently at the floor, concerns me. She turns as I approach, eyes still on the ground as she falls into step with me up the path and past the school gates.

"What is it, Han?" I stop when we get beyond sight of the school.

Hannah stares at the ground, frowning. "I don't want it to be like this."

"Neither do I," I say.

"I know you pulled at the wedding." She's so sure of the truth that she doesn't even look up to check. "And you shouldn't have felt like you needed to hide it."

There's nothing I can say to that.

"I just want you to know that you don't have to keep secrets from me. You can trust me." She glances up and I step closer. "I trust you."

And I know that she is thinking about the one secret that's been so huge that she hasn't been able to tell a single soul. Except me.

"Hannah." I put my arm around her and pull her into a hug, the way I should have done the night she told me that Jay was the father. Maybe he isn't the only one who's let her down. I press my face into her hair for a second. "I'm sorry."

"You're forgiven," she mumbles into my collar.

WEDNESDAY 3RD MARCH

HANNAH

This last week or so has been UNbearable.

I have never been so horny in all my life and I think it might kill me if I don't have sex soon. I almost don't care who it is, I'm that bad. I would jump a reanimated corpse if its eyeballs swivelled the right way at me.

Tyrone. God. I can't stop thinking about the evening we had sex. I'm sure my memory is playing tricks on me with the way it likes to magnify his member, but it's not like I'm thinking straight enough to sort it out.

Fletch … memories of his hands up my skirt and on my skin. I get a hot flush in my nether regions when I accidentally catch his eye as I avoid looking at Mr Dhupam, who is probably the fittest teacher we have. (This isn't saying much, but talk to my pants cos my brain ain't listening. Actually, my pants aren't either.)

I know it's gone too far when I catch myself gazing at Gideon's arse.

But who would have sex with someone whose baby is straining the buttons on her blouse if it's not theirs? Besides, I haven't forgotten the freak-out I had at Rex's party. My body doesn't want sex with anyone else, no matter what it thinks when there's a member of the male species within perving distance.

My body wants sex with Jay. Even the thought of our kiss in the car is enough to cause a mini spasm of desire, and if I let my mind drift back to his party...

This has *got* to be why marriage was invented, so that when you're pregnant there's someone to have sex with.

AARON

In my position as Hannah's closest friend, I am uniquely qualified to notice that she is being an utter pain in the arse at the moment. She pays no attention to a word I say. If she's not staring over my shoulder, then her eyes are glazed over and she's somewhere else entirely. I caught her staring at Rex's crotch the other day when he came over to say something to me about ICT coursework.

Although associating with Hannah has made me as appealing as a cold sore to the basketball lot, Rex still tries to talk to me, smiles and gives a nod of acknowledgement when we pass in the corridor. Unless he's with Katie, in which case he keeps his eyes on the floor. She cut him down the other day at registration and Mark Grey did a whipcrack gesture behind her back. The others smirked but Rex looked miserable as hell. I wonder whether regular sex was a fair exchange for his spine?

When I make this joke to Hannah after we meet up before lunch, she just nods vaguely.

"Did you even hear what I said?" I ask.

"You said something about sex."

"Is that all you can think about?"

I thought I was teasing her but she looks at me very seriously and says, "Yes. It really is."

"Really?"

"I might die if I don't have sex soon."

"*Really*? It's not been that long…"

"If I'd had sex fifteen minutes ago I'd still want it now," she mutters.

"My baby daddy duties don't extend to that, sorry," I say with a grin, but I've failed to take Hannah's epic sense of humour failure into account.

"I know, Aaron. You don't have to spell it out." And with that she gets up and strops off into the canteen.

SATURDAY 6TH MARCH

AARON

If I'd realized where we were going then I would have made every effort possible to get out of a shopping trip with Hannah, Anj and Gideon.

The Clearwater Centre is on the other side of the river from where I live now – the side I am more familiar with. The side I lived on until seven months ago.

None of them knows this and I intend to keep it that way.

I think of what Hannah said when I answered the phone: "If I can't have sex then I will shop."

I should have shagged her myself.

HANNAH

We leave the shop weighed down with bags. I say "we" when I mean "me". Anj says she'll "think about" the jacket she tried on, whereas I went mental and bought the whole shop, or at least the maternity part of it. Robert gave me some money after I had a meltdown midweek and he and I were the only ones in the house. I'd been in front of my wardrobe, wailing in despair at the three hideous maternity things that Mum had insisted on buying for me, the sound carrying all the way downstairs to the study. He hugged me and told me that it was entirely normal to feel like this – apparently Mum had a similar hissy fit when she was pregnant with Lola.

That was when he took out his wallet and handed me all the cash he had – which was *loads*. That was exactly what he did for Mum and he thinks it's the best way to fix a hormonal outburst. I agree.

"Where are the boys?" I say, since Aaron and Gideon skived off the moment we got here. So much for getting a male opinion on my new clothes.

"There." Anj points at a comic shop called Otherworlds. Nerd nirvana – not a shop I've ever paid much attention to. "Gideon drags me in there *every* time we come here."

"Why?" I ask.

"Look behind the counter." Anj nudges me. I peer into the window at the guy serving. If I'm honest, he's a bit weaselly for my tastes, but still. Cute enough. As I'm looking, Gideon explodes out of the door, followed by Aaron. Gideon covers the ground between us in three bounds and links his arms through ours, singing, "He totally has my email address."

But a group of girls blocks our path and I hang back before we get tangled up, which is when I notice that Aaron's missing. I look round to see him standing halfway between here and the comic shop. At first I think he's staring right at me – but then I realize Aaron's looking at the girls walking this way.

AARON

When Gideon suggested going into Otherworlds, I agreed. I'd be safe – only one other person from my past knew the place existed and he wouldn't be there. Walking in was surreal. Different posters, different layout – I didn't go often enough to get friendly with the staff and I didn't recognize the lad Gideon was lusting over. I walked over to the graphic novels, picked up one I already owned and opened it at my favourite part. It's about dreams. Odd given the strained relationship I have with mine.

When I finished it, I turned and walked over to the counter. Gideon took the hint and we left.

I'd been safe there.

Now I'm outside and I am not safe at all.

HANNAH

The other two haven't noticed that Aaron's stopped in the middle of the walkway, so I'm the only one that sees his expression as the girls part to go around me, their bags bumping mine before they clump together as they approach him.

Aaron is terrified.

AARON

Four of them. All painfully familiar. One so much more so than the others. I turn for the side and consider flinging myself over the railing to the level below just to get away. But there's no need – they've passed me by, too busy talking to notice me.

HANNAH

"Aaron?" It's the second time I've said his name, and I rest my fingers on his jaw, turning his attention to me. I want to ask what just happened, but I stop myself. Aaron never asks me too much – I should do the same for him.

I look past him and see one of the girls look back at us. Pretty, blonde, kind of rock chick. Our eyes meet for a second, then she frowns, eyes darting to the back of Aaron's head as if he's someone she might recognize … but the crowd shifts and she's lost amongst the other shoppers.

Only then do I realize that Aaron is no longer leaning on the railing, he's leaning on me.

AARON

There's a box in my wardrobe, one of those plastic ones with the cheap lids that never clip on properly. It's covered in stickers: faded superheroes; blindingly shiny holographic discs; papery white patches where I've peeled off stickers that I tired of and doodled my own picture in biro; newer, bigger, cooler skateboard stickers and band logos. On the lid, I've stuck on some paper and written in massive caps "IDENTIFY YOURSELF CITIZEN" and drawn an intricate image of a thumbprint. The punctuation-phile in me finds a black pen and draws in a comma before CITIZEN. Childishly satisfied, I take the box over to my bed and sit with it for a moment, wondering whether this is really a good idea.

It isn't, but I'm going in anyway.

The box is filled to the brim with envelopes, cards, notebooks, thin cardboard folders and many, *many* fictional blueprints for the Death Star. I pull out almost everything, turning over some of the less familiar pieces, trying to remember why I kept them. I find a project from Juniors and a note stapled to the front of it where the teacher made a joke about me being the next Roald Dahl. I smile at it. I'm not looking for memories this old.

At the bottom of the box are year photos – too big to fit comfortably, they're slightly bowed inside their cardboard frames. I only take out the top one, from the end of Year 9. It's a smaller photo than those up in the corridors of Kingsway, maybe only 450 of us, but I'm only looking for the girl I saw two hours ago: Penny Fraser. She's turning a little towards the girl next to her, a huge smile about to blossom, strands of hair swooshing across her face. I peer closely at her, the crooked nose and the very pierced ear. She looks so *young*. Not as young as in some of the photos of me and her together, the ones tucked away in photo albums that my mother has very carefully left packed up in the loft.

I'm standing one row back, looking suitably ashamed of the God-awful haircut that Mum had inflicted on me the day before. If I squint closely enough I swear I can see the line where my tan stops and my fringe should have been … although maybe I'm just imagining it because I remember being so painfully aware of it at the time. My eyes skip over half-familiar faces to the end of the row.

Chris.

Grief isn't always a knife-sharp twist in your heart or a dull bludgeon in your stomach, sometimes it's a net, cast suddenly and silently over your soul so that you feel trapped and suffocated by its grasp. I feel the loss in the deepest recesses of myself, hidden parts of my mind and my matter, united in missing someone I will never see again.

I turn the photograph over and spend a long, long time looking out of the window.

FRIDAY 12TH MARCH

AARON

I tell Neville about seeing Penny at Clearwater. I give him just enough context to stop him from asking questions.

"Why are you telling me this?"

Obviously not enough context.

"I'm not your therapist and this isn't Jeremy Springer." I don't correct him. "You don't just get to offload and leave."

"I wasn't—"

"You were. I'm old and I'm wise and I've had enough of this bullshit," he says. "You're just taking bits of the jigsaw out of the box. You don't have to put the whole picture together, but you've got to understand it's frustrating, only knowing bits here and there."

I don't say anything, remembering him telling me I needed a friend.

"People who only give away bits of themselves are hiding something."

"You do it too," I say quietly.

"Well, you're not the only one hiding things."

I look up at him, studying his expression, taking in the seriousness of his gaze and noticing the "tch" of his teeth as he works his jaw slightly – something he only does when he's about to wipe the floor with me at cards.

"You know I'm going to ask what things, don't you?"
I say and he nods. "And you're going to tell me that I've
got to tell you something about me in return." Again, he
nods, closing his eyes briefly as he dips his head ever-so
slightly.

I like Neville. I have no idea why. He smells of alcohol
and stale sweat. He's a bad loser and a terrible winner. He
hasn't a kind word to say about anyone and every other
thought he has is lewd. Yet he makes me laugh – at him,
at the world and at myself. There's a lot to be said for
learning not to take yourself too seriously. Neville is more
than the sum of his old wrinkled parts. He's my friend.

He's still watching me, then he adjusts his position,
his hips clicking loud enough for me to hear and I see a
flash of pain in his expression before he settles back in his
chair. "You might be a pansy and you're shite at cards, but
you're not so bad, I suppose. And I trust you."

Which surprises me.

"So I'll tell you mine. And then you can tell me yours."
He doesn't wait for me to agree – he knows he doesn't
need to. "I have never forgiven meself for what I did to
my wife."

There are so many things that I could ask: *What did
you do? Why can't you be forgiven?* But I know what I'd
like someone to ask me.

"What was her name?"

"Alison." Neville reaches into his pocket and hands
me a photo from inside his wallet. It's of Neville – I can
tell that right away. He's a bit older than Dad and he

looks kind of rakish. The woman next to him has her arms wrapped around him and is smiling, rolling her eyes at her husband.

I hand back the photo. "What happened?"

"I cheated on her."

I wished this surprised me.

"Alison knew what I was like before she married me, but I promised I'd take our vows seriously. And I did, for a while, but I struggled once we had kids…"

Kids?

And so I learn about Neville, about his marriage and the strain he felt once he became a father. Parenthood's not something I ever think about – this is a part of Hannah's pregnancy neither she nor I can guess at. Either way, I can't see anyone handling it as badly as Neville. It sounds like he slept with half the staff at his university and most of the students' mums. It's a miracle his marriage lasted as long as it did – twenty-four years. It came apart when one of the women he slept with took it upon herself to break up his marriage, not by telling his wife, but by telling his daughter. On her wedding day. To the woman's son. Overnight his daughters switched their love for hate because of what he'd done to their mother – then, six weeks later, she died.

"What did she die of?"

"Broken heart." Neville is staring at his slippers, so he can't see my involuntary and insensitive eye roll.

"People don't die of a broken heart, Neville."

"What would you know?" he whispers as his shoulders

start to shake. I move to sit closer and Neville refrains from calling me gay when my knee bumps his. He's too busy crying. I sit there with him, staying close, letting him know that I'm there when he needs me and I'm thinking all the while that Neville cannot truly believe that he is responsible for his wife's death.

Not the way I am for Chris's.

It is not the right time for me to tell Neville that.

THURSDAY 18ᵀᴴ MARCH

HANNAH

When I first found out that Katie had told Marcy about the baby, I'll admit I freaked out. Not with anger and shouting. No. I'm above that. I rang up to find out her side of the story. I rang SEVEN TIMES before I was forced to leave a message. It was meant to be all mature and polite, like, "Marcy has put up this post on Facebook and I can't see how she would know…" But it wasn't. It was more like, "You [sob] are my best [sob] FRIEND [sniff, sniff, deep breath] and I TRUSTED [choke on own tears] you and why did you tell Marcy? [sob … goes quiet] I just want to talk to you. [small sniff] You're my best friend. Katie. [little sob] So call me, yeah? [whispered]" And I never told anyone I'd left that message. Not my mum, not Aaron. Not Anj, not Gideon. I just waited for her to call me.

She never did.

It's been two months, and when I see her standing by my locker I guess she's waiting for Nicole, whose locker is two away from mine. I don't say anything to her as I shove my bag inside, take out some money and slam it shut. I reckon I've got enough time to walk to the shop and buy an ice cream before next lesson if I go now. It's not really ice-cream weather, but, hey, hormones don't care about sunshine.

"Where you going?" Katie says, as I shrug on my too-small coat.

I'm so surprised that she's speaking to me I answer by accident. "Corner shop."

Katie looks at me through narrowed eyes, waiting for something. "I'll come with." She pushes herself away from the lockers and heads out of the door. I don't want to go now, but I don't want to look like a coward either. Besides, ice cream is enough to tempt me into danger.

"I know he's not the father," she says, as we pass the gates. "I did the maths."

So this is what it's about.

"Better check your workings, Katie. We both know it's not your best subject," I say mildly. I will not engage in battle. I must not. Katie isn't as stupid as everyone likes to think.

"LOL. Not."

We walk on a few paces.

"Why are you here, Katie?"

"Being friendly."

"You wouldn't know what that means."

But she carries on as if she hasn't heard. "… I thought you should know that I've worked it out." I feel a flush of cold dread in case she names Jay, but she doesn't. "The dates and stuff – four months along in January? It happened before Aaron. If I can work it out, it won't be very long before someone else does."

I stop in my tracks. "Is that a threat?"

She stops and looks at me, saying nothing. Which means it's a threat.

A flood of rage forces itself through my body and I'm trembling as I fight the urge to launch myself at her and slap her and scrape my nails across her face. I want to destroy her with my hurt. I want not to be powerless. There's actually a millisecond of red across my vision as I think about it and I feel my fingers curling into the palms of my hands as I ball them into fists.

I want to scream at her, as if the sound would blast into her bones and cause her to explode into a thousand tiny pieces and then catch every last one and grind it into the ground with my shoes.

I wish with all my heart that I could hurt her the way she did me.

But I can't, because only someone you care about can hurt you, and Katie does not care about me.

I breathe and let the fury fade away. I feel so ... useless.

"You're wrong. Aaron's the father. You can tell him what you like, it won't change anything."

She looks disappointed and I realize she'd been hoping that I would blow up in her face. I'd forgotten how much she likes a fight. She studies me for a moment before her lips curl into an unpleasant smile.

"It might change quite a lot when your baby comes out brown. When he sees it's Tyrone's."

You can tell she thinks this will get a reaction. After our fight, Marcy nearly broke it off with Tyrone, but he's a good liar and a good charmer and he's good in bed. These things count. So she stayed with him. Katie's desperate for me to rise to the bait. Desperate to find out the truth she always suspected. Desperate to give Marcy a reason to notice her again when Katie reveals what I got up to with Tyrone.

Which makes it very easy for me not to react at all. That and the fact that I couldn't give a Rottweiler's turd about anything to do with Tyrone.

"Just fucking admit it's Tyrone's."

I stay silent.

"You won't be able to lie for ever, you know!" She's wound up, lashing out because she's not getting what she wanted. "Aaron's going to find out and then he'll leave you, and you'll be left holding a baby no one wants."

I cover the distance between us in a heartbeat, my face right in hers.

"If I ever hear you say no one wants my baby again then I will tell *everyone everything* about you. I will show them photos I have on my phone of you giving some loser a blow job by the toilets in a bar. I will send Marcy a screengrab of a message you sent me on Facebook when you told me how fat her arse was. I will look through my English notebook and I will find that shag/marry/kill conversation where you said you'd shag Mark Grey, marry Tyrone for regular cock and kill Rex to put him out of his misery."

Katie isn't looking so confident now. "You wouldn't. I've got just as much shit on you."

"Yeah. You have. You were my *best* friend." There's a flicker in her gaze and I wonder if she remembers my voicemail. "I trusted you, but you swallowed it all only to vomit it back in my face. And do you know what? The friends I have are the ones who know how much of a bitch I can be and still choose to hang out with me. No one else matters."

I can see she's thinking it through and that she's about to

say something about Aaron – again.

"Aaron won't let me down, so don't even bother trying. But if you want to push me…"

I leave it open before I hurry away towards the shop. I still want that ice cream. I hear Katie shouting after me, but I'm not going to listen.

FRIDAY 19ᵀᴴ MARCH

HANNAH

I can feel her watching me as I walk out of English with Aaron. We pass her leaning on the wall by the door and I feel her eyes track us as we move towards, past and away down the corridor.

I wonder whether Aaron does too.

AARON

I wonder whether they'll have hot dogs at the canteen for lunch today? I've been trying to work out a pattern to when they give you the good stuff and by my calculations there's a fairly good chance of scoring high today. If not hot dogs, then perhaps something with pastry…

"Did you see her there?" Hannah says, out of the blue.

"See who where?" I look around the canteen as we walk in.

"Katie. Back there in English."

I shrug in response. Ignore Katie and she'll go away, like a particularly noxious fart.

"She was watching us," Hannah says, sliding her tray angrily along the rails so it almost rockets off and I pin it down with the flat of my hand. She's really worked up about this. Last night she called to tell me all about Katie's failed confrontation. It was a long conversation – and a repetitive one. I say the same thing now as I said yesterday:

"So what? I'm not going anywhere – she can tell who she likes whatever she wants. You and me? This" – I gently prod the taut flesh of the bump – "we're all good here. Katie can—"

HANNAH

He stops when he sees me crying and pulls me in for a hug, but I wave him away angrily.

"I don't know why I'm crying, don't give me any sympathy." But I dive in to give him a squeeze anyway – not so quick that someone behind misses a chance to whistle. Tosser.

We sit with Anj and Gideon, who have saved us seats and Aaron's just come back with pots of ketchup for the hot dogs when his phone goes. I nab a pregnant person's share of the sauce (eating for two is the *best* excuse) when I notice he's frowning at the message.

"You OK?" Gideon asks. Aaron seems to have zoned out and I nudge him.

He looks up, still frowning. "It's from the home. It says I don't need to go and see Neville tonight."

"Bonus or bummer?"

"I'm just worried, that's all – it says he's not feeling well."

"Why don't you call?" Anj suggests. "Reassure yourself."

I nod hard. I know what it's like worrying about Gran. "Quick – while Mrs English is looking the other way."

AARON

I duck under the table. This school is ridiculous with its no-mobile policy. By all means carry them around – just never use them.

"It's me, Aaron," I say as soon as Neville picks up.

"Of course it is." He breaks off into a cough that rattles with so much phlegm that I hold the phone away from my ear, as if some of it's going to come out this end.

"You OK?"

"Course I am. Just got a bit of a cough and the staff have put me in bloody quarantine in my room." More coughing. "Don't want the rest of the frail oldies catching it and popping their clogs."

"No chance of that happening to you, though?" I try to sound casual, despite being aware of Mrs English's feet walking towards this table.

"What? You gone soft on me?" A crackly throaty chuckle and more coughing. "Don't be so daft."

"They told me not to come…"

"I know, I told them to tell you. Don't want you getting sick and passing it on to Hannah and the baby. I'll see yo—" Cough. "—u next week."

I slam my thumb on the red button and bump my head as I emerge to see that Mrs English isn't fooled in the slightest.

HANNAH

Robert can't collect me tonight. Lola's going to a party after school and he's helping in the hope it'll encourage other parents to do the same at Lola's party next month. He asked me if I wanted to come too, but I played the pregnancy card. A: It's not something I should be doing in my condition (which is a total lie – none of the books say "No kids' parties!") and B: Does he really want to show off his pregnant teen stepdaughter?

Anj and I are walking to the bus stop when she says, "So, what's Aaron's deal?"

For a panic-stricken second I think she's talking about the whole question mark that Katie's trying to put over his paternity.

"After last week I thought something had happened between you two."

Aaron was a bit withdrawn after we went shopping. He never explained about his mini freak-out and I never asked. So much for the whole trust thing.

"No. We're all good."

"Well, yeah, this week…" She looks at me sideways. "Have you heard what Katie's been saying?"

My insides turn cold. I didn't realize she'd already started telling everyone her little theory.

"What's she been saying?"

"I don't know, but I heard her talking to Nicole about how weird it is that Aaron moved here in the middle of his GCSEs."

I recover a bit. "Not that weird. They moved house."

Although that's all I know. Aaron said that they went to Australia for the summer and came back to a new house. It's as if his life before the holidays never happened.

"Yeah…" Anj tails off. "It's odd how he never really talks about anything before he came here, y'know?"

I shrug.

"Hasn't he talked to you about it?"

"No," and I look up as I say that, so she knows I'm not hiding some mysterious truth that threatens to break me and Aaron apart. Just the lie that holds us together.

"I thought you might know something." She's frowning.

I shake my head.

"… he's, like, your best mate …"

True.

"… the father of your baby …"

False.

"… don't you *want* to know what his deal is?"

The truth is that I don't. Aaron is my rock. My hero. There's some saying about heroes and clay feet… I don't want to discover what Aaron's feet are made of.

TUESDAY 23ʳᵈ MARCH

AARON

After the lesson ends, I dawdle, closing and saving my work. Although the room's usually empty within thirty seconds of the lunch bell, I'm not the only one there. Rex is waiting by the door and gives me a "Hey" as I approach. He even makes eye contact.

"Hey," I reply, walking out into the corridor and into the crush of bodies heading for the canteen.

Rex falls into step beside me, forcing a fast-flowing Year 7 kid to swerve round him. "So. How's it going? With Hannah and stuff?"

I shrug. "Fine."

Rex clears his throat and looks down at the floor. "You been deciding baby names and that?"

"No decisions so far." Which evades the question nicely. "There's still time for you to nominate if you like? It's not due for another three months. Rexina has a nice ring to it…"

The way he laughs at this mildly-amusing-at-best joke, in front of witnesses, is deeply suspicious.

"What do you want, Rex?" I stop to look at him. This time there's no eye contact.

"I told her you'd be suspicious."

"Why's she sent you?" There's no need to ask who he

means. "Is it to tell me that I'm not the father?"

Rex looks uncomfortable. "Look … it's just what people have been saying…"

"'People'?! You mean Katie," I say a little too loudly. A few people glance over. "Tell Katie the same thing Hannah did: I'm not going anywhere."

This gets his attention. It hadn't occurred to him that Hannah would have talked about this. That she and I are a team.

"Come on, Katie and Hannah were really good mates. If anyone knows…" He sees the way I'm looking at him and his words dry up.

"You're not seriously going to try and use the 'good mates' argument after the way Katie treated Hannah?" I seem to have no control over the volume of my words.

"Katie was upset too—"

"Why are you defending her?" I've had enough of this. "Really? Have you not seen yourself? Have you not seen the way she treats you? The girl's poison, Rex."

"That's my girlfriend you're talking about!"

"Stop defending her!" I'm almost shouting in frustration, dimly aware of the clot of people gathered nearby, staring. "Look at how she ditched Hannah. Those two were *best friends*. Instead of doing her dirty work, try looking out for yourself before she fucks you over too."

He's calling after me as I hurry away, but I'm not running from him, I'm running from my loss of control. The knot inside me is made of many things – guilt, anger, misery … and fear. I am frightened that this isn't where

Katie's questions will end. When she finds she can't turn me against Hannah, how far will she go to find a way to turn Hannah against me? God knows she won't have to go far.

THIRD

FRIDAY 26TH MARCH

HANNAH

Twenty-eight weeks along.

The baby weighs about 875 grams. (Although that doesn't sound much for how big I look…)

It can open its eyes, suck its thumb and hiccup. (It hiccups a lot.)

It can dream, apparently. Presumably dreaming and waking are pretty much the same thing if all you've ever seen is the inside of a womb.

If it was born now it would have a ninety per cent chance of surviving, which sounds pretty good to me. Although don't come out yet, little one, you hear me? You stay in there and cook until you're done, yeah?

It hiccupped at me. I will take that as a sign of agreement.

AARON

When Dad drops me off at the home I stand at the bottom of the ramp and think about running away – of course I do – but Neville laid his soul at my feet with his confession and now I owe him mine.

May Neville forgive me the way that I can't.

I sign in and head down to Neville's room, but when I get there, I'm taken aback by the sight of him, diminished inside his clothes – and he's wearing slippers, not shoes. Neville has always despised residents who spend their days in slippers and dressing gowns.

"Nice slippers."

"Sod off." He glares at his feet. "I might have peed in one of my shoes."

I smile. "Let me know if you want me to get you a new pair."

"Trust me, sunshine, your need is greater than mine."

Laughing, I sit down in the other chair and look at him, noticing the bulge of an inhaler in the top pocket of his shirt. "You all right?"

"I'll live." And he coughs. A lot. I hand him the half-filled glass of water from the table, but he goes for the inhaler. "Doctor wants to put me on antibiotics, but I've told him where to go."

"Is that such a good idea?"

"They give me the runs. I'm old, I'm slow. I don't want to shit in my slippers now, do I? Won't have anything to keep me feet warm."

Can't argue with that.

"What you told me – the other week?" I'm looking at the carpet, studying the pattern between my feet. "Thank you."

"What for?"

"Trusting me not to let the truth change anything. For knowing I'd still come back and visit you the next week."

"Only you didn't…" But he's only teasing.

Neville looks at me, his chest shaking with each breath,

but his gaze steady. "Aaron. Whatever it is you're going to tell me, I will still expect to see you next week. There's nothing you can tell me that will change that."

I close my eyes and take a leap of faith. It's time to tell Neville how I killed my best friend.

THURSDAY 1ˢᵀ APRIL

HANNAH

I have just been to my first after-school netball match.
No, that's not an April Fool's (I wish it was – netball is the
most boring sport *ever*, although still better than an evening
watching Aaron and Gideon geek out over retro sci-fi films).
There's loads of our year still hanging about at the bottom
of the grounds and there's a steady trickle of players leaving
the changing rooms and heading down there. I won't be
going – me and Anj are going back to mine to make (and
"taste") party food for Lola's birthday tomorrow – but I'm
waiting in too obvious a place outside the changing rooms
and Tilly from PSHE comes over to chat.

The chat is a formality. Really she just wants to feel the
bump. She puts her bag down and bends over to stare at her
hand as she presses it on my school shirt. "Weird!"

I don't tell her that the baby moving around is way less
weird than her touching my tummy.

When Anj "Player of the Season" storms out of the
changing room, her joy on the court has turned to fury and
she zones in on Tilly. "Why is everyone asking me if Gideon
and Aaron are seeing each other?"

Tilly looks petrified, which is fair enough because Angry
Anj is scary.

"Maybe-because-Katie-Coleman's-been-telling-people-that-Aaron-left-his-last-school-after-he-was-bullied-for-coming-out?" It comes out as a continuous stream and Tilly holds her breath waiting for Anj's response.

"Well, they're just friends."

"OK," Tilly squeaks. "I wasn't the one asking."

"I know," Anj says. "Sorry."

Tilly makes a quick exit, off to find out where the party is. I feel a bit of a loser seeing her scuttling away to hang out with the cool kids when all I've got going on is a six-year-old's party to plan. I guess that's going to be my life from now on – may as well get used to it.

"That's Tilly's bag, isn't it?" Anj is looking next to my left foot.

"Yes."

She sighs. It's not like anyone else is going to take it to her, so we follow the noise, not talking. I'm just piecing together what I think Katie's up to. Spreading a believable rumour that Aaron's gay (because let's face it, that's a conclusion I didn't find it hard to jump to back in the day) kinda brings into question the possibility that he really is the father of my baby. Plus, this place is a bit backwards when it comes to coming out. Why else would Gideon still be looking for his first snog? He's cute. I would. But no one has.

Katie's voice is raised as we approach the crowd by the benches. She's always needed to shout the loudest. She – and Marcy from the sounds of it – are teasing Tyrone, asking him if he's had an AIDS test. It doesn't take a genius to work out what she's on about and I feel Anj tense next to me, her jaw tightening, her hand balling into a fist around the strap on Tilly's bag.

"Seriously. Katie needs to see my mum for an education…" I murmur, but neither of us are laughing as we catch sight of the two girls.

Neither has seen us – we're still on the outskirts. Marcy's laughing so hard that she spills a splash of her drink over Tyrone as she says, "You going to start sweet-talking Gideon? Get him to join the basketball team?"

Anj is powering through the crowd, but man-mountain Mark Grey is in the way and no one's moving for her and I want to be with her, fighting for my friends…

And then I hear Rex telling Tyrone to stop his girlfriend from talking out of her arse.

The crowd shivers out a delicious "Ooooooh!" and I'm standing on tiptoes, trying to see what's happening. Tyrone's looking cross, but it's Marcy who's really riled, though I can't make out what she's saying, because she's kind of screeching… Tyrone's actually holding her back from slapping Rex, I think…

"Rex is just jealous because Aaron's hot for Tyrone!"

And that's when the crowd goes silent. Because the person who says that is Katie. Rex's girlfriend.

I catch a break and dart/barge in to stand next to Anj, peering through the bodies as Katie laughs at her own joke. The others look uncomfortable.

"He warned me." Even though he's speaking very quietly, I don't think there's a person here who doesn't catch what Rex is saying – or the way Katie is looking at him.

All of sudden I feel sorry for him. Rex is not a bad guy –

he doesn't deserve a girlfriend who looks at him with such disgust.

"What are you talking about?" She almost spits at him as she says it.

"You screwed your best friend over and now you're trying to screw Aaron. No one cares who he shags, but you're wanging on like it's something that matters."

It seems Katie doesn't have a comeback for the truth.

"Aaron was right all along. You can't be trusted. You'd stab me in the back as soon as suck me off if you thought it'd score you some points."

Katie opens her mouth, but before she can say anything, Rex has slid off the table and he's walking away from her.

"Don't bother following me, Katie. You're a dirty little shit-stirrer. We're done," he calls, as he shoulders his way into the crowd. When he reaches me, he meets my eyes and smiles, a flat, disappointed smile that tells me that he knows. He understands. I glance back at Katie, who is trying to act like she couldn't care less that she's just been ditched in the most public way possible. But she does care, because she is scanning the crowd where Rex left and she catches my eye.

The thing about being friends with someone for so long is that you know them. And I know that she is thinking the same thing I am: if Katie is no longer Rex's girlfriend, will Marcy still let her hang out with them?

Although I want Katie to fall – I want her to feel a fraction of the misery she caused me – I want her to stay safely in Marcy's good books. If she feels herself slipping out, then there's no telling what she'll do to get back in… No telling whose reputation she'll trash to make herself look good.

Actually, it's pretty easy to tell. Rex couldn't have made the target any more obvious if he'd splashed it in red across Aaron's back.

FRIDAY 2ND APRIL

GOOD FRIDAY

HANNAH

Ignoring the fact that there was a key family member missing, because he decided to fuck off to Scotland with his uni friends instead, I declare Lola's sixth birthday party the best yet. Cake? Check. Sandwiches with the crusts off? Check. More sugar than it is sensible for ten kids, four teens and five adults (and one rabbit) to consume? Check. And so many awesome games. I like how my friends don't pretend to be too cool to enjoy old-school party games – Gideon collapsing with laughter instead of being a statue, Anj causing chaos by whipping away the kids' chairs even when they were sitting on them; Aaron carrying Lola round on his back when she wanted to pretend to be a cowboy herding all her friends in the garden...

I think we used up all the fun in the world today. Which is just as well, because tomorrow I'm going to have to start revising like a bastard and then my life will be no fun whatsoever.

"Hannah?"

Mum's standing in the doorway and, because I'm facing away from the door, she has to wait as I wriggle and flop my way round until I'm facing her.

She comes in and sits on the bed and hands me the phone without saying anything.

I frown and take it, glancing at my clock. It's nearly midnight.

"Hannah? Is that you, love?" It's Gran.

"Yeah, it's me. You OK, Gran?" I'm worried.

"Me? Yes, I'm fine … fine." There's a pause. "Hannah, I've something to tell you, love."

I'm sweaty and panicking.

"It's Neville."

Neville?

"He's died, love."

HANNAH

It took me a ridiculously long time to work out what to text after I found out about Neville. What do you say in 160 characters?

Heard Neville died yesterday. That sucks. Ru OK?

Sorry 2 hear bout Neville, he was a gr8 guy. Ru OK?

Gran told me bout Neville. That must b really hard 4 u. Ru OK?

Death is bad. Ru OK?

R. U. OK?

In the end I settle for something a little less pushy:

Here if u need me. Hx

Maybe a text is too impersonal. Should I call him?

Normally I'm good with this kind of thing, knowing how to care about someone, giving them the right balance of attention. But that's not the relationship I have with Aaron. He's the one who takes care of me.

I sit up. Think, Hannah. What would Aaron do?

It's like What Would Jesus Do.

Jesus would say something like, "Neville's found his true place." He wouldn't say "heaven" because I'm pretty sure Neville is going *down*. He made the seven deadly sins his to-do list, with lust underlined three times.

Listen to me talk. I don't think God's going to be too

pleased if I schlep up to the Pearly Gates before I've done a bit of make-up time to cancel out my misspent youth.

It's no good. I don't know what Aaron would do and this is one thing I can't ask his advice on.

Perhaps I shouldn't have come round to his house? It's a bit stalker-y. Only I can't back out now because I'm absolutely busting for the loo and I'm not sure I'd make it home in time and no one wants to find a pregnant girl squatting behind their front hedge.

Mrs Tyler – I can't call her Stephanie (if I did I'd have to call her husband by his first name and neither of us wants that) – is the one that answers my knock on the door. She looks pleasantly surprised to see me, and tells me that Aaron's in his room. It's only once I've bolted past her to the bathroom and swapped sympathetic "been there, done that" smiles that I notice Mrs Tyler doesn't look like she knows about Neville. Although now I'm peeing in her toilet I might have missed my chance to find out.

When I go upstairs, Aaron's room looks dark, but when I push the door open, I see him lying on his bed in shorts and a T-shirt, watching TV. I walk in and sit on the end of the bed.

"Hey," I say.

Aaron nods and I turn to see whatever he's watching. Adverts.

"Are you OK?" I ask, as if I don't know the answer. I don't even know why I'm asking.

Aaron doesn't say anything.

"Are you just sad about Neville?"

His eyes flicker away from whatever point they were fixed on, but they don't look at me. They look at the leather jacket Neville gave him for Christmas.

"There's no such thing as 'just' sad," he says, before giving me a look that makes me feel the size of an ant.

"I didn't mean that," I say. "Sorry."

AARON

I shrug.

"'Just' saying," I say with a small smile that's not meant for Hannah. I wish she'd left me in peace. Silence suits my mood. She's fidgeting at the end of the bed, trying to find the words that will get me to open up about Neville.

It's a lost cause. I'm not going to talk to her about this. Words can't describe how I'm feeling.

"When's the funeral?"

I suppose that's better than a question about my feelings.

"Week after next sometime. Easter slows things down."

"Are you going?"

I nod, once. Of course I'll go.

"Do you want me to come with?" The question comes at me from the end of a long, dark tunnel so that it doesn't seem real by the time I hear it. I don't answer. I'm thinking about funerals. Too many funerals.

There's a sigh and I come back to the room: Hannah sitting on my bed, meaningless adverts flickering behind her, giving her a halo of sorts. If Hannah's my guardian angel then no wonder I'm screwed.

"Look, Aaron, I know it's awful that Neville's passed away..." I think about how many euphemisms there are for death and I wonder whether I've even heard half of them. "... but I don't think sitting at home on your own is going to make you feel any better about it."

I don't say anything. She's led me back to dangerous territory where we talk about feelings. I am not ready for feelings. I am not ready to feel them, let alone talk about them.

Mum calls from downstairs.

"I've got to go down for dinner," I say, hoping she'll take the hint.

HANNAH

I try and think what I can do to let him know that he can talk to me about it. That I'm here. Not just here in his room, but here in his life. I shuffle closer to him and go in for a hug, but it's the worst thing I could have done. Aaron bends into me at the waist, but he's stiff and cold and he doesn't put his arms round me, just seems to wait until I've finished holding him before he springs back upright.

"How come you came over?"

"I wanted to see how you were."

Aaron waves a hand at his clothing and hair.

"Do your parents know?"

Aaron says nothing.

"You haven't told them?" That's worrying, but I don't want to sound judgemental. "Aaron, you can talk to me."

"I am talking to you."

"Mostly you're just scowling over my shoulder at the stupid TV and waving your hands around. That's not talking."

"I'm sorry. My best friend just died. I'm not quite up to polite conversation."

"I don't want polite conversation." I'm getting upset – not helped by the fact he just called Neville his best friend. What does that make me? "I just want conversation. With you. I'm worried about you."

"Thanks for your concern." He's bitingly sarcastic. "I like the way it's manifesting itself as being irritated with me – that's really touching."

I'm stunned at how mean he's being. But he's upset, he's grieving, I've got to be patient with him. Which isn't exactly something I'm known for. Aaron's still looking over my shoulder and I can see that he's tired. I wonder if he got a call in the middle of the night? Or was it the first thing he heard this morning? I want him to tell me what he's thinking – if he wants to cry, go out, get wasted… I. Don't. Know. And that's the point. I *want* to. I want to do whatever it is he wants me to do.

I wish I was psychic.

AARON

Hannah is struggling at the end of the bed. I know she wants something from me, but I've nothing to give.

"Hannah, I've got to go down for dinner."

She nods, and I hear her try and smother a sniff.

"Are you crying?"

"No." She's lying. I don't even know why I asked. "I'm just sad about Neville."

Her voice is husky with tears and when she looks up I can see them pooling in her eyes.

"Me too," I say, but my words are hollow. They sound like lines I'm reading from a play. They aren't connected with anything that's going on inside me.

"You can talk to me about it, you know. I'm here for you."

She cares more about me sharing than she cares about me.

HANNAH

"Hannah, can't you just let it go?" Aaron stands up. "I don't want to talk about it. I'm not OK. I'm not even fucking *close* to being OK, but that doesn't mean I want to talk about it. Not to you, not to my parents, not to a mental health professional…"

His reaction strikes me dumb. Why is he so angry with me for caring?

"Can't you just leave me alone?"

"No." I surprise myself with my answer. "I can't leave you alone, Aaron. I'm worried about you. I care about you. I want to help you when you need me most – the way you did for me."

"Tit for tat?"

"No, that's not what I meant—" But he's not listening to me.

"Because it doesn't have to be."

"What do you mean?" I'm scared. A dead, dark feeling in my heart.

"If the price of being your hero is having you try to save me like this, then I resign."

"Resign?" I whisper. I feel like I've lost control of everything that's happening around me. Aaron's unravelling and I can't seem to grab the end of the string.

"I'm out. Done. Finished. Go find Jay and get him to do the honourable thing." Aaron looks through me, his eyes hard and glassy. It's like he's someone else. "I'm not the hero you're looking for, Hannah…" Aaron suddenly sits down on the bed, the heels of his hands pressing into his eye sockets. "I'm just not. You expect too much from me."

"I don't expect anything." I move closer and crouch down in front of him, my hands reaching up to his…

"You expect me to let you in." His hands open and he meets my gaze. My hands stop where they are.

"Is that so much to ask?" I'm pleading with him. I don't want him to shut me out.

"Yes. It is." He presses his hands back to his face. "Please. Leave me alone, Hannah. Please…"

AARON

When I take my hands away from my eyes, she's gone – and she cannot see that I'm crying. For Neville. For Chris. For myself.

And when I slide down onto the floor and let go, I realize that I'm crying for Hannah because she thinks she's lost me when she doesn't know the first thing about loss.

HANNAH

I haven't been sick the entire time I've been pregnant. Until now. I'm forced to do it over someone's garden fence, but there isn't much I can do about it, so I just hurry away, wiping my mouth and trying to get a grip on my tears.

Whoever was in that room wasn't Aaron. Not *my* Aaron, not the Aaron who stood by me when Jay wouldn't, not the Aaron who stopped Marcy in her tracks, who called Jay out for being a coward, who turned pretending into reality.

A fake father I can live without, but I've just lost my best friend and I don't quite understand why.

HANNAH

Aaron hasn't called. Three days. I want to break the deadlock, I want to call him, but the last thing he said was to leave him alone. This is what he wants from me and I'm trying to do it. I'm trying to be his hero, even if it means crying myself to sleep every night with worry.

Mum asked if he was coming today, but I said I didn't think so. The date's been on our calendar for ever, but I hadn't mentioned it to him. I wasn't sure whether we'd still be living the lie we created by the time I went to check out the birth centre at the hospital. Did I think I'd have come clean about Jay? That he'd have done it for me?

That would have been very stupid of me.

This place seems all right, although I'm a bit put off by what sounds like a cow mooing in one of the rooms down the hall. When I look at Mum, she pretends that she can't hear it. Instead she makes a fuss of reading out every leaflet she can find on the table, bamboozling me with questions:

Do I want a water birth? (Erm…)

Or do I want an epidural? (Now you're talking.)

Do I want to be on the ward or in my own room? (Surely the answer to that is obvious?)

Who will I nominate as my birth partner for the antenatal classes?

The last one gives me a burning lump in my throat as I try not to cry. Obviously I want Mum there – but the word "partner" makes me think of Aaron. I wish I'd not left it so late to ask him if he wanted to come today. I was going to do it at the weekend, but after…

Oh God, I miss him so much and he's not even the real father.

Go find Jay and get him to do the honourable thing.

Maybe it's time I did.

HANNAH

My source tells me that Jay got back from his Scottish piss-up yesterday. My source is unhappy that his son chose to go to his mum's instead of ours, but, of course, he can't possibly know that it is because his son is scared of what I will do if he does. So. I will take the fight to him.

Jason's mum answers the door. "Hannah!" Huge smile and eyes desperately trying not to stare at my bump. It's an expression I'm familiar with. She calls up the stairs and Jay shouts something I don't hear.

"He says he's in the shower." She doesn't suggest I wait.

"I'll wait."

She walks through to the kitchen, where the walls are coated in photos – the other half of Jay's life: a couple of cheesy school photos and loads of holidays with him and the evil Step Goons plus parents. His mum sees me looking and says something about the twins being out with their dad for the day. Good. I don't need them around to judge me too.

"So, how far along are you?"

"Thirty weeks."

"You're looking big for thirty."

"It's all the ice cream." I shrug. It's probably not, but I try and tell myself it's better to be fat than to have a humongous baby to push out. The mental version of putting my fingers in my ears and singing "LA LA LA".

"Do you know what you're having?"

I resist the urge to say, "A baby," and go for, "Nope."

"Have you got some names lined up?"

I shrug and look at the door, hoping Jay will come and save me from this small-talk torture. I have a shortlist, but I've not told anyone what's on it in case I change my mind – or in case someone else tries to change it for me. When Mum was pregnant with Lola, she had a list going on the whiteboard in the kitchen and me and Jay would wipe off the names we hated when she wasn't looking. She never wrote "Lola" down and if she had I'd have totally wiped it off, yet Lola is *so* the right name for my little sister that I can't even remember what others were in the running.

"Jason would have been called Jasmine if he'd been a girl," Jay's mum says and smiles. "I liked names beginning with 'J'."

I nod. Come on, "J". I've always hated coming here. Jay's mum isn't like mine – she's all cashmere jumpers and pearl earrings. She doesn't have a job and Jay once told me that everything his stepdad earns goes on the twins. The house they live in, the clothes Jay's mum wears – it's all a lie paid for by Robert. The only truth in this place is Jay's shitty old car that he bought himself.

There's thumping on the stairs Lola-style and then he's in the doorway, his eyes looking bluer than usual as if he washed them in the shower too. Jay throws me a tight smile and his mum leaves with a "Goodbye, Hannah."

Jay grabs a can of Coke for me without asking and waves

me out to the conservatory, where the wicker sofa creaks as he sprawls into it. I ignore the can of caffeine I can't drink and take the chair opposite. I don't want to sit next to him.

"In ten weeks I'll be having your baby." I get straight to the point, not giving myself a chance to think about what happened last time we were alone and within kissing distance. The time for wasting is over.

Jay nods, not looking at me, not saying anything.

"I'm due the eighteenth of June." Every time I say that it sounds sooner. Duh. I mean, I know it *is* getting sooner, but it's really starting to *feel* it. Jay is still saying nothing, but I'm going to wait.

I wait.

Wait some more.

He's sipping his drink and not looking at me.

This feels so much like the last time I spoke to Aaron. Misery claws at my heart when I think of him, wondering how he is… No. Not now. This is about me and Jay. And our baby.

Jay sips his drink again. "What do you want me to say?"

"I want to know whether you'll be there for me."

"What? On the due date?"

I swallow. No tears for this one, remember, Hannah?

"I wasn't thinking that specifi—"

"It's in the middle of the exams—"

"Yeah, and? It's in the middle of mine too!"

Jay gives me a look so cold that it freezes the heat of my anger. "This wasn't my choice."

What can I say to that?

Silence stretches out across the room and beyond, into the space between us. I'm on one side of a valley, screaming for help, sobbing because I am all alone over here … and he's on the other side, turning away with a shrug.

"But it's happening…"

"Not because of me." Jay is glaring at the can in his hands and I can see the pads of his fingertips bulge with the pressure of his grip. "You never asked me what I wanted, Hannah. You never gave me a chance to be a part of this until it was too late."

I swallow. "You'd have asked me to get rid of the baby."

"I don't know." He scrunches his eyes shut and shakes his head a little before opening them. He's still not looking at me. "Yes – probably. You're my…"

And we don't finish that sentence, either of us.

"Why didn't you take the morning-after pill? How hard could it have been?"

I stare at him. The boy I was in love with was leaving for university – going a week earlier than he had to because he couldn't wait to leave us all behind. I was tired and I was emotional and the journey from my house to the chemist in town was too much to do on my own. And I was stupid. Very, very stupid. I thought that because he'd pulled out, I didn't need to bother.

"What's the point talking about it? It doesn't change the facts. This baby is yours. And I—"

The way he jerks his head up stops me. He does not want to hear that I love him – and I'm not sure that I want to say it, because no matter how much I might lie to myself,

I know that what I really want, why I came here, crawling on my knees, is to hear Jay tell me that he loves me.

"I want you to be there." My voice sounds feeble and suddenly I feel heavy, like the weight of everything has just hit me. I'm having a baby – Jay's baby – and he's not got it. *Still*. I am sitting in front of him, my bump barely covered between my top and leggings, and I have asked him in every way I know how. There is nothing more I can do.

"You have Aaron for that." Jay is still looking at me when he says this and I wonder if he can see the hurt written on my face because he thinks he can simply pass this on to someone else. And the hurt that cuts deeper: the someone else has told me to hand it back.

I haul myself to standing and Jay looks up as I wait for him to tell me to stay so that we can sort this out. But he doesn't say anything at all as I walk into the kitchen, silently begging him to follow me as I strain my ears for the sound of his steps on the tiles behind me. I try and stride slowly towards the front door to give him time to change his mind. With my hand on the lock, I pause and close my eyes.

Please, Jay.

But I open the door and when I turn to shut it behind me there's no one there.

On the other side of the door lies misery. For the first time since I took the test in my gran's bathroom I feel fear. Raw, terrifying, uncontrollable fear that I have made the biggest mistake of my life.

TUESDAY 13TH APRIL

EASTER HOLIDAYS

AARON

In the back of my wardrobe there is a suit that I have worn only once. It should still fit. I haven't grown that much and it was a little big to start with. I take it out of the carrier and hang it on the back of my door and look for a clean school shirt, then I go next door and find one of Dad's ties – he left early to play golf and Mum's at work. They still don't know. I went out on Friday – walked to Chris's grave and sat there for a couple of hours, long enough to lose the feeling in my toes and fool my parents into thinking I'd been to Cedarfields.

I look at my reflection, and a memory of a boy I thought I'd forgotten looks back at me. I've spent so much time hiding from him that I hadn't realized he was simply lying in wait.

I change my socks. Neville would approve of the slightly subversive bright green ones I end up wearing. I pull on the leather jacket and leave, so focused on where I'm going that it's not until I'm on the bus that I remember I didn't double lock the front door. Oh well. Double locking a door seems pretty small compared to dying.

There is a world outside the window that drifts past me: workmen on a break, their tools on the ground and flasks clutched in hands with dirty fingernails; people waiting to cross the road; a young couple arguing, not holding hands; and a runner, bouncing from foot to foot impatient for a break in the traffic; primary-school kids playing in the park, enjoying a day of freedom…

I turn and look at the passengers: a man talking in too-loud French on his phone; two mums too busy talking to stop their toddlers from pressing their faces to the window and licking the glass; an elderly lady with soft white curls, eyes half closed behind glasses so clean they flash in the sunlight…

I feel so detached. Like I'm watching a TV drama with an especially self-pitying Smiths song playing as the camera pans the scene before me. Even the way the early morning sun shines through the window is casting a slight mist at the edges of my vision.

There's something damp on my jawline and I reach up to touch it. When I take my fingers away, they're damp from tears I didn't know were falling. The mist in the corners of my vision has started to close in.

I get off a stop early. You shouldn't turn up to a funeral crying – it's like turning up to a date masturbating. I push my hands deep into the pockets of the jacket only to discover that there's a hole in the lining in the corner of the lefthand pocket. I push my finger through and stroke the soft side of leather that no one but the manufacturer ever saw, then there's a ripping sound and my whole hand slides through the hole and into the bottom corner of the jacket.

There's something in there.

HANNAH

In the back of my wardrobe there is a dress that I have worn only once. It should still fit.

Shit. It really doesn't.

I slump down onto the bed, supposedly stretchy dress rolled up under my armpits (which is as far as it's likely to get). It's navy anyway and I'm not sure that's allowed at a funeral. I'm not sure *I'm* allowed at this funeral. I asked Gran if she was going, but it turns out they have memorial services on site at the home. Guess that makes sense or they'd have season tickets to the funeral parlour. Mum doesn't do funerals – she thinks farewells should be private – so there's no point asking her to come. It would just be me.

Looking for Aaron.

I don't think I'd find him even if I walked right up to him and reached out for a hug. And if I can't do that, then I don't know why else I would go.

AARON

After the service I wait the rest of the day, sitting in the grounds reading my book until his ashes are ready to collect – they usually take longer, but when they saw that I was on my own, they hurried things up. I never expected to fulfil the promise I made to Neville only a few weeks ago – I'd thought we could work on getting him talking to his daughters before he... I was wrong.

It's late afternoon by the time I catch a bus to the part

of town where the Drunken Duchess resides. It's a poky-looking place from the outside, a run-down Edwardian building with paint peeling from the window frames and brick dust loose enough that a customer's sneeze could blow it off. The sign's new, although it's pretty ugly and you get a flash of the Duchess's frilly bloomers as the sign swings in the breeze. Totally tasteless. Totally Neville.

"ID."

It's the first thing the barman says to me and I haven't even sat down.

"My name's Aaron Tyler," I say. "I'm a friend of Neville Robson." I put the ashes on the bar. They're not in an urn because I didn't know it was BYO on fancy receptacles and had to make do with the only thing the staff could find, but the barman barely reacts to the Tupperware box of human remains and keeps on polishing the glass he's holding.

"Thought I recognized that jacket," says someone to my left. "Come to sprinkle him in the beer garden, then?" I hadn't noticed the old man sitting at the end of the bar, but he looks at least twice as old as Neville was.

"Yes," I say.

"Doing it now?"

I nod, staying firmly where I am. All of a sudden I don't feel very ready for this.

"Let him have a drink," the old man says to the barman.

"How old are you, son?"

"Eighteen," I reply.

"Yeah, when?" he says, picking up a new, less-sparkling glass.

"Yesterday." I flicker a look up at him and we lock eyes for a second.

"Funny, seems like you think I was born then," he says, wrist twisting as he polishes.

I reach into the hole in Neville's pocket and take out what I found there. It's a piece of paper. Actually it's two. I unfold them carefully.

"What was his favourite drink?" I ask, scoring against the creases with my thumbnail.

"Whisky mac," says the barman.

"This should cover a round or so," I say and I lay down Neville's legacy. Two fifty-pound notes.

HANNAH

Mum's back from dropping Lola off at her friend's house – after covering someone else's shifts earlier in the week she's got the afternoon off so we can go through all Lola's old clothes and toys and work out which ones to keep out for the baby. She's in the kitchen picking bits of straw off her jumper and looks up when I go down for a drink.

"Can you sweep the utility room floor? I knocked over a bag of bedding when I was topping up Fiver's water—"

But when she sees I've been crying she steps over, guiding me to the table where I snivel whilst she makes me something warm and comforting to drink. Hot chocolate.

"Caffeine…" I mumble, but the look I get says *"Enough of that nonsense."*

"Talk to me, Han." She's sitting close enough that when

I lean in my head rests comfortably on her shoulder. Mum doesn't hesitate as she puts her arm around me and strokes my hair out of my face the way she did when I was little. I've never seen her do this to Lola and it feels special.

"What's going on with you and Aaron?"

So she *has* noticed. I try not to tell her anything bad about Aaron because she doesn't need an excuse to think less of him – the shag-happy sperm donor who got her teenage daughter pregnant. She's made allowances and he's won brownie points for standing by me, for helping me with school, for quietly becoming one of the family. But it wouldn't take much for that to change. I don't want it to change over this. I *never* want it to change.

So I tell her what I can, that he's hurting, that I tried to help, but he wouldn't let me in. That I thought he might have called this morning to ask me to come to the funeral with him. I don't need to tell her that he didn't.

"You're not going to like what I'm about to say," she says softly.

I hold my breath.

"Not everyone deals with things the way we think they should. You're someone who shares everything. Mostly." She doesn't look at me, but I know what she's thinking. "Aaron doesn't strike me as that kind of person. He's" – she pauses for a few seconds – "I don't want to say 'distanced'…"

Then don't. I want to say. It sounds so cold and harsh. But it also sounds true.

"Robert's like that too," she says.

"He is?" I feel Mum's cheek move as it rests on my head

and I think she must be smiling.

"Robert is a lot older than Aaron. He's learned that depths are better hidden behind a lot of affection and bravado. But there are things I still don't know about him, or understand, and there are times when we fight and I don't know how to reach him."

Mum and Robert fight? I never think of them fighting. Not like Mum did with Dad.

"When Robert's brother died I worried all the time about how he was feeling. I tried to make sure that I was here for Jay, so that Robert didn't feel the pressure too much. I called his sister-in-law, to make sure that she was OK because I didn't want Robert to have to call her and be reminded about losing his brother."

This all makes sense to me.

"But I was doing all of this because it made *me* feel better. I was so involved in being the good wife that I never stopped to offer Robert what he wanted."

"What did he want?" I ask.

"Nothing."

I lift my head off her shoulder and look up. "I don't understand."

"Neither did I," she says, with a sad smile.

AARON

The pub is filling up around me. I've downed three whisky macs and the walls are starting to slide. Someone sits next to me smelling of burgers and it makes me feel a little ill.

"Cider," I say.

The barman ignores me and serves the guy next to me, who walks away with his drinks, taking his burger breath with him.

"Can I have a pint of cider, please?" I say. I know this is what I say because I'm concentrating on making the words sound exactly as they should. Not slurred. Not too careful. I know how to seem sober.

The barman is looking at me.

"What's my name?" he asks.

His name? Oh yeah, we've had a conversation about names, about Neville's brother Greville, and the man at the end of the bar introduced himself and then he made me try and guess the barman's name. Which was ... what?

"Ste," I say in a flash of brilliance.

"Ste-*ven*," he says, watching me suspiciously.

"He knows that," says Old Man at the End of the Bar whose name I actually can't remember. "He's winding you up."

"Cider for him too," I say generously.

"Make that a Bombardiers," Old Man corrects me.

"Bombadoodlers then," I say carelessly. SteVEN the barman looks at me strangely, but serves our drinks.

I drink mine too quickly and feel a hiccup brewing ready to burst. I swallow it down as it rises and I feel the fizz of bile in the back of my nose. I sip more cider and look at the plastic box of ashes on the bar. Someone brings back some empty glasses. There's a half-pint glass amongst them and I sploosh some cider into it and push it next to him.

"Cheers, Neville!" I declare and clink my pint against the mini one I've poured.

The barman wipes up the pool of cider I've dribbled on the bar as he collects the other empties. He leaves Neville's drink where it is.

My pint glass is almost empty. Probably because half of it got poured into Neville's. I need something else.

I can't seem to not want to drink something. My hands need to hold something, my mouth needs to sip something, my throat needs to swallow something.

"Can I buy you a drink?" I say to the next person who walks up to the bar.

"OK." It's a girl. She has big boobs. They are not in any way subtly dressed and they are at eye-level to someone sitting slumped on a bar stool.

Neville would approve.

"Can you buy the drinks though?" I say to the boobs and hand their owner a twenty. "Cider for me. No. A vodka. No. Both. And whatever you fancy."

"You?" she says with a smile.

"Me," I repeat, a bit lost. She orders the drinks and the barman pretends he doesn't know that the vodka and cider are for me. So much for his ethics on my sobriety.

"What's that?" she says, looking past me to the box on the bar.

"Neville," I reply.

"Neville?" She takes her drink and hands me the change. There's not much, but there's lots more in my pocket.

"Neville Robson," I say. "Used to drink here."

When I look at her, I see that her face has slipped in disgust as she realizes that I'm sitting here drinking with a dead guy. Her boobs have stayed pert though, so I content myself with a last glimpse of those puppies before she takes them with her back to the crowd in the corner. What time is it?

It's half past six.

I should probably go and sprinkle Neville in the beer garden. After I've finished my drinks.

Oh. The vodka's gone already. When did I drink that? Whatever. I drink the cider.

I really need a piss. I get off the stool and the floor tilts so that I have to hang onto the bar a moment. The barman hasn't noticed, but Old Man at the End of the Bar has and I see him give me a knowing smile.

I go to the loo. I'm sick in one of the cubicles then I wee on it. When I come out there's a couple of guys at the urinals and I nearly bump into one of them on my way to the sink. He says something but I'm not really paying attention. That's why I bumped into him in the first place.

I wash my hands and look up at my reflection too fast. The toilets rock back and forth in my reality and I have to lean my head on the mirror and close my eyes until it stops. When I open them my reflection is just a slab of skin with a giant Cyclops eye in the middle of my forehead. I alter my focus until I have two eyes, blurry, but less weird to look at. Then I push myself back off the glass.

I don't look good. I'm not wearing my suit jacket any more and my shirt is unbuttoned further than it was when I left the house. Where's my dad's tie? For a moment I panic and pat all my pockets until I discover it in my trouser pocket. I take it out and see that there's a stain on it. Where did that come from?

Looks like mayonnaise.

Oh yeah. I had a sandwich at the bar earlier – most of which is now in the second toilet from the end; some of which appears on be on my dad's tie.

I look back up at the me in the mirror. I don't like what I see. I see someone who lets his friends down. Neville, Chris…

Chris. I miss you so much, mate. I'm so sorry.

Don't be my friend, or you'll die.

I look at the person in the mirror. I wish he was dead instead.

HANNAH

We're in the kitchen and I'm trying to convince Mum we deserve some fondant fancies after the epic sorting we've just done when my phone blings.

"Hannah!" Mum tuts as I stop mid-sentence to pick up my phone. But I'm not thinking about cake any more when I see who's texted and I open the message as fast as I can to find out what Aaron has to say to me.

You dont undwrstNd what it"s liee you do't know wast I

That's where the text ends. He must have sent it before

he finished typing, but my phone blings another almost immediately.

Gor nonone he" a good I lost him. It(s all my faylt!!2

Mum is no longer looking annoyed with me when I look up. She can see something's going on. I text back, worried.

Where ru?

Then I call as well. It goes to voicemail. I wonder if it's a good idea to call again but do it anyway. This time he answers. The last ten days are written off in an instant.

"Hello?" I say, since Aaron hasn't actually said anything.

"Hannah?".

"Yeah, it's me. Are you OK?"

No answer.

"Aaron? Where are you?" I say, trying not to sound panicky.

"Toilets."

He slurs so badly that he still hasn't managed to get the "s" out when I ask, "The toilets where?"

"Drunken Duchess. I lost him, Hannah. Neville. He's not here."

"Neville's not in the toilets?" Could the boy be any more confusing?

"I thought I brought him in here with me, but I didn't and when I got back he was gone. How could I lose him? HOW?!" I flinch the phone away from the shriek he makes.

"Do you want me to come and help find him?" I say, but Aaron's not listening. I think he might be crying. I put my hand over the phone.

"Can you drive me to a pub called the Drunken Duchess?" I ask Mum.

"Why?" she mouths, frowning, but I ignore her and tell Aaron that I'm on my way, although I think he's hung up.

"It's Aaron. There's something wrong—" I'm halfway out of the door before I realize Robert's halfway in, still in his suit, car keys in hand.

"Where's the fire?" he jokes before he sees Mum's face and stops me, hands resting firmly on my shoulders. "Hannah?"

Sometimes Robert's harder to lie to than Mum.

"Aaron's in some pub..." Even though I can see he disapproves, he doesn't say anything. "He's having some kind of breakdown."

I look at Robert and back at Mum. "I've got to go to him – he needs me."

I see a conversation between them, one of glances and sharp breaths – no words, until, "I'll drive." And Robert's turned on his heel, straight back to his car, Mum and me hurrying after. They have a lot of questions, none of which I can answer, and it takes some persuading to get them to stay in the car, but Mum will just stress me out and there's no way I'm walking into a pub like the Duchess with Robert dressed for a boardroom takeover. Me, I fit right in. The place smells like stale beer and pork scratchings and I have to ask people to "Excuse me," before I start shoving bodies out of my way. I've only got fifteen minutes before Mum comes in to find me.

"Hi," I say to the barman.

"ID," he says.

"Er, hello, pregnant?" I say and point at my stomach. "Not about to go on a bender."

"Then how can I help you?" he says in a weird formal tone that makes me think he's taking the piss.

"I'm looking for my friend Aaron. Dark hair, leather jacket…" That's when I see the jacket I mean in a heap on the floor. I crouch down and use the bar to pull myself back up. "This leather jacket."

"He's in the beer garden," the barman says, nodding to a rickety-looking door.

I go outside but Aaron's not there.

Back inside I look round the room. Aaron's definitely not in here, although I check round the corner where there's a dartboard. I push open the door of the Gents and try to breathe as little as possible. Boy wee stinks.

"Aaron?" I call out, grateful that I can't see any strange men in here.

"Ladies is that door, luv." Someone comes in behind me. I glance round to see a man about Robert's age with a tattoo nudging up from the neck of his football shirt.

"I'm looking for my friend," I say and walk further into the toilets, trying to bend over and look for feet in the cubicles.

I push the doors and one jams up against something. "Aaron?" I say, trying to crouch down further. Neck-tattoo man bends down for me and nods.

"Someone's in there." He shoves the door a little harder then reaches round. There's a groan. The man shoves the door open and I see Aaron sprawled on the floor, his face pressed up against the side of the cubicle and his hand dangling in the toilet bowl. There's a stain on his sleeve and when he opens his eyes they're bloodshot. They don't stay open for long.

My helpful stranger stops me from going in and instead he drags Aaron out. He grunts for me to open the door and he takes him all the way out, down the passage and out of the fire exit. The man arranges Aaron into a sitting position on the step and goes back inside, saying he'll get some water. I lower myself carefully next to Aaron and shrug on his leather jacket. It's cold – which should sober him up a bit at least.

I stare at the hair on the back of his neck. He's had it cut – for the funeral, I guess – and I wonder what it would be like to stroke it. And because he is drunk and because I want to, I put my hand on Aaron's neck and brush my thumb over his skin and across his hair.

For a second I think that this is what he wants too … until he shakes me off and I snatch my hand away, annoyed that, even now, in the midst of an alcoholic stupor he still can't let me in.

Then he lurches forwards and retches.

OK, I'll let him off. But I don't reach out to him again.

"You all right?" I ask. He's blatantly not, but what else do you say?

Aaron shakes his head. "I lost him, Han."

"You lost Neville? You mean his ashes?"

Aaron doesn't say anything, but the door behind us opens and my knight in shining football strip hands me a pint of water and a Tupperware box.

"The barman said the lad would be looking for this," he says and gives me a grin. "Just give us a shout if you need a hand with anything, darling."

"Thanks," I say, before holding the box up and looking at it. It's full of ash.

Neville.

"Here," I say and hand Aaron the box first and the water second, like I'm asking him to mix me some cement. He doesn't say anything, but I can see his shoulders drop in relief.

"I need to sprinkle Chris's ashes," he says, putting the glass down and standing up.

"Chris?"

"Neville. Neville's ashes." Aaron sways dangerously and almost knocks over his glass of water as he starts clawing at a corner of the box's lid, trying to prise it off.

"Stop, Aaron." I stand up and put my fingers over his. "We'll come back another time to do this. I don't think Neville would mind."

AARON

When did Hannah get here? I don't remember that.

But she's found Neville.

"Thank you," I say and give her a hug. She looks nonplussed.

"You're welcome," she says and pats me on the shoulder.

My mouth tastes awful. There's a glass of water on the step, so I pick it up and sip some, swilling it round my mouth and spitting it out, then take a proper drink. Although some dribbles out the side of my mouth and down the collar of my shirt, most of it makes it in.

"What are you doing here?" I ask Hannah. "I thought we weren't talking. Are we talking?"

"*You* weren't talking," she says, frowning. "But you texted me. I called. I was worried."

I shake my head. It's not me she should be worrying about. She should worry about her. I'm dangerous to people who care about me.

"I killed him," I say, letting her lead me away.

"Killed who?" Hannah says, patiently.

"Chris."

"Yeah, so, I don't know what you're talking about." She's annoyed.

"My best friend," I say.

"What?" She stops yanking at the stiff bolt on the back gate and looks up at me and I think how pretty she is when she doesn't try. Her hair's all scruffy and she's wearing hardly any make-up but that just means you get to notice her eyes more. Even in orange street light.

"My best friend," I say, echoing something I know I've just said. "You're my best friend."

"You're mine too. Why d'you think I came out here looking for you?" she says and starts working the bolt loose on the gate. "Who's this Chris you keep going on about?"

Chris. Oh God, Chris. I'm so sorry. I miss you, mate. I'm so sorry. I didn't mean to… I should never have… I wasn't…

I slump down on the floor, my head folding into my hands and the tears coming so fast and wet that they almost choke me on their way out. I'm nothing but grief. It doesn't hurt. It's a cold, deep emptiness inside me and I want it to end. I can't face this again. I can't...

HANNAH

Shit. I have no idea what's just happened, but Aaron's gone into total meltdown on the floor. He's making the most awful sound – like a wail – and he's sobbing so hard his whole body is shaking. When he looks up at me his face is like one of those theatre masks with the mouth turned upside down and there are tears streaming down his face. It's like nothing I've ever seen before and it scares me.

But it's not about me, is it?

This is about my best friend.

WEDNESDAY 14TH APRIL
EASTER HOLIDAYS

AARON

I wake up in a strange house, in a strange bed in the middle of the night, feeling sick. There's a plastic bucket next to me on the bed and I vomit into it then put it on the floor. That's when I find that someone's put out a bottle of water and a glass. I drink half the bottle and lie back, feeling like I'm on the roundabout in the park with someone spinning it faster and faster...

I wake up again, and there's light at the window. Someone's cleared the bucket away and given me a new one, and there's fresh water beside me along with a packet of crisps. I scoff the crisps and gulp the water, although sitting up kills me. I feel weak with exhaustion and I need a piss, but... I collapse back onto the bed and pull the duvet up and around me. I can smell myself, which is not a good sign, but I'm past caring. I guess that's not a great sign either.

When I wake up the third time I'm feeling a lot better. A surge of gratitude washes over me – the high the body throws up in relief that it hasn't been annihilated by alcohol. There's noise beyond my bedroom door and I can hear Lola running along the landing. I stand up and stretch then shuffle over to the window and look out. It's afternoon. There's a gentle knock on the door and Hannah's there in tracksuit bottoms and one of her old vests that only just covers the bump.

"Mum wants to know if you're hungry." Her expression is completely neutral. It worries me.

"I could go another packet of crisps?" I say with a smile that is only half returned, before she tells me that I seriously need to brush my teeth.

"Use the green brush. There's a towel and clothes for you as well."

I take the hint and shower. After I've dried off, I pull on the shorts and faded Nike T-shirt she's left out. Jay's, but for me.

Hannah is waiting on the bed next to a tray of food: crisps, biscuits, cold pizza, slices of apple, a Mars ice cream and two cans. One Diet Coke, one lemonade. I don't need to ask who the ice cream's for as I sit down. That baby she's brewing is made of the stuff.

"I'm so sorry. About last week." I apologize from the pit of my very empty stomach before taking a slice of pizza. "And about last night."

"You said some pretty scary shit," is all she says in reply.

I don't remember exactly what I said. I don't remember much at all, only bits here and there, pieces of a puzzle that don't give any indication of the whole.

"Like what?" I say, because it's going to be the only way to find out. Not that I want to.

"You said you had no one." She swallows, concentrating hard on finishing her ice cream. "That you killed your best friend, Chris."

There's a pause. I told her about Chris? I look down at

the duvet cover, desperately trying to remember when I said that, wondering if I told her everything or nothing, or something hashed up and halfway in between.

"You said you wished you were dead."

Hannah's voice breaks and I look up to see that she's crying. Grown-up tears that just run down her face.

I've never seen her look so sad.

"I'm *so* sorry, Hannah," I say, shuffling closer and putting my arms around her. "I don't mean that."

"You did," she says into my shoulder.

I think about lying to her, but how can I?

She squeezes into me so tightly I think she's trying to climb into my soul. And I feel it coming, the choice between shutting her out and letting her in…

"Who's Chris?" she asks.

I hold my breath and close my eyes. I think about a part of my life I've tried to shut away. But I let it out when I told Neville and now it's here in this room, waiting to be shared with the person I most want to hide it from. I can't afford to lose Hannah any more than she can afford to lose me, but if I don't tell her the truth, then it's over.

What the hell. Here goes.

HANNAH

And so I learn who Chris is – and what happened to him. It is the hardest thing I've ever had to hear, but I know it was harder for him to tell me.

It changes nothing. Aaron is still my favourite person in the whole world.

He is still my hero, even if he can't see why.

AARON

Of the seminal moments in my life, Careers Day in the Autumn of Year 5 is my favourite. Everyone had to dress as whatever they wanted to be when they grew up. I had gone in a tweed jacket and a bow tie and when Miss Weston asked me what I wanted to be I told her that I wanted to be the Doctor.

"Shouldn't you be wearing a lab coat and stethoscope like Paul?" She pointed to Paul Black, who was trying to strangle everyone with the stethoscope in question.

Before I could answer, a boy I didn't know from the other class spoke up.

"Paul's a doctor," he explained, giving me a look of approval. "He wants to be the Doctor."

"Who?"

"Exactly," we said at the same time, relieved that she understood.

She didn't. We were sent to the quiet table to reflect on why cheeking teachers was wrong.

"I'm Aaron Tyler," I whispered across the table.

"Chris Lam." Chris checked Miss Weston wasn't watching and stretched over to shake my hand, blinking behind over-sized glasses. "Nice to meet you, Aaron."

I shook his hand and grinned. "My friends call me Ty."

Geekiness formed a firm foundation for friendship and when we studied for the entrance exams for Bart's – St Bartholomew's – it was Chris I studied with, hoping we'd pass or fail together. The day we heard that we'd both got in, Chris came round to my house to celebrate with lemonade and a batch of my dad's legendary brownies. We'd just rolled out our latest architectural plans for the Death Star, holding the corners down with half-full glasses and empty plates when there was a knock on the back door and someone rushed in, waving a sheet of paper.

"I got in!"

My other best friend. The one I'd kept hidden from Chris. The one who knew more about Star Wars than George Lucas, who'd helped me paint all my D&D figures, who I'd known since nursery. Only problem was … she was a girl. Chris didn't like girls.

"Penny – Chris." I turned to Chris, who was sweating so much that his glasses had slid down to the tip of his nose. "Chris, this is Penny."

"Hi!" Penny stuck out her hand and shook Chris's so hard it nearly dislocated his shoulder.

It wasn't exactly the start of something beautiful and I spent most of my first year at Bart's a pawn in their battle for my best friendship, and the second trying to stop them from killing each other, until, eventually, after a thawing in Year 9, we hit puberty and Chris and Penny started getting on a lot better. So well, in fact, that they got distinctly friendly at the Year 10 Halloween disco and six months later, were still going strong when Chris went away to France for Easter.

That fortnight I enjoyed having Penny to myself. We'd hang out, watching DVDs and playing old-school RPG games on my computer, although I fully expected to lose her completely the second her boyfriend returned. It was a surprise when I was the one who received a text from him the day he got back, asking if I'd like to walk into town.

I met Chris at the end of his road.

"You sure you want to walk?" I asked, looking at the sky. Mum had told me to take a raincoat with me, but I'd ignored her.

"It's not far." Which was a lie, but he was acting strangely so I didn't press the point. We'd been walking for about ten minutes, talking about homework neither of us had done, when we crossed the main road by Bart's. The air was heavy and thunder rumbled somewhere miles away – a portent of doom if ever there was one – when Chris cut across what I was saying.

"I need to tell you something." He opened his mouth a couple of times, as if practising forming the words. "I cheated on Penny."

I stopped walking. The sky was growling and I thought I saw a little flash out of the corner of my eye. I didn't know what to say.

Chris stopped a little way ahead of me. "Say something, Ty."

"*Why?*" I ignored Chris's shrug, not wanting to know the answer anyway. "How are you going to tell her?"

He rubbed the back of his neck. It's a gesture I'd seen his dad use when he was about to say something no one wanted to hear. "I'm not sure about that."

I narrowed my eyes. "How much did you cheat by, dude?"

Thunder in the silence. That was when I realized why he was acting like this: he'd slept with someone else.

"Got bored of waiting, did you?" My voice was harsh, but he deserved it. Penny had told him she wanted to wait until she was ready. When Chris had told me this, he'd said he didn't mind and that he respected her for it.

Chris said nothing.

"So … what now? You popped your cherry on your holibobs and now you've confessed it'll magically grow back?"

"Don't be like this, Ty…" Lightning.

"Like what? What did you expect me to be like?"

"Just … don't be a jerk." Chris stepped closer. "I don't want to hurt her… I care about her."

That made me laugh. It came out mirthless and harsh against a rumble of thunder.

"If you really cared about Penny you wouldn't be telling me this – you'd be telling her." I thought of all the things she'd said about Chris in the last two weeks – the confidence with which she'd told me I'd know when I met the right girl… "If you don't tell her, then I will."

Chris looked up at me sharply, eyes narrowing behind his glasses as he absorbed the threat. "You'd sell me out, just like that?"

"Sell *you* out? I've known Penny since—"

"It's not like she'll come running to you because I've fucked up!"

There was a silence between us during which we both registered that he'd gone too far. Fat drops started to fall from the sky and I watched as the pavement turned dark with rain. The dim mustard light of the storm suited my mood. I couldn't believe Chris had just said that.

"Look, I didn't—" Chris started to say, reaching out to put a hand on my arm.

"Fuck off!" I said, slapping his hand away.

"Let's find somewhere to talk." He turned up the collar on his jacket and shrugged into it further as the rain spilled down onto us. "I'm getting soaked."

"So?" I didn't care about getting wet. I was too angry to care about a little rain. Or a lot of rain. My top was already sticking to me.

"Well, I'm not standing around here to get wet and ragged on by you," Chris snapped and edged towards the kerb.

I grabbed his arm and pulled him back. "You're not going anywhere until you face up to what you just said."

He tried to shake me off, pulling away from me. The fact that he was trying to wriggle out of it infuriated me and I grabbed his other arm, twisting him to face me properly.

"Let me go!"

"Don't be such a spineless *twat*, Chris!"

Angry, he shoved both hands hard into my chest, unbalancing me … but I still had hold of his jacket and

I yanked him towards me, accidentally cracking the top of his head with my chin as I tried to stop myself from falling flat on my arse. It was the lamest fight ever to have occurred in the history of fisticuffs. We were more like two kittens tangled up in the same ball of wool until Chris clamped one hand around my shoulder and dug his thumb into the hollow above my collarbone, causing me to yelp as I let go.

Rain streamed down, plastering his hair to his head, rivulets cascading down his glasses. With one arm still rigid, holding me away from him, Chris wiped a sodden sleeve under his nose and checked for blood. There wasn't any and, just like that, he seemed to tire of fighting and turned away to cross the road. Catching his sleeve, I tried to hold him back. I didn't want us to leave it like this, not even for the length of time it would take to find somewhere dry to sit, but he must have thought I was still fighting him the way he whipped round and tried to shrug his jacket off. But that wasn't what I wanted.

So I let go.

Chris wasn't expecting me to do that. He was straining with all his weight, one foot resting on the edge of the kerb, one foot in the gutter streaming with rainwater.

So he slipped.

He twisted as he tried to regain his balance and keep from falling over. It was the wrong thing to do because he stumbled awkwardly and fell away from the pavement.

Into the road.

There's a thousand little things that go into making one

big thing happen. Wet tarmac, a car going a little too fast to catch the green light ahead, a boy who fell backwards when he should have fallen forwards, a boy who shouldn't have let go of his friend's sleeve when he did.

When you see something truly awful happen, you don't process it at all – it's only afterwards that details come to you. The only thing that registered with me was the noise: a sickening crack and *thunk*, both sharp and blunt, the sound of a body hitting a bonnet and breaking. It's the noise I hear in my worst nightmares.

Chris was twisted all wrong on the ground and there was something darker than the rain pooling where his head rested on the road. I was terrified of finding out whether he was breathing, but I still walked out into the road and leaned forwards to check.

I couldn't tell. I couldn't tell anything.

All I could think was that the last thing I said to my best friend was that he was a spineless twat.

HANNAH

I slide my hand into his. I'm not sure if he even notices.

AARON

It didn't hit me until the hospital, when Dad came into the room and whispered something about Chris to Mum. She turned to me and held me, clinging to me, squeezing me as if I was the one who was never coming home. I held her back, let her cry silent, grateful tears into my shoulder, let her whisper to me that she loved me so much.

That was when I started to cry. There weren't any thoughts, just feelings of loss and horror and grief, relief that my parents weren't going through what Chris's parents were, shame that I felt that way. Guilt drove me to cry harder and harder until I could barely breathe for sobbing and I was sick on the floor, but no one said anything, not my dad, not my mum, not even the nurse who quietly came and mopped it up and handed Mum one of those shiny steel bowls. I don't know when they took me home.

During the police interview the next day I stared dully at the tabletop. I didn't want to see the look in the officer's eyes when I told her the truth.

"We were fighting." I felt my dad go very still on the chair next to me. It was the first he'd heard of it.

"And…" The police officer's voice was careful, neutral, non-committal.

"I didn't … mean to." The words seemed to fall out of my mouth, as if I had no control. "He was trying to get away and I was pulling him back…"

I closed my eyes, only to snap them open to avoid the memories waiting in the dark.

"You were pulling him back?"

I looked up at her then and I watched the way her jaw clenched as she looked back at me, waiting.

"I shouldn't have let go." I started crying so much that the interview was suspended and my father pulled me close and told me that he loved me. Told me that it wasn't my fault, I wasn't to blame. I didn't believe him.

I was spared the funeral. When I couldn't get out of the car in my new black suit, my dad simply turned round and drove home. But school was a distraction I thought I could handle. I was wrong. The sympathetic looks and hugs from the girls – except for Penny, who was absent; back pats from the boys; teachers ignoring the empty seat next to mine. But it was the gap in the morning registration, where his name should have been, that got to me most, reminding me of the space in my world that my best friend should have occupied.

At the end of the week I found Rav waiting for me by the main entrance. We'd been mates – the three of us.

"This week's been hard," he said.

I nodded.

"Want to come and get drunk with me and some of the lads?"

I did, and I got very, *very* drunk. Drunk enough that I could forget who I was for whole minutes at a time. Drunk enough to forget who my friends were and to end up sitting with the group of lads who hung out by the late-night supermarket near my house – lads that Chris and I had always been a little bit scared of.

Chris. No matter how much I drank, I could never forget Chris.

At least, not until I blacked out.

The next morning I woke up on the sofa in Rav's room, my host telling me that I wasn't allowed to be sick or his mum would find out what we'd been up to – not that I could remember any of it. For all the pain I was in, I realized that twelve hours had passed like twelve minutes. That night I didn't need an invitation; I went down to the supermarket with enough money for the oldest lad – a guy called Smiffy, who was a Mark Grey of a man – to buy me a bottle of tequila and I drank the lot.

But I couldn't pull the same stunt the next day, not on a Sunday.

The week passed by. Wake up. Remember. Go to school. Remember. Come home. Remember. Go to sleep. And repeat…

Somehow I'd managed to avoid Penny at school. We didn't have many classes together and I'd turn up late and leave early in the ones we did share. Breaktimes I'd hide in the library, picking out a title at random and reading it for as long as I needed to lose myself, then putting it back on the shelf when the bell went. But Thursday night she rang my house.

"Ty. We need to talk."

I told her I'd go to hers. The supermarket was between my house and Penny's – it was seven o'clock and I wasn't surprised to find Smiffy there with a couple of other lads. I handed him the twenty I'd taken from Dad's wallet and asked him to buy me some vodka and cider. If I drunk enough before I went to Penny's then she wouldn't want to talk to me. I didn't have much of a window, so I needed to drink fast and I cut the two together. Too focused on my own problems, I didn't notice that Smiffy was looking for trouble when another group of kids headed into the supermarket.

There was a scuffle by the doors. It didn't really register with me until the lad next to me yanked me up and said that Smiffy needed a hand. Not that I knew what to do with my hands, my brain was blurred with booze and I found myself stumbling into the back of one lad who turned and landed a crack to my browbone.

The world came into focus and it was red with remembering.

My guilt, my misery spilled out into violence and I plunged into the fray, grabbing a fistful of a T-shirt to land a punch so vicious I'd hear the crunch of my own bones, flooring one person to start on the next. Everything in me was unleashed, all the hatred I had for myself... I wanted to *hurt*, lashing out with abandon, incapable of feeling the brutal blows landed in retaliation. The more I fought, the less I seemed to feel, driving me to dismay, spurring me on, desperate to find a way to feel the pain I deserved.

Senseless with grief, I ended up laying in to one of our own.

"What the—?" Smiffy held his nose, arm up to block my next punch, missing the kick I let fly. He doubled over, grabbing me on his way to the floor. I was rabid, flying with my fists, my feet and my head, all of them making contact with something as everyone piled in to try and stop me, to calm me down. Someone shouted out that I was bleeding, but I didn't care and I heard someone else scream – it could have been me – or the guy I'd just hammered in the nuts.

"Stop it!"

It was a girl's voice and the bodies surrounding me started peeling back as the person who shouted pushed through.

"TY!" There was blood smeared across one of my eyes and I was having problems focusing through the other. But I would have recognized Penny anywhere. She'd grown bored of waiting and, when I didn't answer my mobile, she'd set off to find me.

When I opened my mouth to speak something came out, blood and part of a tooth.

Penny called my parents, who drove me to hospital. I was concussed. Badly bruised. One of my teeth was chipped and I had to have stitches in a gash that ran the length of my left forearm and a cut in my jaw where you could see the bone. Although my nose remained miraculously unbroken, I'd broken my little toe and fractured one of my fingers.

No one was particularly pleased with the amount of alcohol I'd consumed but the threats to pump my stomach were just that.

The whole time my mum remained calm, listening to the painkiller doses, writing down how often she needed to wake me because of the concussion and any symptoms that signalled an immediate return to A&E. Dad cried in the car on the way back. He didn't want me to see him, but I saw his shoulders shake and noticed Mum take her hand from the gearstick and rest it on his knee.

The next day was spent in pain. And shame. My parents sat with me, talking to me, telling me that they loved me and that I couldn't punish myself like this.

"Why not?" I whispered. "I deserve it."

Mum tilted my chin up, forcing me to look at her.

"We don't." Mum kissed my forehead, her hand on Dad's. I leaned into her and Dad hugged us both so hard that I worried he would pop a stitch.

HANNAH

The hand that is not in Aaron's has found its way to the bump. I think about the child I don't yet know and I get an inkling that maybe I have more in common with Aaron's parents than with him.

AARON

Penny was waiting for me in the library on Monday. She took in the damage as I sat down – the yellowing bruise around my eye, the patch of stubble where I couldn't shave around the stitches on my jaw, the taped fingers.

"I miss him too, you know," she said, tracing a pattern on the table with a nail coated in chipped navy varnish.

"I know. I—"

"Don't you *dare* say you're sorry, Ty. Don't you dare."

"I wasn't going to." How could *sorry* even start to cover the span of my guilt?

She gave me a sidelong look and a smile. "Of course you weren't."

I said what I should have said straightaway. "I was going to say that I'm here if you need me."

Penny nodded, as if she was trying to shake off the tears I could see were falling. "I need you, Ty."

I closed my eyes and dipped my forehead to rest on hers. I wanted to tell her that this was a bad idea. That I wasn't the person she thought she needed. Only I couldn't do that to her. Or to me. I'd already lost one best mate. I couldn't lose the other.

That was two weeks after Chris died – eight more to live through until the inquest. Eight more weeks in which I hid the truth from Penny. I don't know what I thought would happen after that – I'm not sure I was thinking at all – but when the time came to go to the magistrates' court, I told Penny one last lie about having a doctor's appointment and went with my parents to face whatever judgement was cast.

The purpose of the inquest was to go over the witness statements and confirm the circumstances that led to Chris's death by questioning the witnesses – me and the woman driving the car – on points that had not yet been cleared up. Every word I heard myself say seemed to hammer home my guilt, discussing the fight in details that were only too easy to recall because I relived them every waking second. And I hoped for something to change, that I would finally be exposed for what I was, finally made accountable.

The verdict was death by misadventure.

Death by misadventure. That's a phrase that plays in my head sometimes, the way a fragment of a tune, or a poem might, cropping up to remind me that nothing multiplies guilt like the implication of innocence. As if I've ever been close to forgetting.

As I walked out with my parents I saw Chris's dad waiting by the doors as his wife came out of the toilets, her face blotched red from tears I'd caused. I wanted to tell her that I was so sorry – not just for what I'd done, but that I wasn't about to be punished for it – but she beat me to it.

"You killed him!" A sentence that started in a hiss and ended in a shriek. Out of the corner of my eye I saw a few people turn towards us. "My son is *dead* because of you…"

"I—" But she was sobbing into her hands and I could see her tears spilling out through her fingers as Chris's dad put his arm around her and pulled her into him. I expected him to be angry too – Mr Lam's temper was legendary – but when he looked at me, his eyes weren't blazing with fury, they were dull, deadened with loss.

"Go away, Ty," he said, pulling his wife close as I felt my mum's hand on my arm. "You've done enough damage."

The next day was worse.

When I got to school, I saw one of the lads I sat with in ICT was waiting by the front doors. As I reached them he handed me a rolled-up newspaper.

"I thought you should know," he said as he went inside.

I unrolled the paper to face a photo of Chris on the front page.

There had been a reporter from the local paper at the inquest, one who had given Chris's parents a sympathetic ear. Chris was the fourth "youth" to die on the region's roads in as many months and the paper was at the heart of a campaign to impose lower speed limits in residential areas. That morning the paper had been delivered to every house within a ten-mile radius of our school.

My hands started to tremble as I read the article, littered with quotes from my friend's grieving parents. It told how their son had been fighting by the side of the road with a friend, "a typical bit of teenage rough and tumble", which had turned to tragedy when Chris fell into the path of a car. It led on to say that though the driver hadn't been speeding, the way Chris had fallen... I couldn't see the words, I was shaking so much.

I was scared of going inside. No one in the school needed to see my name in print to know who Chris had been with. My hand looked strange on the door as I summoned up the courage to push it open. The world felt tilted, unreal, as I walked down the corridor. I could feel people looking at me, but I didn't dare meet their gaze.

Penny was waiting by my locker, her friends clustered nearby, kept away by the forcefield of fury that surrounded her. As soon as I was within striking distance she lashed out, the slap stinging my skin. I saw her pull back for another, but she hesitated, fingers curling like a dying flower until her fist fell limply against my chest, fresh tears falling from closed eyes.

I tried to hold her, but she pushed me away.

It's not like she'll come running to you…

"Penny, I—"

"Don't you dare say you're sorry, Ty."

I didn't know what else to say.

"It says you were fighting. What were you fighting about? What could be so important that you'd push him in front of a moving car?"

"I didn't" – I closed my eyes, saw my hand letting go of his jacket, his foot on the kerb – "push him." It was barely a whisper.

"What were you fighting about?"

But I shook my head. I would have confessed to pushing him rather than tell Penny that the boy she loved, the one she mourned so keenly, had slept with someone else.

"Tell me!"

"It's not important."

"How can you say that?" Penny screamed in my face, battering my chest with her fists. I tried to put my arms around her, but she fought me away and ran off down the corridor. I made to go after her, but there was a hand on my arm, a warning, "Leave her, mate."

I didn't want to hear it and I spun round in anger, my fist bunched and flying, remembering how it felt to fight. Wanting something to take me away from what was happening…

I punched Rav so hard that I broke his jaw. And my hand.

HANNAH

"What happened after that?" I ask.

"I was suspended. My parents decided I needed a fresh start and whisked me away to Australia for the summer whilst they sorted out the house." He's staring across the room and his face is gentle, like he's thinking about how grateful he is that they'd do that.

But that wasn't what I'd meant. "I meant with Penny."

Aaron shakes his head, once to each side and the look of loss on his face slays me. "That was it: friendship over. She never spoke to me again and I made it easy for her. I faded out of my own life and when we decided to move I shut down my Facebook account, changed my email address and got a new phone."

I could never have done that, shut off my whole life in one go. "So you never told her why you and Chris were fighting?"

"I've only ever told one person the truth about that." Aaron looks at me and takes a sip of Diet Coke.

"Not even…" I don't say Neville's name, but I see Aaron close his eyes, a gentle "No" formed on his lips.

I find myself staring at his mouth long after his lips have stopped moving.

AARON

Neville might have left, but Hannah's still here, in spite of all I've done to push her away. Now, when I look at her, I finally see someone I trust. Someone I love.

HANNAH

Our faces are close enough that all I can see are his eyes and I see something there. Something promising.

Slowly, I tilt my mouth to his until our lips touch, until there's only a kiss between us.

AARON

I lift my hand up to rest on her hair...

There's a cough in the doorway and we pull apart, guilty.

"Aaron?" Hannah's mum says. "It's your parents on the phone."

THURSDAY 15TH APRIL
EASTER HOLIDAYS

AARON

My parents are – understandably – pretty upset. Mum in particular. Yesterday she blamed herself for putting me in a vulnerable position. Of *course* I was going to get attached to Neville, she should have *seen* it coming, how could she have been so *stupid*? It took me a long time to explain to her that what she'd done had made all the difference. Without Cedarfields, without Neville, I'd never have made it this far. The reason I was so upset about losing him was because he'd been there when I needed him most. I'm not sure she understood, but it was late and we were all tired.

Tonight is a different matter. Tonight she's mad with me.

"I don't know what to do with you." I stay quiet. "This time last year I didn't have any grey hairs. That's impressive for a woman my age, but now…" She leans forward and runs a finger along her scalp, joining up single grey hairs like an astronomer grouping constellations. "Look. I'm nearly as grey as your gran."

Dad and I raise our eyebrows at each other.

"Don't think I didn't see that," Mum says, sitting up again. "Aaron, you have *got* to stop doing this to us. I'm serious."

"Doing what?" But I know.

"Scaring us." Her eyes sparkle with unshed tears. "You don't know what it's like, being a parent ..."

I think about that night in the car with Robert.

"... this time last year I honestly thought we were going to lose you the way that Chris's parents lost their son." It hurts to hear this, but I force myself to listen. "Such a *waste*."

There's a pause in which she glares her tears into submission and Dad rests a hand on my shoulder and waits for her to go on. But she's still not speaking, holding her breath and trying not to cry.

"Aaron," Dad says. "When are you going to start trusting us?"

How can I tell them that I have always trusted them when all I do is lie about the things that happen in my life? It's time I told them everything.

Including Hannah's secret – and how I feel about it.

WEDNESDAY 21ˢᵀ APRIL

AARON

I wave a goodbye to Dad as he heads into the staffroom after a traffic-besmirched journey arguing in German (mostly). He seems to be satisfied by my accent and has stopped griping about an aptitude for languages running in the family, which means all those language downloads on my iPod have paid off. *Gott sei Dank.*

I'm walking down the corridors during that pre-registration lull where everyone's in the classrooms, sitting on desks and killing time until the teacher walks in. Up the stairs and round the corner; our class is the furthest away from the staffroom and I can hear the raised voices from this end of the corridor. The posters pinned on the walls waft as I walk past, but I ignore them. I stopped reading the noticeboards before the end of the first week – no one else does.

My left shoe squeaks annoyingly on the next couple of steps and I stop to wriggle my heel a bit until it stops.

When I reach the door, the noise on the other side is deafening, louder than I've ever heard before. I take my phone out of my pocket to check it's on silent – it is. I've missed a couple of calls from Hannah, probably asking me to pick up an ice cream, and there's a message from

Gideon, but since I'm about to see him I don't bother opening it.

I lean my shoulder on the door, lever the handle down and enter the classroom.

HANNAH

Beside me Gideon turns towards the door and pinches my arm.

I twist where I'm standing and see Aaron.

God, *please*… I don't know what to do.

He smiles, but when he sees my expression he knows there's something wrong – something *very* wrong – because the smile fades as he meets my desperate gaze. I flicker a glance to my right and watch him follow my lead.

A sudden hush has fallen over every one of us as we watch him read it. Beside me Gideon is shaking with rage and Anj grips my arm, holding me back as I strain over the desk towards the bitch who did this.

AARON

All this must have taken some persistence.

Across the top of the image on the whiteboard is the headline from the local paper – FOURTH YOUTH TO DIE ON OUR ROADS – and underneath there's part of a Facebook Chat conversation. One is Mandy, a girl Chris and I sat with in Science. She constantly teased us on our bromance whilst trying to stop us from copying the results from her experiments – someone I'd call a mate.

The other is someone called Katiecakes whose avatar is a picture of some boobs – no prizes for guessing the owner. I wonder how many of my past school friends she tried before someone responded. I wonder if she tried Penny.

The screengrab cuts into the middle of their conversation:

& Aaron woz there wen his mate got killed?

Yeah. It was pretty rough for him – he went off the rails a bit, drinking, starting fights. He even punched someone in the corridor. Broke his jaw.

R WE TALKING ABOUT THE SAME AARON TYLER?! ;) That Y he "left"?

He left after the news article came out.

?

Everyone thought it'd been an unlucky accident, but the article said that Ty and Chris had been having a fight – that's how Chris fell into the road.

WHAT?????!!!!

Yeah. It came as a bit of a shock. Penny took it pretty badly.

Who she?

Chris's girlfriend. Her and Ty had always been pretty tight, but after the accident she was the only person he hung out with. But they had a massive blow-out at school when she saw the paper and after that she stopped talking to him. She'd leave the room if he walked in, stuff like that.

So they were like an item? OMG thats AWFUL! He
pushed his friend under a car & started shagging the girl
he left behind!

And because Katie isn't interested in the truth, because
she wants to cast me in the worst possible light, that is
where she has cut the screen. I'd like to think Mandy
would have defended me, but who knows? Maybe that's
what everyone at Bart's really thought. It's then that I
see the photocopy of the full article on our classroom
pinboard. I think of the overstuffed noticeboard I
passed on the way in. I'll lay money Katie's posted those
around the whole school. In fact I'll be disappointed if
she hasn't.

I walk over and sit at my desk and look at Hannah.
She's staring at me like a puppy on death row. Anj looks
pretty tragic too and Gideon is practically steaming at the
ears, but it's Katie whose gaze I meet.

Her expression is totally impassive. She's watching,
waiting, seeing just how far she's really pushed me.

The door opens and in walks Mrs English.

HANNAH

Mrs English doesn't really know what she's looking at.
She asks Aaron to explain since his was the name she
identified.

Thirty-five pairs of eyes turn to see how he'll react.
Thirty-five pairs of ears prick to hear what he'll say. One

heart (mine) threatening to break if this goes wrong.

"The class has just found out why I left my last school."

She looks confused. Does she know? Aaron's dad must have told the teachers something... You see her glance nervously at the board, her eyes widening as she takes in all the information for the first time.

"Can someone tell me who put that up there?"

AARON

Mrs English isn't looking at anyone in particular – there's more than one Katie in our class, and it's not like our form teacher is able to identify the right one from an inch-square picture of cleavage.

Katie is looking at Hannah and at me as if daring us to say something, but even as Hannah opens her mouth someone else says, "Yes."

For a moment no one knows where to look, but I recognized the voice right away and I'm looking at Rex as he stands up off the desk he was leaning on.

"Katie Coleman did it. I saw her fiddling with the projector when I came in."

Katie is horrified. The colour's drained from her face.

"Is this true?" Mrs English is looking at Katie for an answer but it's the person behind her who speaks up.

"It is. She asked to borrow my laptop – I didn't realize she was going to use it for this." Marcy doesn't even deign to acknowledge Katie as she speaks.

HANNAH

I watch Marcy turn, the way I knew she would. Katie used to be her boyfriend's best mate's girlfriend. Now she's worth no more to Marcy than I was – now she's fair game for Marcy's preferred brand of humiliation.

Katie gambled everything on this – and lost.

Serves her right.

AARON

I owe Anj and Gideon an explanation. It's very hard, telling them, explaining what happened when Neville died – how Hannah saved me. I tell them what I told her, joining up the dots that Katie's little PowerPoint presentation had set out. Anj is hurt, but she listens and, when I finish, she hugs me just as hard as Gideon. They tell me that they understand how hard it must be and that they're here for me, that I'm their friend.

Neville, Hannah, Gideon, Anj… I can't believe I deserve them, but I'm grateful nonetheless. So grateful it hurts.

SUNDAY 2ND MAY
BANK HOLIDAY WEEKEND

HANNAH

My antenatal classes are crammed into a bank holiday weekend that should have been spent in the garden trying to force extra facts into my brain before the exams start. Now I've got something else to revise for. Hurrah.

Yesterday I sat through four hours of questions about baby prep that we should all totally have figured out by now, but the midwife running the class felt we needed to go over. She wasn't wrong – half the people in there make me look organized. I can only assume their older brains are worse affected by all the pregnancy hormones. And they had so many *questions*. Dear God, it was like they thought we had all day. Don't they know that when it comes to revision lessons, the faster you let the teacher tell you stuff, the more likely you are to get out early? Don't they have better things to do with their weekends than sit in a room that's all windows, melting in the heat as the midwife answers yet another question about the first stage of labour. THE *FIRST* STAGE. We didn't even get to the second – the important bit – before the end of the session.

That's what we'll be talking about today. Giving birth.

Yuck.

I lean forward and nab a cup of lukewarm water and three biscuits. I need to keep my energy up. Five a.m. wake-up calls from my bladder are better than any alarm invented by man and if you sit me down somewhere warm there's a ninety per cent chance I'll sleep – I already snatched five minutes in the taxi over.

I don't want to be here. Mum came with me yesterday, but Lola's sick today and Robert's away on a business trip. I couldn't ask Mum to come with me – not when I could hear retching echoing from the toilet bowl. Poor Lolly. I called Gran, but she can't sort it out at such short notice.

So it's just me. Fifteen, pregnant, single mum. All the others are a sensible age, with jobs that give them maternity leave and husbands that know more about pain relief than the anaesthetist who's going to be giving it. I can't help but feel resentful towards all of them – hey, I'm fifteen, I'm meant to be angry at life, right? Isn't that what people twice my age think it's like to be me? Isn't that what they remember themselves being? Only I'm not them and I'm only angry because I want what they have and I don't understand why I can't have it. Why can't Jay be un-shit? Why can't he be the boy I've been in love with all my life? Why can't he just man up and deal with this? It's not like I want him to marry me. All I want is for him to come clean so I can stop lying to everyone.

I gnash my teeth to distract myself from the thoughts running riot around my brain. The woman next to me must have heard – she's looking at me oddly.

"Hannah, isn't it?" the midwife asks me and I nod. "Is your birth partner on her way?"

Birth partner? Lame.

"My mum can't make it today. My sister's sick." I bite my nail and stare at her, daring her to say anything more. I can almost see her thinking that my mum's a single parent and look where it got me… "My dad's on a business trip."

I can't believe I just said that. I just called Robert my dad. The rush of love I feel for him overwhelms me. I do love Robert. Loads. I moan about him all the time. I'm jealous of how he's always boasting about Jay and Lola's school stuff… But I'm starting to get how he loves me too: when he gave me the money for new clothes; how he's never once said a word about me supporting myself or moving out; that time he came with me for a midwife appointment I'd forgotten to tell Mum about; driving me and a vomit-covered Aaron back from the Duchess. I think about the closed account in my heart that used to belong to my father and I realize that without noticing, I've been transferring all that credit to Robert – and some.

The midwife claps her hands and the murmuring of mum-to-be bonding quietens down. I shift in my chair and it makes a farting sound. Charming. Even the chair is against me. I shove in a biscuit and glare at anyone who dares make eye contact.

Ten minutes in and I'm tempted to walk out. So far I have heard too many men ask questions about lady parts that make even me – the owner of actual lady parts – feel queasy. How are these people ever going to have sex with each other ever again? Not that sex is the first thing on my mind when I see the midwife push a plastic doll through a frighteningly life-sized rubber vagina.

One of the men actually asks if the doll is to scale.

It can't be. Babies aren't that big except in hospital shows where they don't have minutes-old babies on standby for the end of a birth scene.

You can almost hear all the women let out their breath when she says no.

"This doll's head is proportionally smaller than a baby's."

Shit.

In that silence there comes a quiet knock on the door. The midwife looks up, pleased to have something to distract the fifteen women who want to tear her face off. I don't bother turning round as it would be way too much effort – instead I watch her frown and say the name of the class like she thinks the person there is lost.

"What is it that you're looking for, love?"

"It's OK, I've found it, thanks." I recognize that voice, but before I have a chance to turn, Aaron's sitting in the seat beside me and giving me a hug. "Your mum texted me."

That boy. Best. Fake. Baby Daddy. Ever.

Fact.

AARON

There are some things it is best not to repeat. I think I heard most of them in that antenatal class.

SATURDAY 8TH MAY

HANNAH

He calls at 11.17 on a Saturday night. I shouldn't answer it.

"Jay?"

"Did you tell Katie?"

I don't understand what he's going on about and my brain's too slow to form the right questions.

"Did you tell her?" He's almost shouting and I don't like it.

"Of course not! Do you know *anything* that's happened in my life the last six months? We fell out. And stop shouting," I add as an afterthought.

"Well, she sent me a text saying she knows I'm the dad."

That makes a twisted, Katie-Coleman kind of sense. Her plan with Aaron backfired, so she's come back to the identity of the dad. She knows it's not Aaron, not Tyrone ... somehow she's finally worked her way round to Jay. Good job she didn't start there. I wish she'd just leave me alone, but that isn't Katie's way – once she starts, she finishes and she hasn't finished with me yet.

"Katie knows nothing," I say, although there's a little niggling doubt in the back of my mind. After all – she's right. Maybe she's just trying to get a reaction out of him and then she'll *know*... "You haven't replied, have you?"

"No. Why do you think I'm calling you?"

That sentence is so disappointing. Why would I think

he'd call? He hasn't so much as emailed since I saw him at Easter.

"Just tell her she's mental or something. No one else knows."

"Aaron does."

I close my eyes. Jay can be so difficult. But when I picture him, I still fancy him. Hate my stupid hormones – now is not the time to get horny again. Besides, why am I giving him advice on how to hide the truth when I want him to face up to it? I'm such an idiot.

"I don't care what you do, Jay. Goodbye."

"Wait." And like a muppet, I do. I shouldn't. I should hang up right now. "Hannah?"

"Yes?" I try to sound like I don't care, but he knows he's scored a point.

"She really doesn't know?"

"Not unless you tell her."

"Good. It's Dad's birthday coming up and I don't think he needs to find out like this…"

"It's not like he's ever going to find out, is it?" I say viciously and hang up before I can hear him tell me not to.

Jay calls back instantly but I reject it. He sends a text.

Ure not doing something stupid right now ru?

I text back.

Did something v stupid a long time ago. ANYTHING is a shitload more sensible than that.

He texts back: *Dont tell them now, Han. Not now.*

When?

But he has no reply to that.

And neither do I.

AARON

There's something in the air as we gather outside the hall. No one's in uniform and it's interesting looking at some of the people I've never seen at the park or a party. There's one guy who's not in any of my classes, but I've seen around and always thought he looked pretty cool – the kind of person that in another life I might have ended up mates with. Judging solely on his faded Joy Division T-shirt, I come to the conclusion I was right.

Katie is wearing something that is meant to be Juicy Couture – only "Couture" is spelled with a double "O". For a moment I feel sorry for her. She isn't the person she wants to be and no matter what she wears or who she sleeps with, it's not going to change that.

"What you looking at?" Katie mouths off and all my pity evaporates. I heard she tried to tell Nicole that Hannah's stepbrother was the father. Nicole told her she was pathetic – oh, how the bitchy have fallen. It doesn't matter that she's telling the truth.

Everyone turns when the front door bangs against the wall as someone pushes it with too much force. It's Hannah.

The word "radiant" springs to mind. It's a pregnant woman cliché for a reason – Hannah is glowing. Her skin is clearer than Marcy's and her dark hair looks model perfect. Everyone's used to seeing her in an oversized school shirt that makes her look blousey and fat, but today she's wearing her favourite outfit – a skin-tight khaki dress that displays her curves to full effect. Flip-flops show off perfectly painted toenails (courtesy of Anj) and pale curved calves lead up to her half-length leggings.

I watch other people as she approaches, the way they reassess the girl they've been sidelining since January. Fletch's eyebrows hit his hairline and even Joy Division boy frowns, pondering a moment before remembering who the pregnant girl is.

"I'm bricking it."

The spell is broken. This isn't some fecund goddess. This is Hannah Sheppard. Only the Hannah in front of me isn't the same one I met back in September – that one would have been hyper-aware of the glances her way, would have swung her hips a little and made eye contact with a minimum of three boys before reaching me.

Dad pulls open the door to the hall and calls us inside. There's a pause, a gathering of breath, a steeling of minds and then the rustle of nerves personified as plastic bags and pencils as we make our way into our first exam. As we pass Dad, he winks at me, then at Hannah, who gives him a nervous smile.

On the way to our desks, I manage to catch her hand and give it a squeeze.

"Good luck," I say.

"I'm gonna need it!" Hannah says in a rush. "Do I have

to wish you luck too or can I keep it for myself?"

"You can keep it." I squeeze her hand one more time, my fingers brushing across her palm as we part.

Week one:

English Lang.

Biology

French x 2 (Reading and Writing)

I'm finding this harder than I thought I would. Not the papers – which are exactly as hard as I thought they'd be – but the being pregnant at the same time. I thought all that stuff Mum said back in January about deferring was her hoping to give me more time to cram and the "You're going to be very uncomfortable by then … won't be getting much sleep … feet will swell up…" were all just excuses.

I was wrong.

Every night I wake up to go to the loo three times. *Three* times! I wouldn't mind peeing all night if it meant I got back to sleep right away – only after piss-take-two I usually stay awake for ages. I can't switch off. If my brain isn't whirring over all the things it doesn't know about whatever exam is coming next, then it's wondering about Jay.

It's a ticking time bomb of a problem that different parts of my brain keep chucking about faster and faster and faster, until I feel dizzy with worry. Then I think something like, "Stress isn't good for the baby", and I kick off another whole world of worry. I'm petrified of what happens next. In a month's time I'm going to give birth and all the antenatal class taught me was that giving birth is the most painful scary thing in the whole entire world and I might die from it. (That and the importance of doing your pelvic floor exercises.) But that's not the point because it's not the giving birth I'm stressing over – it's the bit that happens afterwards.

I, Hannah Sheppard, will be responsible for another human being. Not one I get to carry about conveniently in my tummy, but one that can wriggle and cry and be dropped (I'm *so* scared of that), who will want to eat *all* the time – and eating is breastfeeding because bottle-feeding sounds like a lot of faff and they say if you breastfeed you lose weight but the idea is totally freaking me out because that's just not what I think my boobs are for, except they are and…

That's usually when I fall asleep. I think it's my brain short-circuiting and making me pass out.

Then I wake up for wee number three and pick up where I left off.

I nearly fell asleep during my first French exam on Tuesday. You know when you're reading something and you just totally haven't taken it in? So you start again and then you just sort of zone out? And you think, "I'll just close my eyes for a sec. I'm not gonna sleep, just rest and then I'll be fine." Only you don't rest. You fall asleep and slump forward and hit the desk with your face… Unless you're so fat that this is a physical impossibility so you end up sliding down the gap between your chair and the desk until you get wedged.

I woke up when someone threw a ruler on the floor. It was Gideon. He'd seen me snoozing.

Katie would never have done that. She'd've just told me later about how I drooled out the corner of my mouth or said something embarrassing in my sleep. If phones had been allowed in then she'd have taken a photo and put it on Facebook. She used to do anything for a laugh – I never realized I'd only ever be the butt of her jokes.

But I miss her. Or I miss the Hannah I was before all this – the one who went out drinking and dancing, the one who was allowed to be hot. I miss being sexy. I really do. No one finds a pregnant person sexy, not even the person who's pregnant. After this what will I be? A saggy bag of stretch marks and pregnancy weight with lady parts like an over-stretched elastic band?

Will I be someone anyone wants?

HANNAH

There's been a lot of thumping and banging going on downstairs and it's totally ruining my concentration. I slam the book shut and look at the cover.

Fuck it. If I don't know the difference between centrifugal and centripetal by now I'm never going to. Besides, I'm hungry.

When I get downstairs I see several pairs of shoes in the porch – one of which looks suspiciously like Aaron's. I walk towards the kitchen like a girl in a horror movie only, when I push open the door, I'm not greeted with an axe murderer, but the sight of Robert and Lola and my three best mates arranging a tower of presents.

My hands fly up to my face to cover my mouth, but I'm grinning so wide I can barely hold it. As everyone comes in for a hug, Lola tells me that there's a cake, but we can't cut it until Mum gets here.

"Where is she?" I ask.

Robert looks at his watch and tells me she'll be here in a minute. I don't know where she's gone, but a little voice suggests something I really want to be true, but suspect isn't.

Maybe she's picking Jay up from the station?

Ssh, voice. That's just silly.

You know what he's like about grand gestures. Maybe he's going to step through that door and give you a big hug and then, with all your friends here, he'll hold your hand and say that the time for pretending is over and that he's the father of your baby.

He wouldn't do that and, anyway, why would Mum be the one to pick him up?

Because you'd guess if Robert was missing, duh.

I swallow and smile at my friends and try not to listen to that little voice.

That's the sound of keys in the front door! I turn, not looking too excited, not looking too hopeful. Mum walks in, smiling, and says she hopes we haven't started without the guest of honour and I hold my breath, not yet able to see him.

Because he isn't there, is he?

It's Gran. And I feel like crying because, instead of being genuinely overjoyed at seeing her, which I should be – which I *would* be – I'm crushed with disappointment. I let myself cry, but force a smile and bounce around and hug her really tightly. All the tighter because I know that really I *am* happier that it's her and not Jay. Gran has stood by me all the way. When no one else knew, she was the one who didn't judge and just let me do the right thing. Jay wouldn't have done that.

And I'm squeezing her, hearing my voice saying how pleased I am to see her, how I'd no idea about any of this, but I'm not hugging her. I'm clinging on. If I let go too soon I'm going to fall apart.

AARON

There's something wrong with Hannah. Since her gran walked through the door she's been overexcitable, mirroring Lola, and I can see Paula biting her tongue because she doesn't want to tell her fifteen-year-old daughter off in front of her friends. Gideon and Anj are laughing along – they don't seem to see that Hannah's mood is brittle, ready to snap under stress. Her smile is wider, brighter, toothier than ever, like she's trying hard to convince us – to convince herself – that she's happy.

She *loves* the presents. LOVES. THEM.

Her mum's given her a bundle of baby towels and a bath set. Robert's given her a piggy bank and we watched him slide a fifty in once it was out of the box. Lola handed over a cuddly lion that she immediately tried to reclaim once Hannah opened it. I see Hannah take an envelope from her gran as well as a present. She opens the present – a traditional-looking baby book – but pockets the envelope.

The cake is lovely. Paula's an even better baker than my dad, and it's light and fluffy, filled with whipped cream and strawberries and dusted with icing sugar. Lola's written "BABY" in chocolate chips on the top. She started too far over and the "Y" is squashed along one side of the cake.

After we've eaten so much cake and sweets and home-baked party food that we're approaching a collective diabetic coma, Hannah's mum says she's got to take Ivy back to Cedarfields and there ensues a teary goodbye. Gideon and Anj start carrying stuff up to the baby's room and Robert takes Lola to go and feed the rabbit as I help Hannah clear up. Only Hannah's stalled, staring at something on the kitchen calendar.

HANNAH

In today's square Mum has written "BS" – code for baby shower, in case I'd bothered to look. Underneath I can see that she's rubbed something out.

I take the calendar off the wall as Aaron comes and stands next to me.

AARON

Someone has rubbed out the words "Ask Jay?" from today's box. There's a quiet sniff from Hannah and I rest my hand on her shoulder.

"I thought Mum had gone to get him earlier."

Suddenly her mood makes sense. Hannah's fingers catch on the paper and she accidentally flips over to the week after next. In Saturday Lola has written "DADDY BIRTHDAY!" Again, the last few letters are squashed together to stay within the box.

HANNAH

And that's when I get the idea.

HANNAH

Mum picks me up after Physics.

"How was it?"

"Meh." It was meh minus mc² but she can wait until results day to find that out. Watching *The Big Bang Theory* with Robert was a waste of time. "Mum?"

"Ye-e-s?" She suspects something straightaway. Not a good sign.

"What are you doing for Robert's birthday?"

"No. You can't go out that night."

"That's not why I'm asking." As if I *ever* go out these days. "I was just wondering."

"*We* are having a nice family dinner."

"We being?"

"The family. The clue is in the phrase 'family dinner', Hannah."

FFS. "So Jay's coming?"

I see her frown. Of course he's not. Yet.

"He's pretty busy. I asked him up for your party but…" she says.

"Robert's birthday'll be more his sort of thing, won't it? He could just come up for the night. I bet if you paid his petrol…" I'm thinking that I'm pretty good at being crafty when I notice Mum's looking at me and not the road ahead.

I look at her and she looks back to the road.

"Miss him, do you?"

I hadn't expected that. What do I say? "I suppose…"

"Of course you do. You two were very close."

Oh God, what is she saying? Just stop, Mum, please.

"You could give him a call…?"

Nononononono… "You know what he's like, Mum. If I call him he'll make an excuse about his exams or something." Good one, lay the groundwork early. "If *you* ring, you can explain how much Robert's missed him and he'll understand."

Mum swings the wheel round as we turn onto the main road and we sit in silence as she concentrates on merging into the traffic. Then, "That's a good idea. Let's do that."

Nailed it.

AARON

At ten o'clock I get a call from Hannah.

"You should be revising History," I say immediately. It's her weakest subject after English and I know Dad has his concerns as to whether she'll pass.

"For your information, Mr Tyler, I have been. Now can you put your son on? I need to talk to him."

I smile. "He's very busy watching videos of pugs dressed as superheroes on YouTube. This had better be important."

My smile fades as she tells me why she called.

SATURDAY 5ᵀᴴ JUNE

HANNAH

I've been standing under the stream of water for nearly fifteen minutes. I am clean and pink. The baby is awake and trying to get comfy inside my too-small body and I rest my hand on my belly and smile at its efforts. Water runs from my hair, down my shoulders, between my breasts and cascades over the bump. I don't see the silver splashes where it hits the shower floor because my belly is so big that I can't even see my toes. I hope the nail varnish Anj did before the exams isn't too chipped and if it is, well, what am I going to do about it? I can barely reach my feet to put my shoes on and I'm not trusting Lola to paint them. I could ask Mum, I suppose.

I twist off the tap and stand, dripping for a moment, slicking my hands back over my hair and wringing out the ends before I get out, taking *loads* of care – I have proper paranoia about slipping and falling on the wet tiles. I wrap the towel around me and stand in the patch of sun from the window, snug inside my warm, soft cocoon. The baby presses a limb against something and I wince but it's still on the move so it passes quickly.

I'm dry and wearing my favourite dress and leggings. I haven't bothered with make-up. I predict tears today and I don't want panda eyes – it's bad enough I'm going to have puffy eyes. I have puffy everything at the moment. My ankles are a weird shape and my fingers are pretty swollen too. In some ways I'm looking forward to having the baby – at least then I might get my body back, even if it is different from how it was when this started.

I hear a squeal of laughter from the sitting room and psych myself up for what's ahead. I stand on the top step and think about running back into my room, slamming the door shut and refusing to come out, like some diva who's had the wrong champagne delivered backstage. Can I run away and hide? Please?

But running is all I've been doing and I'm tired. Time to stop and take a stand. There's no justice in Jay getting away with it any longer – he's the father. He doesn't get to opt out. That's all there is to it.

Pausing outside the door, I look round the frame, ready to see Jay and my little sister having fun without me. Robert's there too, his two kids standing either side of him, showing him something on the Wii. Lola's pretty party dress is tucked into her knickers so she can move around more easily, and a suit jacket I suppose must be Jay's is lying on the sofa. Mum comes up behind me and rests a hand on my shoulder and I turn to see her watching them too, a warm, happy smile on her face.

Can I really do this?

There's a knock on the door and Mum frowns. She's not expecting more guests and I duck under her arm, beating her to it. I open the door to Aaron, dressed as if he's come for dinner, although he should have come dressed for war.

I say nothing, just step into his arms.

"This is it," I say and Aaron kisses the side of my head.

AARON

I can feel her quaking as I hold her.

"This is it," I say, wishing it wasn't. When she lets go I have to fight the urge to pull her back and tell her that she doesn't need to do this. She doesn't need Jay.

But needing and wanting are different things. She can pretend that this is about ending the lies, but it isn't only that, it is because, even after everything he's done, Hannah still wants Jay.

HANNAH

Mum's gone into the sitting room to join the others so when we walk in it's to face all four of them.

"Aaron!" Mum sounds as surprised as she looks. "We weren't expecting you."

"Happy birthday, Robert," Aaron says and hands him a card and a bottle of whisky – good stuff that I reckon he's nicked from his dad. We both know Robert's going to need that later.

"Er … thank you." Robert looks baffled.

All this time I've been avoiding looking at Jay, but I can't hold it off any longer. His lips are pressed so tight together they've turned white and with his short hair and stubble he looks dangerous. And he's looking at me.

AARON

Paula looked at the clock when I walked in and when she turns back to me I can tell that she thinks I'm intruding.

"I didn't know you were coming over, Aaron. We're about to go out for dinner…"

"Aaron can come too!" Lola bounces over to hug me, knocking into a vase of flowers, spilling water all over her dress and the carpet. I bend over and right the vase as Hannah's mum fusses over Lola, telling her to go and get changed whilst she cleans this mess up.

Lola bounds upstairs saying she'll choose something Daddy would like and I feel Hannah tense as her mum comes back in with a tea towel.

"Honestly, I don't know what's got into that child today. She's been mad with excitement about you coming, Jay—"

HANNAH

"Jay's the father."

Oh God, there must have been a better way to do it than that. Mum's looking at me as if she has no idea what I just said and Jay's looking at me with nothing but fury in his eyes. I daren't look at Robert. I daren't.

I open my fingers and Aaron's hand is there almost before I knew I was reaching for it. Is he trembling too, or is that just me? It's me. I'm terrified.

"Hannah?" Mum. Her eyes are pleading when I meet her gaze, as if she's asking me to take back the words, swallow them as if they never existed.

"Jay's the father of my baby," I say again, quieter this time.

"Aaron?"

I just shake my head and feel his thumb brush the side of my hand. We agreed he should stay quiet, he's here to give me the strength to do this myself.

"Jason?" Robert's voice. I look up and he's looking at Jay, who is still looking at me and not at his father. When Jay says nothing, Robert repeats his name. "Jason, what's going on?"

I look at Jay. Don't just leave this to me, Jay. Please don't. Say something, say anything.

"I don't know what she's talking about."

"What?" I hear Aaron's voice chiming in with mine.

"Hannah's lying."

When I said "say anything" I didn't mean *that*. The horror of what I'm hearing has sealed my throat and frozen my face. He's saying I'm a liar? He's telling them I'm making this up? How can he do this?

I step forward straight onto a soggy patch of carpet.

"Sit down, Hannah," Mum says, then calls up the stairs to Lola to tell her to practise her birthday dance for Daddy before she comes down. I sit on the second sofa, Aaron next to me, Mum and Robert on the other one and Jay on my favourite armchair. He and I used to fight over it, sitting on one another, trying to crush the other into submission, until we'd give up and squash into it together. Bet I'd win if I sat on him now.

"Why are you saying this, Hannah?" Mum says. I don't

know whether that means she believes me or that she doesn't.

"Because it's true. Jay and I ... we ... and..." I look at her and hope she understands what I'm saying.

"You two slept together."

"Yes."

"No."

I stare at him, but his eyes are narrow and sharp and ready to cut through my soul.

"Why are you doing this?" I whisper, the words catching on my tears as they come out.

"Why are you?" Jay says, but there's no sadness in his voice that I can hear. Just anger.

I have no answer to this and I look at him, tears flowing down my face. Does he know how much he's hurting me? Can't he *see*?

"It's Dad's birthday and you're saying all this. Why, Hannah? Why would you do that to Dad?" Jay's warming up now and I can hear he thinks this is going to work.

"Jason—" Robert puts a hand on his arm, warning him to stop, then turns to me. "If this is a joke, it's not very funny."

Even though I'm dreading it, I manage to meet his eyes. They're hard and bright, like Jay's, but they're not unkind, just lost, disappointed in me for making up such lies about his beloved son.

"It's not a joke," Aaron says. Robert and Mum look over at him as if they'd forgotten he could talk. "Hannah slept with Jay and now she's about to have his baby."

Jason looks at Aaron with loathing. "You're not going to

listen to him – he's just trying to worm his way out of it, isn't he?"

Mum and Robert glance at each other. They might have a hard time thinking Jay's the father, but they'd have a harder time believing this is Aaron's idea.

"The due date is the eleventh of June. I" – Aaron glances at me apologetically – "got to know Hannah properly in October."

"These things aren't accurate…" Mum says, but she goes out to the kitchen and fetches the calendar, flicking back through the months. I watch when she flips from October to September, but Robert's not looking at her, he's looking at me.

"When?"

"Jay's leaving party," I say quietly, wanting not to meet his eyes, but knowing I've got to.

"She's lying! Hannah's slept with loads of boys." Jay's almost shouting.

"That's not true," I whisper.

AARON

No one else hears Hannah say that it isn't true. But then she says something that we all hear:

"You were the first."

And I feel her gripping my hand so tight that my fingers turn cold, but I'm squeezing back, telling her that I'm here for her.

Jay was her *first*?

I never realized.

HANNAH

All I can feel is Aaron's hand in mine as I look at Jay struggle to understand what I've said. He didn't know. How could he, when the girl in his bed was pretending, the way she'd been pretending all summer – to her friends in the park, the boys she pulled? The way she'd pretended to her best friend.

"It's not true!" Jay's voice is loud with indignation and I want to slam my hands to my ears and shut out the noise. "Tell them about the others."

No one says anything. We're all looking at Jay, who's looking at me and at Robert and Aaron, across at Mum. Beside me, Aaron says quietly, "'Others', Jay?"

Robert looks at Aaron and then at Jay, his face pale as Mum walks back over to me, the calendar open on September, finger resting on the nineteenth, the night of Jay's party, eyes wide with a question she doesn't want to ask.

AARON

At last Robert says something.

"*Others?*"

Jay doesn't seem to understand. So much for university education.

"You slept with your *sister*."

"Stepsister," Jay tries to say, but Robert isn't listening.

"You slept with *Hannah!*" Robert's shouting and when he steps across the room Jay actually flinches, but it's

Hannah his father reaches out to, a hand on her shoulder. "She's *fifteen*. You slept with your—" This time he can't even say it – the horror is insurmountable.

Jay starts, "I didn't—"

The look Robert shoots him stops Jay's protest dead. His father turns to look at me. "And you? October..." His eyes widen as it dawns on him. "You knew all along."

I want to shake my head. I want to say no. "I didn't know it was Jay until—"

What is it that I'm going to say? But I don't get the chance to finish the sentence.

"You need to leave," Robert says, quietly.

I look at Hannah, her eyes tear-glazed and swollen, but it's her mother who answers.

"You lied to us, Aaron." Eyes as anguished as her daughter's. "How could you? You must have known this would—"

"It's not Aaron's fault," Hannah tries, but it was never going to work.

"Get out." Robert once more. "This is a family matter. You are not family."

And I leave, walk down the road to where my mum has been waiting in the car. We say nothing as she pulls away and I rest my head on the glass, thinking of the way the family I'd become a part of threw me out of their brood.

It's done. I'm no longer the father of Hannah's baby.

AARON

It's important to give people space. I understand that, which is why I have only sent one text, one email and called her mobile once. No reply. I draw the line at calling her house phone; I don't want to risk speaking to Paula or Robert. Or worse, Jay.

Whether I get through or not, I don't for a second doubt that Hannah knows I'm here for her. But what Hannah needed was the father and now, finally, she's got him. If Jay's still around, does it really matter where her best friend is?

HANNAH

Mum has put my life on lockdown until something is worked out. I don't know how taking my phone away and disconnecting the Wi-Fi is going to help, but no one in this family is thinking straight at the moment. For some reason Mum seems intent on stopping me from talking to Aaron – as if he's to blame for any of this.

When we get to school that afternoon, Mum tells me that she'd prefer it if I waited in the car before my exam.

"Why?"

The sigh she lets out sounds as if she's so tired of talking to me that any more words will drain her completely. "I don't want you distracted."

Mum watches me watch Aaron walk past with Gideon. How can I describe to her – to anyone – how I feel? Aaron's not someone who churns me up the way Jay does – he calms me down, keeps me sane. Can't she remember how hard it was when we fell out in the holidays? Doesn't she know that seeing him look at me as he walks past, hurt that I'm not getting out and waddling over, is breaking my heart? Worse – it's breaking his. Will he know that I think about him all the time, when I'm meant to be thinking about a thousand other things?

He is my best friend in the whole wide world.

Surely he knows that without me sending a text?

But Aaron's not like me. If he were in my seat, he would unclick the seatbelt, swing open the door and run across the tarmac, shout my name and tell me, to my face, that I am his best friend. Just to remind me. Just in case.

But I'm not as brave as Aaron. Despite my track record, I cannot bring myself to disobey my mum. Not on this one.

AARON

All I need to know is whether she's OK. That is all.

Even as I tell myself this, I know that I am lying. I need to know whether she needs me because *I* still need *her*. Hannah and her baby are a part of my life now. I don't want them to slip out of it.

I'm the last person to take my seat in the hall. I look over at Aaron, but he is looking at the clock. I look at the paper on my desk and the pens and instruments I've brought with me and I look at the back of the person in front. You can see her bra through the top she's wearing – the slightest hint of back fat nudging over the top of the elastic. I run the flat of my fingertips up my own back, as if I might be scratching it, but I can't tell what my back looks like. For all I know I could have a full-on back boob to match the pair at the front.

I look at Aaron again, taking in everything about his face, the lashes, the lips, the scar on his jaw that I now know came from a night he would rather forget – from a life before this one. I want to tell him about my communications blackout. I have screamed, I have cried, I have punched the wall – I could show him the grazed knuckles – but I have not been able to escape.

"If you set foot outside this house without my permission, you will not be allowed back." And I can't risk that being true – for my baby's sake, not mine. I haven't even been allowed to see Gran in case she smuggles Aaron in for a meeting. Instead I had to watch as my paranoid mother called her and told her what had happened. I was crying with shame – why couldn't she have let me tell her? Eventually Mum handed me the phone.

"Hannah? Are you OK?" Gran sounded worried.

"Not really."

"Do you remember what I said? That you're a brave girl and I love you?"

I'd thought she was about to tell me that she was taking it back, but she didn't.

"I should've added that you are the strongest girl I know. The strongest person. Remember that, love. This'll sort itself out and I will be here for you as soon as your mother comes to her senses, which she will. She always does."

"I love you, Gran," I sobbed, but Mum was hovering close, beckoning for the handset once more.

At least Mum and I are talking, if you can call screaming matches talking. Robert and Jay aren't speaking. Jay's still at his mother's – Robert told him that if he ran back to university he may as well stay there and, like me, Jay's not prepared to put that threat to the test. And Lola, my rock, is gone. No one knew how to tell her what was happening, so they've sent her to Robert's parents until everyone stops shouting at each other and we've worked out how to patch up our fallen-apart family.

None of them seem to realize that, for me, Aaron is family too.

AARON

I am here to do an exam. I am not here to worry about Hannah, or think about what's happening between us.

I look down at my paper.

I've to bisect an angle.

Best get on.

HANNAH

It's the end of the exam and I reckon I've done worse than I did in my mocks. I'll be lucky if I don't get a minus grade. So much for my mum's theory about distractions.

Sitting this close to Aaron, not being able to speak to him, is killing me. As soon as my paper's collected, I'm ready to leap up and out of my seat. Now is the only chance I've got to see him, to talk, to explain...

My bump knocks into the edge of the desk and I bounce back into my seat awkwardly. *Shit*. I'm wedged now and one of my flip-flops has come off. Fuck the flip-flop. Aaron's already walking up the aisle. I've got to get out of here. I twist out of my seat and hobble after him with only one flip-flop on.

"Hannah Sheppard," Prendergast calls out and I'm forced to turn back and collect my flip-flop. And my bag of pens. And my calculator. And my bottle of water.

I scuff my way out of the hallway, trying to slide my foot into my footwear, because I can't bend down to do it or I'll never get back up again, and I'm searching the crowd for him...

There's no sign of Aaron, just my mum, standing outside the school doors, waiting to pick me up and take me home.

AARON

I walk slowly. *Very* slowly. I walk so slowly that Gideon and Anj have reached the end of the road before I'm even halfway up the hill. They get so bored waiting for me that they turn back and meet me halfway.

"What's wrong with you? It's just a Maths exam," Gideon says, but I see the look Anj gives him. I haven't told them what happened at the weekend – it's definitely Hannah's place to tell them about Jay and the baby – but Anj noticed Hannah's absence pre-exam and she knows it's not a good sign.

A car drives past and we all watch in silence as Hannah's mum's car stops at the end of the road and pulls out into the traffic.

"Could've at least offered us a lift," grumbles Gideon and he starts trudging up the hill with Anj once more. I stand there for a second, mastering my disappointment, before I follow them.

WEDNESDAY 9ᵀᴴ JUNE

HANNAH

Surprise, surprise. I am awake. It is …

… late o'clock (or early o'clock, if you like) at night and everyone is asleep except me. And I need to pee. Padding quickly across the hallway, I sneak into the bathroom. I hear something over the noise of the flush, but I jump when I step outside and see a shadowy figure in the hall. Instinctively I lash out with a slap, batting whoever it is away, my mouth open ready to scream—

"Shut up, Han!"

It's Jay.

"What are you doing here?" I hiss, but he shakes his head and guides me back to my room, where I elbow his arm away and step back to face him across the carpet. He looks rough, his eyes are small in a tired-looking face and he hasn't shaved since Saturday. This time nine months ago, I'd've wanted to reach out and brush my thumb across the stubble on his skin. Every part of me would have wanted to get close enough to tilt my head up to his, to feel the promise of what might happen before I touched my mouth to his. There is nothing I wouldn't have done for him to notice me. Now I mostly want to punch him. Repeatedly.

"I've got to go."

"Robert doesn't know you're here, then?" I say, crossing my

arms over my chest, aware that my ugly maternity bra is visible above the neckline of my vest. I try and tug it out of view.

When I look up, I catch Jay watching me and I see a shadow of the boy I fell in love with. Still want to punch him though.

"I wanted to see you," he says, surprising me by coming closer. We've not been alone since he came home – every conversation has been uncomfortably played out in front of one of our parents, with both of us desperately skimming over the details of what actually happened between us.

Jay reaches out slowly and rests his hands on my shoulders so that I can feel him tilting me into the light that falls in through the gap in my curtains. He's watching me closely and a more romantic me would dream of him sweeping in to kiss me like I'm the only thing he wants in the world.

The fat, pregnant, permanently disappointed me expects no such thing, remembering exactly how Jay's kisses turn out. But she's a little less punchy.

"I didn't know," Jay says, quietly.

"What? Could you start making sense sometime soon?"

"That I was, you know … your…"

Oh. That. I shrug. "First. Yeah."

"But you were so…"

"Amazing?" I give him a cheeky grin and he shakes his head, letting out a quiet laugh.

"You're impossible." Jay looks at me, serious once more. "The way you talked I just assumed… But if I'd known…"

It's not really important. I know everything is fucked. My

life. His. But that night with him was something I wanted. Not that I wanted it to turn out like this, obviously. Jay's hands are still on my shoulders and I wonder what he's here to say – or is that it?

"Shit." He takes his hands away to press them over his eyes and rub his face. "Hannah. I've got to go."

"You said that already."

"Back to Warwick."

"What? When?" My brain can't process this.

"Tomorrow."

I can't find the words to express the way I'm feeling. *"Get out."*

"Let me explain—"

"Not much to explain – you're running away!" I push him towards the door.

"I am not running away, not this time. Me being here isn't helping anyone. My exams start the day after tomorrow and what good will it do if I fail the year?"

I stop, giving this pause for thought. But he hasn't stopped trying to convince me.

"What good will it do the baby?" Which is *so* the wrong thing for him to say.

I grab the nearest thing I can find – a lever-arch folder of Biology notes – and hit him with it. "Don't you start talking about what's good for the baby *now*! You've had *months* to do the right thing." I hit him again. Harder. *"Months!"* I'm screaming and he's desperately trying to shush me, too much of a coward to face his father if I wake him.

"Hannah – stop – ow!"

I swing again and the clips burst, sending sheets of paper flying across the floor.

"Get out!" I use the half-full folder to bulldoze him out onto the landing, as our parents emerge from their bedroom. I carry on pushing Jay towards the top of the stairs, where he turns and hurries down, pausing halfway.

"I wanted to tell you myself!" he shouts up at me. "Doesn't that count for something?"

"No, it fucking doesn't!" I hurl the folder at him and it cracks against his shoulder.

It doesn't count for anything whatsoever.

AARON

When I get up there's a letter for me on the table. It doesn't have a postmark and, anyway, the post hasn't been yet. I pick it up and turn it over.

"Normally people open them to find out what's inside," Dad says from his spot leaning on the counter.

"Just testing my prescience." But in all honesty I have no idea who could have delivered this to my house. Tucking my finger under the corner, I tear it open. There's a second envelope inside with a Post-it note on the front. I peel the note off and see that the second envelope is addressed to Hannah.

Aaron
I know you don't like me. Just understand that it wasn't always like this. And I'm not running away.

*I'm coming right back after the exams. But since
you're the one who'll be around, can you give the
other letter to H when the baby's born?*

 It's a lot to ask.

 Thank you.

 J

 P.S. Take care of her. As if I need to ask.

I hold the sealed envelope in one hand and tap it against
the table thoughtfully.

HANNAH

I am holding Jay responsible for the fact that we are
running so very late, disturbing Mum and Robert so that
both of them slept through the alarm. Mum is so flustered
about getting me to my exam that she actually runs through
an amber-to-red light and spends the next three minutes
of the journey worrying whether she'll get caught. I twist
in the too-small space in the passenger seat, trying to stop
my back from feeling so bruised and tell her not to worry,
loads of people do it every day and never get caught – she'd
be very unlucky to get nabbed the one time she did. When
she mutters something about having the worst luck of any
woman she's ever met I fall silent.

 I'm bad luck, am I?

 My belt is unclicked and I'm ready to leap out the second
the car jolts to a halt, the door swinging shut behind me,
cutting off my mum as she calls out my name.

AARON

I'm hanging back by the entrance hall, waiting, when I hear the creak of the doors to the foyer and I see Hannah walking in.

"Aaron, get in here, please." Mr Dhupam steps out and ushers me into the exam.

HANNAH

I am wickedly uncomfortable. I had a bit of backache when I woke up and, now I'm sitting at my desk, it's worse than when I was in the car. Maybe it's all the stress? The lack of sleep? I thought I saw Aaron waiting for me, but I'm finding it hard to focus on anything else other than the pain in my back. I hear the call to turn over our papers and I scan through the list of questions. This paper looks rock hard. Shit. I've got to *try*.

My back is killing me.

I can't even make sense of these questions. Perhaps I shouldn't have chucked my Biology notes at Jay when I needed them this morning for some last-minute cramming?

Why is my back so bad? Maybe I've been sleeping funny or something.

Focus, Hannah. You need a not-entirely-shit grade today.

I'm trying to get comfy and concentrate on making sense of at least one of the questions, but it's hard because THEY MAKE NO SENSE.

I shift in my seat, but that's not helping. I glance over at Aaron and see that he's finished one page and now he's looking at the next. I watch as he curls the top left corner of the page he's reading between his finger and thumb.

Shit. That hurt. I rub my back. I'm wondering whether I've pulled a muscle sitting funny when I feel something damp between my legs.

Oh God. I don't need to look down to know what that is. Waves of back ache plus wetting myself can only mean one thing: I'm in labour.

Mr Dhupam comes over with some more paper when he sees my hand in the air.

"My waters have broken," I hiss at him, trying not to panic. I'm due any day now but everyone told me first babies come, like, two weeks late and I feel wildly unprepared. This might be totally normal, this might be what's meant to happen, there might be nothing to worry about, but I'd feel a lot better in a hospital surrounded by midwives instead of in an exam hall packed with stressed teenagers.

"You OK?" It's him. Aaron. He's crouching beside me, his hand on my back as if he never even noticed the silence between us. It makes me want to cry with relief. Only, hello? In labour. Crying with relief is not a priority right now.

"I think this is it," I say and we look at each other. We have trained for this.

"My dad'll drive us," he says with less than a heartbeat's hesitation. "Come on."

Aaron helps me up and guides me down the aisle. I hadn't realized exactly how much my back was hurting until I stand up, and I'm aware of the wet footprints I'm making on the floor. Anj is frantically trying to attract my attention, but she catches me during a twinge and I just sort of flap at her. I hope she doesn't think I'm rude. I hear whispers as I go past the others, Mr Dhupam desperately calling for silence.

Aaron shouts at a kid hanging about in reception to go and get his dad from the staffroom and I call Mum on Aaron's phone. It doesn't matter how mad I am with her, she's still my mum and I still want her to be there. It goes through to voicemail. I don't think it's right to leave a message, so I try Robert instead.

"Hello?"

"Hi, Robert. It's Hannah."

"Whose number is this? I thought you had an exam. Is everything OK?" I can tell he's on the handsfree in his car.

"Um. I think I'm in labour."

"What?"

"My waters broke during Biology." There's a lot of swearing on the other end of the phone and I almost have to shout for him to get my hospital bag from the baby's room. "Can you ring Mum?"

"I'll go and pick her up. Or…" A pause then, "I don't think Jay's set off yet. He could…"

You can tell he's thinking that Jay could fetch Mum on his way to the hospital.

"I don't want Jay," I say, glancing up at Aaron, who's chewing the skin on the side of his thumb as he watches me. "Aaron's with me."

Another pause. "OK then. I'll see you in a bit."

"Don't worry, Robert. I'm fine. The contractions don't hurt that much."

By the time we get to the hospital I'm thinking that contractions hurt a shitload.

AARON

Hannah is behaving as if she's calm, but you can see she's terrified, even now they've hooked her up to a monitor, which she's watching like a particularly thrilling episode of *EastEnders*.

"Han?"

"Uh-huh?" She looks at me, back at the baby's heartbeat, then at me.

"So when your mum gets here I'll call Dad and see if he can pick me up after lunch." She looks bewildered. "Before lessons start this afternoon."

She closes her eyes and frowns. That's a contraction. She's been going silent and frowning about every five minutes since we got here. I wait.

"Can you stay here?"

"What in the visitors' bit? I'm sure—" She's shaking her head.

"With me. Please?"

I don't know what to say. We never talked about me being here for the actual birth – it was always going to be her mum, Paula, who I've just discovered confiscated her daughter's phone so she couldn't even speak to me... "Your mum will be coming soon—"

"She'll just have to get over it. I need you."

I look at Hannah for a while. She looks determined –

and vulnerable. I think about Jay's Post-it note: *Take care of her*. Standing up, I lean over the bed to kiss her cheek and press my forehead to hers. Jay was right – he didn't need to ask.

"I want to be here." So much that I can't find the right words. "If you want me to stay, then I will."

She screws her face up again and nods.

"Stay north side though, yeah?" she says through clenched teeth.

"I went to the antenatal class, didn't I? I don't need the live rerun." And, in spite of her discomfort, she laughs.

HANNAH

I am in a world of pain. Contractions are unbearable. There is nothing I can do to get comfortable. If one more person tells me that it's not going to be too long now then I will tear their face off. Seven centimetres dilated is nothing. I'd like to rip them a seven-centimetre dilation and see whether they agree. No, I don't want to fucking eat – that would require I actually had a second in which I could unclench my teeth. If Aaron tries to stroke my hair again, I swear I will break every single one of his fingers. I want to be left alone but not too alone. I got angry when Aaron went to get something to eat and even angrier when he brought back snacks for Mum and Robert because I wanted to be left in peace for a change. I have walked, I have squatted, I have bounced on a stupid bouncy ball, I have kneeled on all fours and laid on my side and NOTHING MAKES IT FEEL ANY BETTER.

HANNAH

There's a lot of noise around me. Mum's weeping and Robert's hugging her and squeezing my shoulder. The midwife is telling me well done and that I'm a good girl and I feel like my eyes have tripled in size from all the pushing.

There's a scratchy kind of a wail from somewhere in the room and I reckon that's my baby. I don't know if it's a boy or a girl – they showed me its bits, but I'm tired and confused and I didn't really know what I was looking at. Someone's giving me an injection to prompt the afterbirth, which is a thing I really do not want to see. It's like there's an army of people in pink scrubs – is that to disguise all the blood? There's more blood than I thought there'd be…

My eyes sting from sweat and my arms and legs feel like the muscle's been sucked out and replaced with jelly.

"Aaron?"

"Here." And he is. He's standing beside my head, his hand resting lightly on my sweaty hair. "You OK?"

"Where's the baby?"

"They're just grading it or something." He points to a huddle by an incubator. "Weighing, checking, marking out of ten."

"Is it a boy or a girl?" I whisper, not wanting everyone to know that I don't know.

"Erm, I didn't see and they're not really saying much."

"It's OK, isn't it?"

"Yes. Definitely OK. No one is looking worried except you. CTFO, all right?"

I grin. Aaron never uses letters when words are an option. He's looking at me weirdly. "What?"

"Nothing."

"Mummy, are you ready for your baby?" The midwife, who may or may not be called Nicky, is holding something in a white towel. She's holding my baby and then she's laying it on my chest.

OH MY GOD, THIS IS MY BABY! I HAVE A BABY. THIS IS INSANE.

I think my face is going to break in half from smiling. I don't care that this little person is purple and funny-looking – he? she? is AMAZING.

"What are you going to call her?"

"Her" – Nicky just said "her". I have a little girl. A LITTLE GIRL!!! I want to scream with happiness. I have a daughter. I AM A MUM.

"Hannah?"

I look up at my mum and Robert, who are peering over my shoulder at the baby resting on my chest. I can feel Aaron's hand stroking my hair the way it has been stroking my hair for over twelve hours. I look at the baby, just for a top-up, then at Aaron and grin.

"What's she going to be called?" he asks.

I look down at my baby and see her tiny fingers uncurling and I watch as Aaron puts his little finger in her grasp. I stroke her cheek and she turns towards the feel of it. Look at the amazing little person that I made! I think about all the trouble she caused, the heartache, the lies, the betrayal. But she didn't cause any of that, did she? Not this little person. Her life starts with a clean slate – the way Aaron's did.

I glance up at him and smile, then I look back at my baby. I will name her after the most important person in her life. The most important person in mine.

"Her name's Tyler. Baby Ty."

AARON

I stare at Hannah.

I once told Neville that I needed to do something that mattered – I guess I did.

"Here." She lifts her baby towards me. "Cuddle your fake daughter."

ACKNOWLEDGEMENTS

I never used to see the point in acknowledgments. (I know, what a douche.) Fortunately I'm a better person these days and I've learned that you need to tell people when they've been awesome, just in case they don't realize.

Thank you to Denise Johnstone-Burt and Annalie Grainger – not only for being my favourite editors, but for being two of my favourite people. You have made *Trouble* the book I wanted to write. And to everyone at Walker Books, including but not limited to Daisy Jellicoe for being thorough and lovely, and Jack Noel for being visionary and creating "The Sperm One". At S&S US, thank you to both Alexandra Cooper, who spotted this, and Christian Trimmer, who ran with it so unbelievably awesomely. A writer can never have enough editors.

The biggest of all possible gratitude to my awesome agent, Jane Finigan – for finding a title, for finding the right deal and for loving this book more than I do. And for being brilliant on email. And in person. And generally. Actually, the whole Lutyens and Rubinstein crew are pretty brilliant.

Thank you to my beta readers: first and foremost Laura Hedley for not hating it; Liz Bankes, whose reaction I read when I'm feeling blue; Conrad Mason – I pretty much owe you my firstborn for this; and Freddie Carver, who does not deserve this credit whatsoever, given that he failed to read the manuscript.

For the erstwhile BWC crew, Cat Clarke and Kate no-longer-Knighton – I miss you both. Writing chapters without the reward of a pint in the pub isn't quite as rewarding.

A huge shout out to the book bloggers who I met online before I met in person. You are all proper champions, but I would specifically like to thank Kirsty Connor for suggesting Neville's favourite drink and making sure I get invited to things and Liz de Jager – no longer a blogger, but for ever a friend, one who's held my hand as we walked the path of publication together.

It makes sense to thank my family right about now. Mum – you've got a dedication, which makes the whole book an acknowledgement really. And Dad, who understands that being there has nothing to do with geography.

And Pragmatic Dan – thank you for all of the things, but especially the patience.

Enjoyed this book? Tweet us your thoughts.
#Troublebook @WalkerBooksUK @NonPratt